POISONED PARADISE

USA TODAY BESTSELLING AUTHOR
LUCY SMOKE

Copyright © 2021 by Lucy Smoke
All rights reserved.
No part of this book may be reproduced in any form or by any electronic or mechanical means, including information storage and retrieval systems, without written permission from the author, except for the use of brief quotations in a book review. All persons, places, and events in this book are purely fiction. Any relation to real persons, places, or events are purely coincidence.

Editing by Heather Long & Kristen Breanne & Lunar Rose Editing
Cover Design by Cassy Hallman
Alternate Cover Design by Quirah Casey
Formatting by Dez Purington at Pretty in Ink Creations

DEDICATION

To Cassy and Josi,
With love from your Side Hoe

"There is a charm about the forbidden that makes it unspeakably desirable."

— Mark Twain

AUTHOR'S NOTE:

PLEASE READ IF YOU NEED TO KNOW THE EXACT TABOO ASPECTS

Hello there! Thank you so much for picking up *Poisoned Paradise*. Before we start on this journey, I understand that there are readers who need to know the circumstances of any taboo/forbidden tropes. If you are one of these readers, please understand that this author's note contains spoilers. If you are not one of these readers and start reading only to come across the "taboo/forbidden" aspect without having finished this author's note and you feel that this book should be banned, I recommend coming back and finishing it before you continue.

This book is labeled as Taboo/Forbidden because the male and female leads believe that they are twins. **SPOILER ALERT:** They are not REAL twins. In fact, the two main characters are not related by blood **at all**. There is no real or fictional incest present in this work—just a complex backstory and misunderstandings. With that said, I hope you enjoy the twists and turns to what I like to think of as my latest trauma drama and finding out just how things got so messed up to begin with.

PLEASE DO NOT REPORT THIS BOOK. EVERYTHING CONTAINED INSIDE IS A WORK OF FICTION. THERE IS NO INCEST. NONE. NADA. ZIP. ZILCH.

PROLOGUE

RYAN

15 years old

I STAND THERE, completely silent, just staring at her. With her upturned face, and her beautiful brown eyes, and those flower petal lips, all I can think is … *why her? Why does it have to be her?* Any other woman in the world, I can see, but her? What the hell had I done in a past life for this one to torture me so?

"Ryan?" Her voice is trembling. No, it isn't her voice. Her whole body is trembling. She's a mass of shaking nerves and fear and it comes out when she speaks, but even so, she's stronger than me. Far stronger than I've ever been or ever will be.

This can't be happening. I thought I had more time. I thought I could just pretend a bit longer. She's ruining it. She's ruining everything. Those three words—so simple, so gently said—had just shattered the façade I'd built ever since I realized I was in love with her.

"Ryan, did you hear me?" she asks.

I hold up a hand when she moves to reach for me. "I heard you," I croak. "I just..." *Can't believe all of my dreams are coming true,* my mind finishes for me. Is it wrong to be this fucking lucky and unlucky at the same time?

"Do you..." A blush rises to her beautiful face, staining her pale cheeks pink and making me want to do more to see that gorgeous blush go all over. I want to peel away the layers of her clothes and dive into her and see what I can do to make her cry out and writhe against me. "Do you feel the same?" she asks.

I take another step back, bumping into the wall as I cover my mouth. *Lie,* I urge myself. *Lie, damn it!*

Sweet, innocent, Willow. What the hell had I done? Had she sensed my attraction? Had she somehow come to view my presence in her life, the one constant either of us had—each other—as something more when it could never be? This is all my fault. I have to fix it.

"No," I force the word out, my voice tight and harsh. "No, I don't. That's disgusting."

Her blush disappears in an instant as her skin drains of color. Willow pulls her hand back. Her eyes widen. Big brown, luminous eyes that so often smiled up at me as she'd brushed my hair back away from my face and told me stories. I'm not much for stories, but I didn't mind hearing them when they came from her.

"Ryan, I-I..."

I can't stay here. I turn to go even as she stumbles through a response. My cock pounds in my jeans, knowing that she feels the same way I do. The sick, twisted part of my mind that has wanted her since I was old enough to understand that my love for her isn't fucking normal is celebrating. So many scenarios run through my head. We can keep it quiet. I can have her. I can fuck her and love her and keep her close to me. I can make her dependent on me. I can make it so that she'll never want to leave me, that she'll never look at anyone else the way she's looking at me now.

I have a very short window of opportunity now. I need to fix this and fast. If I don't, if I stay—if I think about it, I'll convince myself that I can have her. Even though it's wrong. Even though it's sinful, my heart doesn't care. My fucking teenage cock doesn't care either.

If only she were anyone else. If only I was. "Wait!" I ignore her call and duck out of the back room that we'd been in when she dropped that bomb on me. "Ryan!"

There's only one way out of here. One way to get the hell away from her. I need to get away from her. If I don't, then I'll end up telling her the truth. I'll end up dragging her down into my hell. Miranda Carson has threatened to send me to juvie often enough. Now I just have to make sure she follows through and I know exactly how.

I can hear Willow following me at a much slower rate as I storm through the house. For a foster home, it's nice enough, though the Carson parents are more inclined to their own offspring—a weaselly, rat-faced little asshole a year or so older than me. Connor Carson. Piece of shit, small dick pussy that he is. Whether he realizes it or not, I'm aware of the way he stares at Willow and how he feels about her because I feel the same—I want her even if it's wrong. It's excuse enough and the perfect crime.

Willow's gaining on me. Panting, flushed, feeling like my whole world is spinning out of control, I find Connor in the kitchen with his mother. Perfect. He looks up from where he sits at the table while she fumbles with one of the burners on the stove.

"What are you looking at, shithead?" he snaps with a scowl.

That's all it takes. One second, he's sitting—high and mighty—at his mother's wooden table, and the next, he's on the tiled floor with my fist in his face. A scream echoes up the walls. Willow's or Miranda's, I'm not sure, but it doesn't matter now.

I whale on him, throwing punch after punch until cartilage cracks under my knuckles and blood stains my hands. I have to get out. I have to leave her. And this is the only way to do it. She'll be fine without me. I'll be out in a few years, and once I am, everything will go back to normal.

She can be normal.

I have to give her that.

"Ryan! Stop!" Willow's cries are followed by

her tear-stained face appearing in front of my field of vision right before something hard whacks me in the back of the head, sending me toppling off of Connor.

"Oh, my baby!" Mrs. Carson screams, diving down onto the floor as one of the other foster kids comes running into the room. "Call the police!" she commands. "Call them now!"

I drag air into my lungs, filling them with the stench of blood and sweat, and pain. "Oh, Ryan..." Willow's soft sobs reach my ears, pricking at both my protective instincts and my darker, more sinister side. I'd made her cry.

Good. Maybe now I can start the process of her hating me. I need her to hate me. Because no matter how much we love each other, there's no way a love like ours can ever be allowed.

I lay there like that, listening to the sounds of her tears and the cruel venomous words coming from Mrs. Carson, telling me she'd known all along that I was bad. That I was evil. That I was full of sin and wickedness.

I don't even have the strength to tell her that I know.

When red and blue lights fill the windows and a hard knock sounds on the front door, I know my time's up. I lift my arm away from my eyes and meet Willow's gaze.

"Fucking forget me, Willow," I say. "Pretend I never existed because from this moment on, *you* don't exist to *me*."

Her mouth drops open, shock registering across her features, but before she can reply, an officer is led back into the kitchen. I'm hauled up by strong arms belonging to a man nearly twice my size. I don't even flinch. Without saying a word, I'm led out of the house, handcuffed, and then pushed into the back of a cop car.

Everything in me wants to turn back and look. My inner turmoil screams and scratches and demands that I see if she's watching, if she's looking. But if I look at her one more time, my resolve might falter. I might change my mind and come after her—even after I get out.

So, I suck it up and stare straight ahead, refusing to see if Willow is coming out to stand on the porch as the same officer who'd cuffed me climbs into the front seat.

"You're in a lot of trouble, son," he says.

I dip my head and stare at my knees as the car lists forward and begins to roll down the street.

He has no fucking idea how right he is.

One

WILLOW

6 years later

"LOVE IS HEAVY and light, bright and dark, hot and cold, sick and healthy, asleep and awake—it's everything except what it is!" I listen to the girl read the passage out loud and try not to sigh in frustration. The cadence of her voice, the drama, all of it is far too over the top. She must be a theater major. Professor Bradley, however, seems to be eating it up. He watches her with a light of excitement in his eyes—obviously overjoyed that *someone* is at least taking his class seriously. Or as seriously as anyone can take it on the first fucking day.

More than anything, I wish I could've gotten out of this beginner's literature course. There are a million other classes I would've rather taken. Hell, I'd have even settled for one of the specialized Physical Education classes if they hadn't filled up so fast. I don't mind the literature, but of all of the stories and dramas to read on the first freaking day,

Romeo and Juliet makes me want to blow my brains out all over the classroom.

A slip of folded paper lands on the desk in front of me, and I lift my head, turning it in the direction it'd come from. Lana, however, is already looking back at her book. Sneaky girl. I smirk and, with a wary look back up at the professor to make sure he's still focused on the performance coming from the back of the classroom, I unfold the paper and read the contents.

Who the fuck makes us start reading on the first day?!

It's as if she read my fucking mind. When I glance back at her, she's rolling her eyes as the girl in the back of the room launches into yet another monologue. I stifle a laugh and crumple the note, shoving it quickly into my pocket when Professor Bradley coughs, catching my attention. His eyes meet mine and he frowns in disapproval.

Heat assails my face, and I yank my head down, staring into my book before he can call me out. I'm not sure how professors act at Trinity University, but at my last university, they made no qualms about embarrassing their students. Thankfully, though, a few minutes go by and he seems to be refocused on the student reading. Relief fills me, and I resolve to keep my attention away from my best friend—I might not like this class, but I do need it to graduate.

The rest of the class period ticks by in exceedingly long increments, and as soon as the clock on the wall clicks close to 3 p.m., the students grow restless. The second that little hand clicks into place, we're out of our seats, only half listening as Professor Bradley calls out reminders about papers and homework.

I hit the hallway and start walking, only stopping when I reach the door to the building and feel a familiar presence creep up behind me. "What the hell was that?" Lana grumbles. Her arm lands over my shoulders as we head down the front steps of the English department.

"A performance?" I offer.

Lana blows her bangs out of her face, the jet black strands flying up and then falling right back into place as she rolls her eyes. "It was something alright. Performance is a … well, that's a kind way of putting it."

I shrug. "What can I say, I'm kindness personified."

She snorts. "You weren't kind when Harley broke up with me," she says. "In fact, if I remember right—you were ready to take a baseball bat to her legs."

"But I didn't," I remind her. "Besides, I think you're better off without her. She was a bitch and she never liked me."

"It's not that she didn't like you," Lana says. "She thought I was fucking you."

"Well, I suppose if I ever switched to girls, you'd be my first pick." I laugh.

Lana shakes her head and chuckles right along

with me. "Yeah, well, I appreciate that, but I think I'm taking a break from girls right now, anyway," she confesses as she removes her arm from my shoulders and strides ahead. She turns on her heel and walks backwards as we both head towards the cafeteria building.

"Taking a break from dating altogether?" I guess.

She nods. "Yeah, it's nothing but trouble anyway. Almost all of the girls I end up with don't want to be with me full time, and it's really getting on my nerves. They all eventually end up back on the dick side."

I snort. "Don't you mean the dark side?"

She arches a brow at me. "I said what I said."

Another laugh bubbles up out of me, and for some reason, once I start, I can't seem to stop. By the time it finally subsides, Lana's long since turned back around, and we're standing before the Thompson cafeteria hall.

"That's right, you haven't eaten here since you moved in, have you?" she asks as we swipe our cards at the doors and then once more at the front counter.

"Nope," I reply. "But I'm more than ready to start." My stomach growls as the scent of food cooking reaches my nostrils.

Lana and I waste no time. We grab our meals, find an appropriate table that manages to avoid the louder sections, and scarf down our food. It's too loud, too hot, and too fucking crowded for us to stick around.

By the time we're finishing up, there's a new crowd coming in. "Come on," Lana says, snagging my arm. "Let's go out through the back door."

"There's a back door?" I ask.

She grins. "We've all got one," she replies. "I hear they're fun to play with."

"I swear to god if you offer to peg me, I'm going to scream."

Lana laughs. "Pegging is when you fuck a guy in the ass with a strap on," she replies. "Doesn't count if you're a girl."

"Well, you don't exactly have the equipment to fuck my ass with the real thing," I reply.

"Point taken," she concedes. "Come on."

I let her drag me towards a second exit across the cafeteria. As the volume inside the hall grows louder, we escape through a less crowded second lobby and head out the double glass doors across from the dining area, nearly colliding with another incoming group.

Everything happens so quickly, I almost don't notice him. I almost don't see. The second I do, however, the world seems to still. "Will?" Lana's voice sounds like it's coming from far away, but I know that's not right. She's right next to me. It's me that's wrong. My whole world is wrong. He's not supposed to be here.

Something smacks into my ankle and I go down hard, crying out as my knees scrape against the pavement and the bag on my shoulder tumbles to the ground. Books spill out and pages fly off down the street. "Shit," I hiss, reaching for the first ones. I should've fucking zipped the damn thing up, but I'd been in too much of a hurry to get out of the cafeteria.

Don't notice me, I plead silently. *Please don't fucking notice*—a familiar hand reaches down and grabs a book.

"Hey, are you—" My face tips up and I see it the second that he recognizes me. Six years, but there's no way he doesn't fucking know who I am. My book slips from his fingers. No, it doesn't slip. He opens his hand and lets it fall as a scowl overtakes his face, and he steps back.

"Oh my god, Will, are you okay?" Lana's at my side in a heartbeat, but I can't make myself respond to her. My chest tightens until it fucking hurts—until it feels like someone is driving a knife between my ribs. I don't react as Ryan takes a step back and circles around me. It isn't until he's out of my line of sight that I realize I don't want him to be. I turn and watch as he jogs to catch up with the group we'd nearly collided with as they wait for him by the glass doors.

Someone says something to him and he just shakes his head. Will he look back? No, he doesn't. The doors open and they disappear inside. "What a fucking jerk," Lana mutters. "I thought he was going to help you, so I hung back."

"He was..." I say. *Until he saw my face, that is.*

Lana frowns at me as she helps me pick up my

books and papers. My ankle throbs as I try to stand back up, making me wince. I'd hit the freaking stairs leading up to the street, apparently, and there's a big gash not only on my ankle but on the opposite knee as well.

"Do you know him or something?"

I freeze at the question. "Know him?" I repeat. Even to my own ears, my voice sounds higher than normal. "Who?" I brush off the worst of the dirt and debris from my skin before heading up the staircase.

Lana follows. "You know who," she presses. "That guy who came over looking like he was going to help you. He was all smiley and nice. I thought he was gonna hit on you or something, plus he was cute, so I just—took a step back. It's weird, he just … dropped your shit and left." She rounds on me, stepping in my path, and forcing me to stop. "So, I'll ask you again—do you know him?"

I clutch my bag to my chest, feeling my books inside. Over her shoulder, I spot a few of the scattered pages that had blown away flitter off further down the street. There's no hope for them now. I pray the campus maintenance folks won't hate me because I really don't have time to chase them all down. I can't be late for class on my first day. If it's between being hated by professors or maintenance staff, I'll take the maintenance staff any day. Professors can ruin my life before I even start it.

"I don't know what you're talking about," I lie,

trying to step around Lana's body. "Come on, we're gonna be late."

"Uh uh, no way, missy." Lana's hand latches onto my arm and pulls me up short. "Don't fucking think you can fool me. We've been friends for three fucking years. You think I don't know when you're trying to weasel out of an answer?"

"Please." I don't know what to say. I don't know how to tell her the god-awful truth of who Ryan is. Not just who he is—but who he is *to me*. "Can you just ... let it go?"

Her brows furrow. "Will, is he an ex? Was he abusive?"

I shake my head. "No, it's not that, I just—yes, you were right. I know him. We're ... it's complicated."

Complicated. Ha. That's an under-exaggeration if I ever fucking heard one. I start walking and she steps out of my path to let me go, but moments later, she catches up to my side, walking stride for stride right along with me. "If he wasn't an abusive ex, then ... does it have anything to do with why you were in therapy?"

I bite my lip. "Sorta," I confess.

"Is he ... bad for you?" she asks.

She has no clue how bad Ryan is for me, but it's not just him. I'm bad too. Disgusting. Dirty. I close my eyes as we come to a stop at a red light. Across the street, the red hand on the walking sign flashes, telling us to wait. I'm the one who ruined things. Not Ryan. I don't even blame him for avoiding me.

He has every right to. If I could go back six years and take back those words I said to him, I would in a heartbeat.

"He's my brother," I finally confess. The words feel like horrible knives being ripped from my throat.

Lana's jaw drops. "You never told me you had a brother!" she says. "Is he older or younger? He looks older." She turns halfway and blatantly stares back the way we came as if Ryan will magically materialize right behind us on the sidewalk.

"Neither," I say. *Here it comes. The sick truth.* "He's my twin." *And I told him I fucking loved him.*

Two

RYAN

FUCK. FUCK. FUCK.

It's her. It's definitely her. There's no fucking mistaking that heart-shaped face or those rich auburn eyes or those lips. Fuck. I want to scream—pound something, throw curses to the wind, anything that might relieve me of this God awful riot inside. Instead, I unclench my fingers and let the book I'd been in the process of picking up when I thought she was just another girl, fall from my grasp.

She's not just another girl. She's the one girl I prayed I'd never see again.

Her eyes, so wide and open, follow the movement as the book hits the ground, spine first, and flaps open—pages fluttering in the wind. She doesn't say a word. I can't tell if she's just as shocked by my presence as I am by hers. It doesn't matter. I just need to get away.

Move, I urge myself. *Get up and walk away.* I don't know how I manage it, but I straighten up and circle where she's crouching down on the cement, and stride back towards Tanner and a few of the other guys from the football team. They are all waiting for me by the doors.

Tanner arches a brow at me, his gaze sliding from me to where Willow remains with her back to me. I look up, my eyes immediately locking on the reflection of her in the glass doors. Her friend hurries to bend and help her. The second I let my gaze linger on her image, it becomes difficult to rip myself away. I stare at her back, narrow and slender, the length of her hair curling over her shoulder until I'm on the other side of the sliding doors as they shut behind me. The very moment I'm on the other side, I feel air rush back into my lungs.

I hadn't even realized that I'd been holding my breath until a tightness panged at my chest. I'm fucking stupid. I shouldn't let her affect me this much. She's the past and this is my present. It doesn't matter if she's here. It's a big campus, so I'll just have to avoid her—pretend she doesn't fucking exist … just as I have for the last six years.

I plaster a smile on my face and follow after the rest of our teammates as we hit the cafeteria. Despite my resolve, my mind can't seem to catch up with what just happened.

What the hell is she doing here? Did she recognize me? Of course, she recognized me. There's no way she'd forget my face just as I hadn't forgotten hers. I'm shaken—to my fucking core. All over one little girl that I thought I'd left in the past and that I've been running from ever since.

I'd fought and bled to keep from going back to her. I had caused even more trouble until it finally convinced my social worker that it was better in the long run if they kept us apart. They hated doing so, especially since we were *siblings*—but I needed to be sure they wouldn't try to ship me back. I needed to be away from her.

"Did you know that girl?" Tanner's voice hits my ears a split second before I realize who he's talking about. Will. He's talking about Willow.

Tipping my head back, I frown. "What girl?"

Tanner arches a brow my way. "What the hell do you mean, what girl?" he snaps. "The girl back there. I thought you were gonna make a move or something, but the second you saw her face, you dropped her shit like it was poisonous."

Like it was poisonous? Yeah, she is poisonous. Dangerous and deadly. Beautiful and stunning. The worst person I could've ever run into in a place like this.

"No," I lie. "I don't know her. She said she didn't need help—she's probably a stuck-up bitch."

"Oh?" Tanner looks like he doesn't believe me, and honestly, he probably doesn't. For an athlete who gets his head knocked around quite a bit, he's not stupid. "Well, she was kind of hot." His tone is light, casual, but his words make my whole body freeze. My fists clench at my sides. "Even if she's stuck-up—you know all girls chill out with a little Vitamin D in them." He tilts his head, a mocking grin on his lips. I know what he's doing—the asshole.

It takes physical effort to place one foot in front of the other, but somehow, I fucking manage it. I stride forward, stopping at the back of the first line I come to. I don't know what they're serving and I don't care. "She wasn't that hot," I say through gritted teeth.

Not that hot? Six years had done nothing but fill her out. She's hotter than she'd ever been in high school. Her hair has grown out. She has it cut so that it frames her face perfectly and that ass—I hadn't thought anything of it. Hell, I'd stopped myself from thinking about her as much as possible since I'd gotten out of juvie. It never occurred to me that we'd end up at the same college. It's almost like the universe is against me.

"Not that hot?" Tanner drops his mocking grin and gapes at me like I've lost my fucking mind, and he'd be right, because I fucking have. I feel like a fire has ignited beneath my skin. It's hot and achy. Six years, I'd managed to convince myself that I didn't need her, that I didn't want her, that she was nothing. I'd just been confused and curious. "She was banging, hell if you don't want her, I'm gonna find out what department she's in. Maybe she can be my date for the party next weekend. Her friend wasn't bad either."

It takes every single ounce of self-restraint in me not to turn around and slug Tanner across his face. "I'd go with her friend," I force the words out, hoping it sounds casual. "She was way hotter."

"She wasn't, but if you don't want to talk about it, you don't have to."

"You sure about that?" I mutter. "Seems like you're trying to get me to talk about it even if I don't want to." I glare at him.

Tanner blinks up at me innocently. "Me?" He feigns ignorance. "I would never..."

"Next!" He jumps forward, cutting in front of me when the attendant speaks. I don't even care. I let it go without complaint as the line moves forward. By the time we get to the front, Tanner's back on the party idea.

"Are you coming to the party next weekend?" he asks.

"Which one?" I take the plate I'm handed and shuffle along. "It's the first month back, there's bound to be a couple for the next few weekends."

"Peter's," Tanner replies, glancing back. "He's supposed to be throwing a rager at the frat house."

I grimace. "Peter's a fucking douche."

Tanner shrugs. "Yeah, but his parties are good." We leave the line and cut across the cafeteria until we find the rest of our teammates. "So, are you coming?" he presses.

I sigh as I take a seat and look down at what I'd gotten. It's some sort of chicken dish with a light brown gravy drizzled over it. I grimace. At least it looks healthy. "Yeah, fine," I say. "I'll go."

Tanner whoops and slings an arm around my shoulders. He leans in close. "Maybe I'll catch up with that chick from earlier and see if she's free too," he says in a low voice.

I stiffen, a growl slipping out before I can stop it. My hand clenches against my fork, and I resist the urge to stab him in the face—but only just barely.

I've been running from Willow for six years, but I guess no one can ever truly outrun their past.

THREE

WILLOW

LANA DOESN'T UNDERSTAND why I refuse to talk about Ryan. I don't want to tell her the truth. A part of it—fine. Knowing her, if I had refused to give up any information, she would have hounded me. So I told her the bare minimum. Ryan is my brother and he hates me. What I didn't tell her was *why*.

I trudge across the campus with my backpack dangling off of one arm, heading towards the library and my newest part-time job. The doors are automatic, so as soon as I swipe in, they swing open and I stride forward, making for the main circulation desk.

"Hey," I greet the girl at the counter. "My name's Willow McRae. I'm here for the work-study program position. I was hired last week. Mrs. Maes asked me to come in today."

The girl, not much older than me, glances at me from over the top of her wire-rimmed glasses. She looks like she'd rather be anywhere else but behind the counter, only further proving my assumption when she pops her gum and then glances past the no-eating sign sitting not but six inches in front of her towards the hallway to the left.

"Go down that way," she huffs. "Mrs. Maes's office is the last one on the left."

"Oh, okay. Thank ... you ..." I don't even manage to get my thanks out before she's already focused back on the screen in front of her.

With a sigh, I turn towards the hallway and start down it. Just as the girl predicted, I find a door at the end on the left with the name *Minerva Maes* scrawled in black letters across the nameplate just to the side of it. I politely knock and wait to be admitted.

"Come in!"

I crack the door and peek inside, catching a glimpse of the head librarian.

"Willow, I'm so glad you're here." Mrs. Maes is a tall, slender woman with a head full of puffy, curly black hair and a beautiful smile. "I've got all your new hire paperwork here. I just need you to sign a few things, and I'll show you the ropes."

I plaster a smile onto my face and take a step further into the room. "Awesome."

For the next half hour, Mrs. Maes runs through a list of requirements and policies. No smoking, eating, or drinking in the library. The library hours. Employee entrances and key card instructions for opening and closing. And finally, my schedule.

"Now," she says, "I'm sure you're aware of the

new regulations when it comes to the work-study program, but your hours cannot extend past forty in a two-week period. No overtime. So if someone asks for you to take their shift and you're already at your allotted hours, they'll have to ask someone else. There are no employees allowed after hours, and of course, as I'm sure you understand, you must maintain your grades at a 3.0 if you want to keep this position."

Considering I'm still averaging a 3.7 GPA from my last university, that won't be a problem. "I think I can handle that," I reply.

"Great." She claps her hands. "Do you have any questions for me?"

I shake my head.

"In that case, let me show you where you can store your things." Mrs. Maes shows me to the employee breakroom as well as a small lounge with cubby holes for student employees to put their things. "We've never had any issues with theft," she explains as she shows me a lockbox at the end of each row. "But if you're concerned, you can stow all of your valuables in one of these. There are only six, but no one uses them, so we've never had any complaints about not having enough."

"Got it," I say.

"Wonderful," she replies. "I knew you'd catch on quickly. Let's go to the second floor next; I can give you the grand tour."

Following behind Mrs. Maes is like chasing a hurricane. By the time she's given me a tour of the library and answered my questions, I'm left feeling sucked dry of all of my energy. "For now, we'll just have you return books to their rightful place. I assume you're familiar with the catalog system, but if not, I've made this helpful little sheet." She hands me a small piece of paper with a list of numbers and letters. "You'll find that the first two letters and numbers on the spine of each book will correspond with the letter-number combo of each row. Once you're done returning this cart of books, you can head home for the day." She gestures back to a cart so full of books it's nearly toppling over. My eyes widen as I take it in. It almost looks like someone had tried building the Leaning Tower of Pisa out of texts. "We'll have you work on the online system next time. Think you can handle it?"

I stare at the veritable mountain of books and glance from it to Mrs. Maes, and then to the girl at the front desk with her nail file. I'd bet my entire work-study paycheck this is also part of her job too. I don't say anything, though, and instead, give Mrs. Maes another fake smile. "Of course," I agree. "It's no problem."

"Wonderful. Here's your name badge. Always keep it on while you're working so it lets people know that you can help them. If you have any other questions, I'm sure Roquelle here can help you." Just as she's about to turn away, Mrs. Maes pauses and glances back. "Oh, one more thing, dear. I know some students can get a little excited, and they think they can sneak into the back of the lesser-used sections. If you catch any of them, just ask them politely to leave. I'm sure I won't have to worry about that with you."

Heat steals over my face. "N-no ma'am," I assure her. "I don't even have a boyfriend."

Mrs. Maes gives me a sweet smile, nodding once before disappearing back to the hallway. "Loser," desk girl—Roquelle—mutters.

I freeze with my hand on the book cart and slowly turn my head towards her. "What did you say?"

Roquelle ignores my question and continues filing her nails. With gritted teeth, I start pushing the cart and head off down one of the longer aisles. It doesn't take me long to figure out that whoever stacked this cart had used no such filing system. The books are out of order and a freaking mess. Trying to scan each spine to match the corresponding aisle is hopeless. So, I stop and start to unload the whole thing. Stacking up each book on the floor, as I bend down and scan their spines to readjust them in order before putting them back on the cart.

I've managed to restock one whole side of the cart when a familiar masculine voice calls out from down the aisle. "Excuse me, do you work—" I pop my head over the cart, and my eyes widen.

The second Ryan sees that it's me, a scowl forms across his face. "What the fuck are you doing here?" he growls.

I'm completely and utterly dumb. Stupid,

really. I should have it actually tattooed on my forehead, because like the dumbass that I am, I stand up and point to the nametag on my shirt. "I work here."

His eyes drop to my chest and linger there for a brief moment. Then his gaze darkens and shoots back up to my face. He glances over his shoulder and then whirls on me, storming forward. I gasp and jump back, my spine hitting a bookcase as he brings one arm down above me and crowds my whole body until I feel the edges of the shelves stabbing me through my t-shirt.

"Six years," he hisses. "Six years, I thought I'd finally gotten away from you."

My chest tightens. "I-I..." What can I say to that? Every letter I'd ever sent him had been returned, and when I'd opened them, each and every one of them had been ripped to shreds. All of my phone calls had been denied. But hearing those words are like knives digging straight into my heart. My head drops and I stare at the ground, where his boots and my sandals are almost toe to toe.

"What do you want, Willow?" he growls.

I close my eyes. What do I want? I think. I want a lot of things. I want to turn back time. I want to take back the words I'd said to him. I want to hide the truth and pretend. I want my best friend back.

"Nothing." The word scrapes from my throat, barely a whisper.

Ryan's heat rolls off him in waves. I don't need to open my eyes to know he's leaned in closer because I feel it against my skin. "You're a fucking liar," he says.

I know I am, but what else can he expect me to say?

"Don't fucking expect things to be the way they were, Willow," he says. "Don't tell people about us, and don't you fucking think that your disgusting little desires will ever see the light of day."

I ball my hands into fists and jerk my head back, nearly smacking it into one of the shelves. I don't care. "Why the fuck are you so angry at me?" I snap. "I stayed away after I got your message. I stopped calling and writing. I didn't fucking intend to run into you like this, but I sure as hell don't deserve your vitriol."

"You think not, Princess?" My stomach clenches and something wicked unfurls within me. That disgusting desire he accused me of is still there, I realize. My breath saws in and out of my chest as he leans forward. I try to back up and scoot away, only for his other arm to come down, his palm slamming into one of the shelves and making them rattle against my back. "You think I don't know what kind of person you are?"

Turning my head to the side, I suck in a sharp breath. "I don't know what you're talking about."

"Oh no?" Hard fingers grip my chin and bring my face back around. Ryan's heat encapsulates me as shivers chase down my spine. Dark brown eyes, only a few shades lighter than my own, stare down at me. "The last time I saw you ... you told me you loved me, Will." My heart rate picks up speed. "Are you trying to tell me you didn't mean it?"

"No." I can't lie. I'd meant each and every word. But the feelings of a fifteen-year-old girl who'd never known anything but him weren't to be trusted. I wasn't to be trusted. "But maybe ... we can forget about it?" I peek up at him, hopeful, curious. "Start again?"

He scowls down at me. "Start again?" he repeats. "What is this a fucking video game?" Ryan leans back and shakes his head, and the next words out of his mouth make my blood run cold. "There is no do-over for you, Willow. What you want is disgusting. It's sick and you know it."

He's not wrong. That's what gets me. I can't even deny the truth. I am everything he thinks I am. I'm the one who thought I saw—no, I'd just seen what I wanted to see. I was wrong. Ryan never thought of me as anything more than what I was supposed to be; he never saw me as anything more than his sister.

Placing my hands against Ryan's chest, I push him back—forcing it more when it doesn't feel like he's going to move. His eyes widen and he stumbles back a step, and I bend down, picking up some of the extra books that I still haven't gone through. It doesn't matter. I just need to get away.

"I'm sorry about the past," I say. There's no point in even lying about it. I'm many things—sick, disgusting, fucked in the head—but I'm not a liar. Never that. "If you don't want to start over, fine. I'm just here because Trinity gave me a scholarship that covered everything, and my previous university couldn't offer the same. I didn't follow you here, I swear. I ... know you don't want me like that." The last words are rocks in my throat, weighing my voice down with nothing but brokenness that I hope he doesn't hear. He's right to hate me. So very right. I should be grateful, but it's hard to be when it feels like my heart is shattering into a million pieces.

I pivot away from him, returning the books to the cart with slow, jerky movements. Like my arms aren't my own, and I'm watching someone else set them down and slide them back into place.

"It doesn't matter if you pretend that you didn't tell me you loved me—and not like a brother." His voice is deep, angry. It makes me pause. "You brought this upon yourself." I jerk upright when I feel his chest right up against my spine. All at once, a hot feeling consumes me. My face. My chest. My legs. It's everywhere—burning me alive. It's wrong. It's immoral. Yet, it's there nonetheless—the feeling that had only begun to blossom six years ago. Desire. "But I'll give you this one warning, Will." His lips graze my ear. My breath saws in and out of my lungs, rapid, untamable. "Stay away from me, or I'll fucking ruin your life." A masculine hand sweeps down my back, pushing my hair forward over my shoulder. A brief flashback enters my mind—an old memory of this exact situation. It was something—one of the many things—that he'd done that made me think ... but I was wrong. I was so very fucking wrong.

With one last touch against my back, he pushes me forward into the book cart. Several volumes drop over the other side and thud against the floor, their pages splitting open.

"Try me, Princess ... and I'll make your life a fucking nightmare," he promises, and then he's gone.

I don't even have any breath remaining to tell him, it's too late. My life already became a fucking nightmare the day he'd left.

Four

RYAN

I'M A FUCKING liar. A liar and a bastard. I snag the football flying towards me out of the air, turn it around, and throw it back. *Ruin her life? Turn it into a nightmare? What the hell was I thinking?* The answer: I'm not. I'm just fucking scared. Terrified. She's close—closer than she's been in years. Trinity is a medium-sized school. It doesn't matter if we don't have similar classes, there's going to be times when I can't avoid her.

All around me, the grunts of my fellow teammates as they run their obstacles, toss footballs, and time each other echo across the field. I finish my football tosses and jog towards the next course. She's different than I remember. I'd read each of her fucking letters right before tearing them up and dumping them back into their envelopes to be shipped back to wherever she ended up. I'd tried to get the message across.

Willow and I were done. We were nothing. We weren't friends, and we certainly couldn't be more than that. I was her twin brother, for fuck's sake. Twisted is too kind of a term for the feelings she elicits in me. Morally reprehensible can't even come close.

Maybe there really is something wrong with my brain because no matter how much time has passed, seeing her there—up close—with her eyes looking up at me, her throat bare, her t-shirt gaping open to reveal the creamy expanse of skin just above her collarbone ... It was like waving a delicious, bloody steak in front of a starving animal.

And I am starving—for her.

"Anderson!" Coach calls. I lift my head and turn towards him, following his finger as he points to the obstacle course set up. "Get a move on!"

I nod and take off. My feet slam against the perfectly packed dirt and well-groomed grass as I dodge and weave, jumping over the sets the managers have laid out for us. This is nothing, just training, and it's certainly not enough to keep my brain occupied. My mind keeps going back to *her*.

She grew up. We both did. Where I'd become a lying bastard, though, she'd grown into someone beautiful. She was on a scholarship—an academic one. Of course, she'd be the smarter one. She had always outdone me in grades.

By the time I finish the course and round back to where I'd first started at the football toss, I'm sweating and still nowhere near done thinking about Willow. She thinks I hate her, and yeah, maybe a part of me does. She'd been brave enough to say it—what I'd been thinking. That it wasn't fair. Maybe the system was wrong. Everyone always commented on how alike we looked—but I don't see it, I can't see it. Brown hair and brown eyes make up how much of the population? I don't know, but I know it has to be a lot. It's the most common hair and eye color. Doesn't mean shit about genetics.

As I pass the field, slowing my stride, I know the truth, though—all of my doubts ... they're just conjecture. It's merely wishful thinking on my part, a way to see around these depraved desires of mine.

"Dude." I glance up as Tanner jogs towards me, football in hand. "You're not paying attention at all. I've been calling your name for fucking forever. What's up with you?"

"Nothing." I hold my palm out, waiting for the football, but he frowns at me and holds it out of my reach.

"Hell nah," he says. "I ain't giving you this until you tell the truth. You've been acting weird since the first day of class."

"Give me the fucking ball, jackass." I reach for it, but Tanner laughs and dodges to the side.

"Or what?" he taunts. "Gonna kick my ass?"

I grin. "I mean..." I begin, narrowing my gaze. "If you're up for getting your ass beat, all you had to do was ask." I don't give him time to evade me this time. Before he realizes my plan, I duck under his arm and wrap my free one around his waist. Even with the extra pads and weights we've got

35

strapped to us, it's no trouble to lift his heavy ass up and body slam him to the grass.

"Fuck!" Tanner curses, dropping the ball and flipping me over until it's my back against the ground.

I laugh as he throws the first punch. It's all the encouragement I need. I bring both of my hands down against the back of his head, cupping it in my palms before settling my foot firmly on the ground and rolling us to the side. One arm slips towards the front of his head and lowers, curling around his throat until I've got the fucker locked in a chokehold.

"What was that, man?" I ask as Tanner slaps my forearm. "I'm sorry, I can't fucking understand you."

"You ... win ... asshole..." he wheezes.

Immediately, I release him.

"Anderson! Striker! No fighting on my goddamn field. If you've got time to fuck around, then you've got time to run ten more suicides!" Coach screams at us and then proceeds to blow his whistle.

Tanner flops onto the ground with a grunt. "You fucking suck, Ry," he mutters. "I just finished my fucking suicides."

That doesn't appear to matter to Coach. He doesn't give up blowing that damn screechy whistle of his until both Tanner and I are back on our feet, running the length of the football field, back and forth, our arms and legs pumping. We retrace the obstacle courses in record time, tossing our footballs and catching with little effort then returning to push weights across the field, side by side.

The rest of the team, done with their training workouts, goes off to grab waters and sit on the sidelines, watching and heckling us as Coach has one of the managers fetch a damn go-cart and drive it onto the field so he can follow after us like the lazy fuck he is.

"Don't stop, boys!" Coach yells. "You're giving me one more before you fucking drop your asses for fighting on my field."

Tanner leans his head back as he gasps for breath alongside me. "Fuck you, Coach!" he calls out.

I almost stop right there and turn to kill the bastard. "You dumb motherfucker," I shoot under my breath.

"Alrighty then!" Coach calls out, sounding amused through his speakerphone. "Then let's make it *five more* suicides for both of you bitches!"

"I'm going to fucking kill you," I growl Tanner's way.

He merely shakes his head and laughs. "You won't have the energy," he replies, and he's fucking right.

Fifteen extra suicides across the field leave my legs feeling like a trembling newborn calf. The second Coach gives us the leeway, the two of us collapse on the ground, panting and gasping for breath.

"Maybe that'll teach you a lesson not to talk back during a punishment, Striker," Coach chuckles as he passes us on his damn golf cart.

Tanner doesn't even hesitate to lift one shaking arm and flip the bird at Coach's back. I turn over, feeling the cool grass against my burning skin. It hurts to fucking breathe. "You're crazy," I grumble.

Not long after the two of us collapse, Tanner gets back on his trembling legs and ambles off. I'm half-convinced he's left me here to rot just like the rest of the team. Despite watching from the sidelines, after the tenth suicide, there'd been fewer and fewer shouts from the stands. They're probably gone—off to the showers and back to their dorms and frat houses. Lucky assholes.

Something thumps against the grass on the other side of my head, and I glance to the side, my eyes landing on a bottle of water and Tanner's cleats. "Here," he says with a grin, lifting his own and downing half of it in one go. "Thought you might need it."

I push myself up into a sitting position and reach for the bottle. I pop the cap and start swallowing, not stopping until the whole thing is empty. Even that doesn't feel like it's enough.

"So," Tanner says, "you gonna tell me what's really up with you now or not?"

I glare up at my friend and groan. "Not today," I tell him. Probably not ever. "But thanks for worrying about me."

Tanner arches a brow. "Well, fine then," he says. "Be like that—but in return, you should come out with me tonight."

My jaw practically unhinges. "You just made us both run fifteen extra suicides," I point out, "and you want to go to a bar?" I'd always known he was a psycho, but this just solidifies it.

"Hell, yeah, we just burned all those extra calories. Now, I don't have to feel guilty about pigging out on cheese fries and beer."

I eye him. "Was that your plan all along?" I ask

Tanner shrugs. "Maybe it was," he hints, tilting his head to the side. "And maybe it wasn't. Who can say?"

"You." I deadpan as I struggle to my feet. "You can fucking say."

"Yeah, guess you're right," he replies as we head off towards the locker rooms. "I could—but I'm not gonna. So, bar?"

"Yeah, fine," I mutter. "I could use a drink after this last week."

"Great!" Tanner snags my bottle and dumps both it and his into the recycling as we pass by. "Then get showered and dressed, my friend, because we are trolling the Trinity nightlife tonight. Who knows, maybe we'll get lucky. I heard there's a special tonight for chicks."

Trinity nightlife, huh? I think. Doesn't sound all that bad. Finding a bar bunny might be just the thing I need. Maybe that'll clear my mind of the one fucking girl I can't have. The one I'll never be able to have.

Five

WILLOW

"NO," I STATE. "Absolutely not."

"Come on, Will, it won't be that bad." Lana's wheedling tone is doing nothing for my complete and utter revulsion of the scene in front of me. "You said you wanted to hang out tonight," she reminds me.

"I specifically remember saying I wanted to *relax* tonight." I gesture to the bar before us, with its door propped open and the scent of smoke and cheap perfume drifting out into the night. "I don't see how this is supposed to help me relax."

Lana rolls her eyes. "Alcohol relaxes everybody, sweetheart. Come on." Despite what I thought was a vehement rejection of her proposed idea of 'relaxation,' she grabs my arm anyway and pulls me in after her.

The bar is packed—bodies lining the walls back to back. There's some guy up on a stage in the corner crooning love songs that don't really seem appropriate for the atmosphere, but then again, it's not like anyone can actually hear him. The music pouring from his mic and guitar are being drowned out by the loud voices of people trying to talk over one another. I can feel a headache coming on, but I know Lana, and I know her motto.

Try it once, and if it sucks, at least you tried and now you know for sure.

So, fine. I'll stay for one drink. I'll try not to feel so uncomfortable. Who knows, maybe with a few shots in me, I won't be uncomfortable at all.

We slam up against the bar at the back of the expansive room and Lana leans over, pushing her breasts against the countertop as she waves down the bartender. When she catches sight of the one handing out drinks, her eyes light up, and she looks down to adjust her cleavage. I can't help but snort. Guy or girl, it doesn't matter to her. Yet every time she breaks up with someone—or they break up with her—without fail, she's guaranteed to focus on the opposite sex for a while. If her last relationship was with a woman, her next will probably be with a guy and vice versa. At least she's predictable.

"Hey, handsome," she says as the bartender approaches, "can we get a few drinks?"

"Of course, ladies." He smiles my way for a brief moment but then returns his attention to Lana. "What'll it be?"

"Screwdriver and a Blue Moon?" She looks at me for confirmation, and I nod. The bartender takes Lana's card and then strolls off. "Jesus, did you see the jawline on that man?" she asks as soon as he's out of earshot.

"Yup," I say. "Sharp as hell." I scan the crowd. I'm not surprised it's so crowded since it's a Friday night, but even for a weekend, it's a little much.

"Here you are, ladies." The bartender returns and drops our drinks down, handing Lana back her card. If she can make some excuse to come back here and flirt, there's no freaking way she's gonna start a tab.

"Thanks!" Lana takes her screwdriver and I pick up my beer, and we're off again.

"I think I saw a pool table in the back," I yell over the noise of the crowd. "Do you think it'll be less crowded over there?"

"Probably!" she yells back. "They've gotta have room to shoot. Let's head over."

Squeezing through the crowd is hard work. We're halfway through the room, and Lana's already spilled her drink twice. Just as we finally reach the opening, I feel someone graze my ass. Heart racing, I turn around and scan the nearby area, but no one's paying me any attention. It must've been an accident. Shaking my head, I push the rest of the way out of the group and slide over to one of the open barstools lined up against the wall where people sit and watch the pool game.

Lana's already there, swinging her legs against the stool as she snags a straw from one of the containers sitting nearby and sticks it into her drink, taking a sip. "So," she says after a long swallow, "what's gotten up with you lately?"

I grimace and look away. "I don't know what you're talking about," I lie.

The feeling of her intense gaze, however, burns into the side of my face. "Sure, you don't," she says sardonically. "It wouldn't happen to have anything to do with the fact that you just transferred to the same university your *brother* goes to—a brother, I might add, that you never mentioned you had. I thought we were better friends than that."

I tip my head back and take a good long gulp of my beer. "We haven't seen each other in six years," I confess. "There wasn't really much to tell. We were both in foster care and..." Do I tell her? My fingers dig into the sides of my beer bottle as indecision wracks me.

"And?" she prompts. "Did he go to a different home? You got adopted and he didn't?"

"He ... beat up one of our foster parents' kids and got sent to juvie," I admit. "I didn't get adopted by the McRaes until later. He probably doesn't even know about them."

Her eyes widen. "I can't believe social services would've kept you guys separated even if he was in juvie. You never called or—"

"He hates me," I blurt out, cutting her off. "I did something ... awful. He wouldn't answer my calls. I never got the chance to tell him about them—before or ... after."

Silence stretches between us, pulled taut on a string. It isn't until one of the pool players shoots to break the rack and the balls make a particularly loud cracking sound, that I jump and come back to myself. Lana reaches over and touches my thigh just below the cut of my shorts. "It's going to be okay, Will," she assures me with a smile. "They wouldn't want you to be sad about the wreck. They'd want you to move on with your life."

"Yeah..." The mouth of the beer bottle touches my lips, and I tip my head back again. I really don't want to talk about my adoptive parents. They had been such good people. Older. Kind. They'd even tried to find my birth parents. I wonder if I should've mentioned that to Ryan before promising to stay away from him.

"Can you do me a favor, Lana?" I ask.

"Sure, what's up?" She takes another sip of her drink.

"Can you not mention to anyone that I'm related to Ryan?" I wince even as the words come out.

Her head turns back towards me. "I mean … I don't have to tell people, but you know I'm gonna ask why?"

I refuse to meet her gaze as I focus on the game in front of us. A blond-haired guy circles the pool table and then bends over, lining up his shot. "It's … complicated," I admit. "Like I said, I did something, and now he hates me. I don't want to cause any drama. I heard that he's a football player, and I know what you've told me about the Trinity team—"

She nods. "Yeah, they're treated like fucking gods here." She scoffs. "I bet they're not half as good in bed as most of them claim to be."

"Yeah, and I'm sure he's probably got a lot of groupies or whatever." Knowing how he'd been in high school, it wouldn't shock me. He'd never been short on female companionship. Watching that day in and day out had been the worst. I'd never felt as jealous and possessive of him as I did in the months leading up to telling him my true feelings. "I just want to keep a low profile," I say on a sigh.

"Yeah, okay." Lana continues eyeing me. "I can do that. No problem."

"Thanks." As we sit there—with the music that doesn't quite fit the place and the loud conversations along with the cracking of balls on the pool table—I start to drift. The thoughts I always kept inside, usually buried after what happened six years ago, come spiraling back.

What if I'd just kept my mouth shut? What if I'd just smiled and pretended like I didn't hate it when girls touched him? What if? What if? What if? Would we be in the same place? Would he have guessed eventually? Could I have been able to take being just his sister and his friend ... or is it better now that the truth is out and neither of us is pretending?

As if she senses my declining mood, Lana launches into an amusing rant about her latest psychology class experiment. I drain my beer and watch the pool game in front of me as I listen to her rage about her stuck-up professor, who's apparently threatened by other females in the department. She could be right, or she could be projecting—I wouldn't know, though, I'm not the psychology student; she is.

"Ugh." The scratchy sound of Lana trying to slurp up the last of her drink hits my ears, and she shakes the glass slightly. "I'm still thirsty." She turns to me and holds up one finger. "One more?" she asks beseechingly.

I laugh and take her glass. "Yeah, sure," I agree, but when she reaches for her card, I push her hand down. "You paid last time, I got this one."

"Shit, girl. You better be careful, or I'll think you're expecting me to put out tonight."

My shoulders tremble as I repress another laugh, shaking my head, as I snag my now empty beer and then head off back towards the bar. She's obviously forgotten all about the hottie bartender. She's got the memory of a goldfish.

I squeeze back through the room and head for the bar, but unlike Lana, I don't seem to be able to grab his attention right away. After several minutes of waiting on the side, I finally spot an open seat at the actual bar top, and I jump on it.

"Hey, sorry, that's—oh hello there." I turn my head at the sound of a masculine voice next to me. I don't recognize the man, but he seems to be familiar with me as he smiles down at me. *A classmate?* I think. He holds out a hand. "I'm Tanner." Guess, I don't know him.

"Willow." I take his hand.

"It's lovely to meet you, *Willow*." The way he

says my name sounds off. Carefully, I pull my hand back from his and give him a wan smile. "Oh." He grimaces. "I wasn't trying to be creepy or anything, I swear."

Yeah, buddy, keep telling yourself that. I hope the bartender hurries up. Lana is way better at dealing with pushy guys.

"It's just," he continues, "you remind me of this girl my friend has a crush on."

"Your friend?" I arch a brow, but before this Tanner guy can respond, the bartender comes over.

"Hey, can I get another beer and another screwdriver?" I ask, holding up two fingers and handing him the card between them.

"Sure thing."

"Yeah," Tanner continues, his smile brightening suddenly. He glances behind him and then hops off the stool he was previously occupying. *Is he leaving? Huh. Guess he's not actually hitting on me like I thought.* "In fact, I think you're totally his type. Too bad he's kind of a dick and absolutely hates to admit anything."

"Sounds like a real prize..." I offer, confused. *Is he trying to set me up with his friend or warn me away?*

"Oh, he's a total douche," Tanner says with a nod, "but he's my best friend. What can you do?"

That, at least, is something I can relate to. Lana is crazy as hell, but she's loyal too. The bartender returns with my drinks and card, and I thank him. "Well, it was nice meeting you, Tanner," I say as I slide back off of the stool and start to back away.

"You too, Willow." Tanner lifts a hand and then turns and disappears into the crowd as well. What a weird guy.

Six

RYAN

THE GIRL IN my arms is moaning as I shove three fingers into her pussy, curling them up as she shudders through an orgasm. Her inner walls are squeezing against my hand as she pants and releases another loud moan. Her hair smells like some sort of cheap perfume, and it makes my nose itch. It's a relief when she pulls back and grins at me as I remove my fingers. She lifts my hand and sucks two of the fingers into her mouth, licking up her own essence before finishing on the third one. I watch her movements and unnecessary moans with a mixture of dissatisfaction and irritation. I should've turned her down when she first approached, but we're already here.

Without hesitation, the second my fingers pop out of her mouth, I cup the back of her skull and push her down. She flashes me a smile and slips down, her knees hitting the tiled floor as outside the door, the bar noise rages on. At least with my dick in her mouth, she'll shut up with all of that moaning of hers.

Warm, wet lips wrap around my cock and suck it down. My head slumps back against the bathroom wall. When Tanner said we might get lucky, I hadn't really thought it'd be this easy. Then again, with how sore my muscles are, maybe it's better just to take the blowjob and then bounce.

"Do you like this?" the girl—Sarah or Sally or something like that—asks.

"Yeah, baby," I lie, cupping the back of her skull and directing her lips back to my dick. "Just keep doing what you're doing." It's not even fully hard, but she doesn't seem to think that's a problem.

She smiles and reaffixes her mouth over my head, sucking me down as she hollows out her cheeks. For a cock sucker, she's pretty experienced. That much is obvious. She doesn't hesitate to grip the base of my dick and stroke me as she licks and sucks over my shaft. Her free hand moves beneath, cupping and squeezing my balls. Perhaps to someone else, it'd feel like passion, but to me, it all feels methodical—like she's done this a hundred times before. At least, it makes me feel better about using her to get some stress relief. The hard suicides Coach had made Tanner and I run might've made my physical muscles lax and loose, but it hadn't done shit for my mind.

"Are you sure you're enjoying this?" Sarah-Sally asks, popping off my dick. She looks up at me with a furrowed brow.

"Yes." I cup her head again with both hands this

time. "Just fucking suck it."

Her mouth opens, and I don't give her time to say anything else. I shove the head of my cock between her full lips and push until I feel the scrape of her tongue on the underside. All it takes is the image of Willow in my head to make my cock spring fully to life. As soon as I do, the girl below me lets out another moan that rumbles around my shaft.

She slurps and slobbers over it like a prized dick-sucking champion. I close my eyes and imagine that it's not this chick on her knees before me, but someone completely different. Someone with eyes wide and so full of innocence. I wonder if she ever dated after I was taken away. The very thought makes me squeeze the head between my hands and pound my dick into the back of her throat. No, I don't like that. I don't like that at fucking all.

Sarah-Sally chokes on my cock as I thrust into her throat. I don't pay her any attention. In my mind, it's Willow I'm punishing. It makes me a fucking hypocrite, for sure, but I don't really give a fuck. I squeeze the sides of the chick's head—picturing Willow's mouth flowered open for me, her tongue jutting out waiting for my cum. It's wrong … so fucking wrong, but it turns me on and before I realize it, I jerk out of the warm mouth and erupt across the girl's face.

Panting, I sag back against the wall and lift a hand to wipe the sweat from my brow. "Didn't know you would be so rough," Sarah-Sally says with a grin as she gets up and reaches across me for the paper towel dispenser. "If you'd like, we can take this back to my place."

"Yeah, no thanks." I tuck myself back into my waistband, buckle up, and push her to the side, ignoring the way her jaw drops at my rudeness. "It was fine. No need for a repeat performance, sweetheart."

"Asshole!" she shouts as I unlock the door and stride out. For how packed the bar is, I'm actually shocked there isn't anyone out in the back hall waiting to use the bathroom. The second I get back to the main hub of the building, however, the crush returns, and I have to push through to get to the counter. Halfway there, I see a familiar head of hair pop up above the rest.

Tanner catches my attention, lifts his arm, and points to the side. I follow his gesture, nod, and the two of us push through everyone else—though I suppose it's not as hard for us as it is for others. I'm at least half a head taller than the majority of the guys here and well over a foot over the chicks. By the time we reach the edge of the crowd and Tanner has met back up with me, two beers in his hands, I'm sweating more than I was when I was in the bathroom.

He hands me my beer before taking a swig. "Saw something cute while you were preoccupied," he says with a grin.

"Yeah?" I ask, tipping my own beer back. "You

gonna find a girl to go home with?"

"Maybe. I have a feeling you'd be a little put out by it, though."

I roll my eyes. "Do whatever," I snap. "I don't care who you stick your dick into."

He points at me. "I'll remember you said that, man."

"Why'd you give up our spots at the bar, anyway?" I ask, changing the subject. "I don't want to stand around if we gotta be here. I already got mine, so go find yours, and then I can take off."

Tanner arches a brow. "You sure you got yours?" he asks. "You seem even crabbier than when you went off with Serena."

Her name was Serena? Damn. Probably a good thing I didn't try to guess.

I shrug. "She was fine. Got the job done, but I'd rather go back to the apartment and chill. I'm just here to hook you up now."

"Awww, what a friend," Tanner replies with a sly smirk. "In that case, I think we should head over to the pool table. I saw a few hotties that way."

"Fine, whatever you say. Let's go."

The reason for Tanner's sudden decision becomes all too clear the second I spot her across the pool table. She's with the same friend from before, a thicker girl with dark hair and almond-shaped eyes. She laughs at something the other girl says, her head going back, revealing the long expanse of her throat. A beautiful throat that would look so fucking good in my hands as I fucked into her tight, sweet pussy. Just like that, my cock is rock fucking hard.

"What the fuck?" I snap to Tanner. "Did you plan this?"

Tanner shakes his head. "No, but it can't be a coincidence, can it?" he asks. "Maybe you two were meant to meet. It's obvious you think something of her."

"You don't know what the fuck you're talking about," I say, trying to inject some form of disgust into my tone.

His head tilts to the side and his gaze becomes suddenly serious. "Are you for real?" he asks. "You really don't like her? Did I read you wrong?"

"It doesn't matter if I like her or not," I growl. "I'm not—" I don't get to finish my sentence because a split second later, a loud squeal erupts.

"Oh, my gosh! Tanner Striker? Ryan Anderson?" Tanner and I turn towards the excited female voice of a very petite blonde that rushes up to us. "I'm Harley, from the school paper. How awesome that I ran into the two of you. I was actually hoping you guys would be interested in being interviewed for the sports section next week."

Tanner leans down. "What's the interview about?" he asks with a smile, eyeing the chick's cleavage.

I leave him to answer her questions and look back to where Willow sits on a stool against the far wall, but there's a new presence focused on her. Cordin Calhoun. A scowl overtakes me. That frat boy fucker has no business hanging around her. Instant rage slides through my veins when his eyes drop down and stare blatantly at the slight dip in Willow's shirt.

My fingers clench around my beer and the conversation between Harley and Tanner fades into the background, as an idea forms in my mind. It's mean. It's cruel. But it will no doubt get that fucker as far from my girl as possible—no, not my girl. Just Willow. He doesn't deserve her, and if she finds out I'm the one who set this up, maybe she'll finally get the hint. Maybe she'll stop being so sympathetic and truly hate me the way she should.

I turn and leave Tanner with the newspaper chick and seek out the first waitress I can find. There's a fifty in my pocket with her name on it. All she needs to do for me is one tiny favor.

Seven

WILLOW

"YOU SAID YOUR name was Willow?" The guy in front of me grins down, his attention falling straight to my cleavage. There's no possible way for me to adjust my shirt now without making it completely obvious that I'm trying to cover myself. I'm not sure why I don't want him to know that I can see the way he's staring at me—like I'm a slab of meat and he's a starving animal—but I don't. I wish I was too stupid to get it or maybe even too oblivious, but I'm not. I see him, and I'm grossed out.

"Yeah." I turn away slightly, but the asshole just follows and so do his fucking eyes. I sigh. "I'm gonna go to the bar real quick," I say, looking towards where Lana's sitting a few feet away, already surrounded by a bevy of guys. I don't know what happened, but after the last game on the pool table, they'd descended on us.

Lana waves me away. "I'm good," she calls out, lifting her still full drink. My beer isn't even half empty; I'm just looking for an excuse to get away from the creeper currently glued to my side.

"I'll come too," he says.

The groan that ricochets through my head almost slips out of my mouth—almost. I don't wait for him to let his friends know; I just start walking. Halfway across the room, however, my head lifts and I catch sight of someone unexpected.

My whole body tightens. My heartbeat doubles. Sweat pops up along my spine.

Ryan.

His cool gaze is on me, but unlike the guy trailing behind me—no doubt staring at my ass—he's not looking at me like he wants to devour me. No. He's looking at me like he'd like to wring my neck. Angry, he's fucking angry. A deep scowl lines his lips and there's a fire behind the look in his eyes.

Heat attacks my face. The warmth burns across my cheeks and down my neck. I suck in a breath and pause, wavering between continuing on to the bar where he's currently sitting or going back just to avoid him because it is, after all, what I'd promised to do. Then again, I'd also promised to pretend like I didn't know him and if I didn't know him, I wouldn't be standing here arguing with myself about going to the bar.

Come on, Will, an internal voice urges. *Just fucking go. If you turn around now, he'll know you're intimidated.*

But I am *intimidated by him,* I think.

"Hey," the guy behind me taps me on the

shoulder, "what's the hold up?"

Just as I turn to tell him I'm heading back, a waitress saunters by, hand held high with a tray balanced on it as she tries to work her way through the crowd. I see it a split second before it happens, she moves, her hips swaying, someone bumps into her, and she stumbles. Fuck. The glass she had balanced on her tray tumbles down.

Cold liquid splashes down over the top of my head and then down my shirt and chest. I scream and jump away immediately, slamming into the guy at my back, but it's too late. My shirt's soaked and ... see-through. I cross my arms over my chest as the waitress quickly adjusts and snatches her now useless tray down from where she was holding it over my head.

"Oh my gosh!" she says, reaching for me as I feel two firm hands on my shoulders. "I'm so sorry."

"It's ..." I'm halfway through telling her it's okay when I feel two sets of gazes on my skin. No, it's not just two sets of eyes. It's multiple. People are staring at me. Some are whispering behind their hands while others are chuckling at my predicament. My heated skin burns hotter. My throat closes up. I pull away from the guy behind me and shake my head as the waitress tries to apologize. "It's okay," I say. "It was an accident."

It was an accident, right? There's no way it hadn't been. My eyes trail over to where Ryan is sitting, watching the scene. His scowl has now deepened, but his eyes are no longer on me. They're trained on something behind me. I refocus on the waitress again as she reaches down and picks up the glass—hard plastic, at least, so that explains why I hadn't heard it shatter on the ground.

"Please, I'm so sorry, let me—" she tries to say, only to be cut off, as the guy at my back puts another hand on my shoulder and turns me towards him.

"What the fuck were you thinking," he growls at the waitress. "You could've hurt her."

"I'm fine!" I insist, but he doesn't listen to me. Why? I wonder. It's not like I'm his date. What does he think he's going to gain by getting upset like this?

"You did this on purpose," he accuses, ignoring me. "And you got it all over me too, bitch. Do you know what brand this is?"

This is so fucking humiliating. I can feel the crowd around us getting antsy. Like social hyenas, they smell blood and are drawn towards it. I want to go. I want to get out.

"I said sorry," the waitress replies. "I promise, it was an accident—"

"Well—"

"Stop!" I snap, cutting off the guy as I back away, keeping my arms placed firmly over my chest. Air washes across the back of my neck, making me shiver. Shit. I can feel my nipples pebbling beneath my shirt. It was so hot. *Why does it feel cold now? Because everyone is backing away from us?* I wonder. "She didn't do it on purpose," I tell the guy. "It was an accident and if you were that concerned about what brand your shirt is, maybe don't wear something that expensive to a bar."

The guy's eyes widen and then he frowns at me. "The hell is your problem?" he demands. "I'm defending—"

"I don't think she fucking asked you to defend her, asshole." Lana's voice reaches my ears a second before she appears out of the crowd, a scowl on her face. She moves between the guy and me, blocking his path. "But she's right. If you've got such a problem with getting a little wet, then maybe you should go dry off. We're leaving."

Relief floods me as Lana turns and strips off the light jacket she'd worn in tonight, putting it over my shoulders. "Come on," she mutters as she pushes through the crowd and gently urges me forward. Maybe it's her charisma. Maybe it's her expression. I don't know, but whatever the case, when Lana moves, people get out of her way.

We're almost to the front door, and I know my face is beet red, but when we pass Ryan, my eyes can't help but look up and meet his. There's no warmth there. No sympathy. No pity. Just emptiness and disgust. I turn my eyes away and stare down at the floor. I don't look up again until Lana and I are outside, but it appears our bad night has taken a turn for the worse yet again.

"Shit," Lana hisses when we see that while we've been sequestered in the bar, it started raining, and not just a little either. It's a heavy downpour.

"Wait here," she says, "I'll go grab the car."

"It's fine," I tell her. "I'm already wet."

Lana shakes her head. "No. Don't worry about it. I'll be right back." She doesn't give me another opportunity to protest; she takes off running towards the back of the parking lot.

The door behind me opens, and I stiffen. "I warned you, didn't I?" Ryan's voice is a low rumble. The sound of it shoots straight to my chest. I pivot to face him, clutching Lana's jacket tighter to me.

"W-what?"

"I warned you," he repeats.

I blink up at him. "Did …" I don't want to ask, but I can't help the question stirring in me. "Did you do this?" I ask. Did he … no, there's no way he planned this. Right?

Ryan doesn't answer, though. He stands there, that same cruel glint in his expression, and slowly scans the length of me. When his eyes land on my chest, I look away and hunch my shoulders inward. When he doesn't say anything for several long seconds, I glance back at him.

His teeth are gritted, and his hands are balled into fists at his sides. When my gaze lands on him once more, it seems to push him to move. He stalks forward, and I stumble back, stopping at the edge of the overhang when I feel the wash of rain mist down my back. Ryan hovers over me like a monster in the night in the dim lighting of the single lamppost halfway down the rows of cars, as well as the neon sign above the umbrella overhang the only sources of light in the nearby area.

"I fucking warned you, Willow," he growls. "I told you to stay away from me."

"I-I didn't come here looking for you," I reply.

"Doesn't matter." He leans even closer, and the scent of his cologne reaches my nostrils. Fuck ... he smells good. Tears burn at the backs of my eyes. *Why?* I wonder. *Why is it like this? Why is he like this? Why am I for that matter?*

"You poison everything you touch, Will," he says. "Your wants and desires are wrong."

A single tear escapes and falls down my cheek. I know. Doesn't he understand that? I fucking know. "I wouldn't have pushed you," I whisper back, my voice croaking. "I just thought ..." *What had I thought? That he'd understand?* No. No one could understand me, but of all the people in the world, I'd wanted him to.

Headlights flash against the front of the building, and Ryan takes a step back. "You thought wrong," he replies, and then he turns and walks back into the bar, leaving me feeling the rot of humiliation and agonizing rejection.

I WANT TO hate Ryan, and I even think about forcing myself to as Lana drives the two of us back to campus. Thankfully, she leaves the radio off. I don't think listening to music right now would do anything but give me a headache. That, however, leaves us in awkward silence. At least, it does until we reach the front of my dorm.

Lana pulls into a parking spot and shuts off the car before turning to me. "Are you okay?"

It's on the tip of my tongue to lie, tell her I'm fine, get out, and go inside. Once I'm alone, it'll be easy to let go. To cry. To break down. But this is Lana. She's my best friend and she knows me better than anyone. She's seen me at my worst—three years ago when we'd first met to be exact. When I'd lost my adoptive parents.

"Willow?" She turns to me. "Did your—did Ryan say something to you?"

I inhale a shaky breath and press two hands over my face. "Yes," I admit through my fingers. "And no, I'm not alright."

When the tears come, they overwhelm me. They streak down my face and soak my palms. Seconds later, Lana's arms encircle me, and in the tiny space of her front seat, she holds me while I fall apart.

There's just something about Lana that can calm a person even when they feel like they're shattering into a million pieces. I don't know why she'd thought to approach me after the McRaes' funeral. She'd been no one to them, just the daughter of one of their friends. She'd arrived with her mom, seen me afterwards, and decided right then and there that we were going to be friends. She'd been honest and sunny, and so warm when all I'd felt was alone. I needed her then like I need her now.

She lets me cry and sob. When it feels like I can't shed one more tear and I'm done, she rubs my back. Finally, I feel like I can breathe again. "I love him …" I say.

"Who?" she asks.

I squeeze my eyes shut and pray like hell I'm not making a fucking mistake. "My brother," I admit. Her hand stills over my back.

"Ryan?" she clarifies. "Was he like your foster brother then? I thought you said he was your—"

"Twin," I finish for her. "Yeah. He's my twin and I told him I loved him six years ago." The seatbelt I never took off digs into my stomach; I sit up and reach down to unbuckle it.

"Will … that's—"

"I know." Shame fills me. Disgust fills me. "I know." The burn of her stare slices into the side of my face. I don't turn to look at her. I don't want to see what kind of expression she's wearing.

"Did you …" She drifts off as if she doesn't want to say it, but it doesn't take a genius to figure out what she's asking.

"No." I shake my head. "We've never done anything. As soon as I confessed my feelings, he went away. He did it *because* I confessed. Him going to juvie—it was my fault."

Lana sighs. "That's seriously some fucked up shit, girl," she says. Shockingly enough, though, there's no disgust in her voice.

I sneak a look at her. "That's all you have to say?" I ask.

She leans back into her seat and shrugs. "What do you expect me to say?"

"That I'm disgusting," I tell her. "That there must be something wrong with me."

Lana's lips press firmly together and twist from one side to another. It's what she does when she's thinking. "Well, sorry to disappoint, but I think it's natural for you to latch onto someone who feels safe. You didn't actually get adopted until you were almost aged out of the system, Will. How many foster homes did you go through? Six? Seven? More?" She reaches forward and flicks the keys dangling from the ignition. Though the car's off, they hang there, jingling back and forth beneath her fingers. "What you felt for him probably wasn't the romantic love you think it is. It's okay to care about your brother. It's okay to love him, but I think you were just confused."

There it is. Lana's logic. It makes sense and coming from anyone else it might sound condescending, but I know she doesn't mean for it to be. The truth is, I don't agree. I know that my love for Ryan is not normal. It's the ultimate taboo. Lana's words make it clear, though, that it doesn't matter what I think. No one would ever believe me. She's a friend, my best one at that, but even she doesn't get it. An ache blossoms inside my chest.

"Yeah," I say. "You're probably right." My words taste like sand.

"What concerns me, though," Lana continues, "is that it seems like he still hates you. I know you said it was your fault he went to juvie, but honestly, he made his own choices. You didn't force him to do what he did to get sent there. You were just mistaken. It's normal, especially for people who were in your situation, to cling to someone who was a constant for them." She smiles at me and pulls her keys from the ignition. "This isn't a big deal," she assures me.

I feel ice coat my spine.

She clamps a hand on my shoulder. "He'll get over it eventually, and he'll realize that you were just a young girl who mistook familial love for romantic love. Right now, you should just try to move on with your life. If he acts like a jerk, don't pay him any attention. Maybe, he'll see that you're not that young girl anymore. You've grown up, and you know that you can't love him—not like that."

I nod, but she doesn't release me. I have to say something, I realize. She's waiting for a verbal response. I lower my eyes and squeeze my hands into fists in my lap, and for the first time in my life, I lie to my best friend. "You're right," I say. "Ryan's my twin, and I don't love him—not like that. I never have. It's just … familial love. Like you said."

"Good." She squeezes me and then lets go. "Now, come on, it looks like the rain has let up a bit." She pops the door open and steps out.

In my heart, a fissure forms. My ribcage

tightens, squeezing until I feel like I might burst. *Familial love,* I think. I always wondered if that was truly what I felt. Maybe that's what I'd told Lana. Maybe that's what I sometimes try to tell myself, but I know the truth deep down—in this corrupted organ of mine.

Ryan was right. I poison everything I touch.

EIGHT

RYAN

I THOUGHT I'D feel relieved after signing Willow out of my life. I thought I'd feel some sort of accomplishment for paying that chick to dump something on her, embarrass her, and make her fucking leave that stupid bar. Although it had taken care of one initial problem—the guy who'd been hitting on her and staring at her tits—in the weeks following, it's done nothing but make her an even bigger issue.

Tapping my fingers against my thigh as students walk into the classroom and slowly begin to fill up the seats, I can't stop considering the things I've learned about Willow since that first weekend. Six years changes a person. The Willow I'd known in high school had been a shy creature. Always sticking to me. She'd had a few friends here and there, but considering how many times we'd moved foster homes, they never lasted.

But here, at Trinity, she doesn't seem to have any problems making friends. She's not as loud and obnoxious as some girls. She's quieter, but no less present. How do I fucking know? Because Tanner has made it his fucking mission in life to update me on Willow's actions on campus. The bastard knows it irritates me, but in a way, I'm grateful.

Willow has friends—like that chick from the bar, Lana Coleman, or whatever the hell her name is. She has a life ... just like I'd always wanted her to have after I left. The only issue is me. There was a reason I never went back to her, why I never answered her letters or calls. Because when it comes to her, I'm weak. And when it comes to me, I know she is too.

No matter what I do to make her hate me, I wonder if hate is even an emotion she understands.

The chair next to me scrapes against the floor as it's drawn back, and Tanner takes his seat. "What's up, man?" he says, setting his giant-ass water bottle down right on top of my fucking notebook.

"Nothing," I say. "Just dreading this fucking test."

He eyes me like he knows better, and fuck him, he probably does. The door opens and his attention slides away. "Well, well, well, look who's here."

I already know without looking. I'd recognize Willow's best friend anywhere by now, and I'm already well aware of who she is now that she's auditing this class.

Tanner raises his hand and waves down to her. "Hey, Lana!" he shouts.

Her head tips up, and she lifts her hand in greeting. I wait for the inevitable. She lowers her arm almost at the same time as Tanner, but instead of moving towards her seat, she turns her attention to me for a brief moment. She eyes me with a narrowed look and pinched lips. Yup. She definitely doesn't fucking like me. I don't blame her, but it makes me wonder what—or rather how much—Willow told her.

Lana turns away and continues towards her seat. Tanner releases a slow whistle. "Man," he chuckles lightly. "If looks could kill…"

Yeah, I know. If looks could kill, then I'd be a dead man.

Thankfully, Tanner doesn't get an opportunity to say anything else because in the next moment, the instructor arrives and starts passing out exam papers. As I wait for my test to arrive on my desk, my mind wanders back to what happened at the bar. It had been stupid and petty of me to pay that waitress to embarrass the shit out of Willow, something a true asshole would've done. What's worse, she knows. I might not have answered her, but my lack of a response was probably proof enough. I was the one who humiliated her.

I close my eyes as I think about how she'd looked, those big brown eyes of hers staring up at me as she'd tried to pull her friend's jacket closer to her. She'd been dripping with whatever liquid the waitress had used. There'd been no added color or smell, so maybe it'd just been water. Whatever it was, it had thoroughly drenched her shirt. My throat closes from the image of that water sliding down her throat and into the neckline of her shirt.

Had she even been wearing a fucking bra? I could have sworn I'd seen her nipples. They'd been so fucking hard and perky beneath the fabric of her shirt. Were they light pink or rose-colored? Small? Bigger? It didn't matter. I bet they'd be fucking delicious ... just like the rest of her.

"Ryan—*shit*," Tanner's hissed comment brings me back to reality. He nudges me and my eyes open and I realize the problem.

I'm fucking hard in the middle of a test, thinking about ... Willow?

I look up as a paper lands on my desk, and I nearly jump out of my seat. What the fuck is she doing here? But here she is, standing there in a pleated green skirt and white button-up, looking like a Catholic school boy's wet dream.

"What—" I start to ask, but then the professor says something and Willow takes one look at me and hurries up, passing out the rest of the papers before she rushes back down the aisle towards the front of the classroom.

Is she his TA? No. That's not possible, not unless Professor Roderickson has gotten a new one. But can she be a TA if she's working in the library? What the fuck is going on?

I look to Tanner for some explanation, but he's staring at me like I'm fucking crazy. "What is wrong with you?" he mutters, jerking his gaze down meaningfully towards my lap.

God. Fucking. Damn it.

The test seems to take forever. I studied, but it's impossible to focus with *her* in the room. The second the last question is answered, I grab my bag and storm down the aisle, slamming the paper down on the professor's set up in the front and head for the hallway.

Minutes later, the door opens again and Tanner rushes out just like I expected he would. The second he sees me, he pauses and sighs. "I thought you'd leave without me," he admits, rubbing a hand down the back of his skull.

"We've got practice," I say. "I just didn't want to be in that fucking room."

"Yeah, I know." He heads towards me and the two of us move for the staircase. "You were surprised to see her."

I don't have to look at him to know he's grinning like a cat. I reach out and punch his shoulder. "Shut. The fuck. Up."

Tanner laughs. "I can't believe you got a boner in class," he snickers. "Wait 'til the guys—"

I drop my foot out in front of his, cutting him off as he trips right over it. The smack of his palm hitting the wall next to us, as he stops his downward momentum, resounds down the hallway. "Hmmm. Maybe you should watch where you're walking, *man*," I suggest coolly.

Tanner shakes his head. "Touchy, touchy," he replies. We hit the staircase and descend to the first floor. "Oh, hey are you going to Bowser's party on Friday?" he asks.

I scowl. "No," I say immediately. "I don't do frat parties."

"Liar," Tanner says. "You've gone to a few."

Yeah, but that was before Willow went to Trinity, before I could run into her anywhere and everywhere. "I'm not going," I snap. "Let it go."

Tanner arches his arms back, crossing and interlacing his fingers behind his neck as he walks. "Fine, fine," he agrees with a sigh. "Do you mind if I ask your girl to go?"

"Fuck off."

He laughs again. "I'm kidding, man, geez, you need to lighten up." He drops his arms and then reaches over to clap me on the back. "Or you just need to get laid. I wasn't planning to ask your precious little Willow."

She isn't my precious little anything, I think. *Not anymore.* But I don't say anything. I just keep walking.

"I was planning to ask her hot friend, though," Tanner continues. "You don't mind if I do that, do you?"

I close my eyes and huff out a breath before reopening them. "Do whatever you want."

"Funny—you only say that when it has nothing to do with the other girl."

"Tanner..." Clouds roll overhead. In the distance, thunder rumbles. I stop walking and wait for Tanner to as well. It takes him a few seconds to realize I'm no longer beside him, but when he does, he pauses and looks back.

"What's wrong?" he asks, frowning.

"Can you drop the Willow thing?" I ask. "Please. I don't want to talk about her. I don't want to be around her. I just want to stay the hell away from her."

At first, he doesn't respond, and then he tilts his head to the side and speaks. "Why?" he asks.

I scowl. "What?"

"Why do you hate her so much?" he asks.

"I don't hate her."

"Then why do you fucking act like it?"

Isn't that the million-dollar question? I suck in another breath and release it. "I have to," I admit. "I can't say more than that. I can't give you a reason—not right now—but it would … it would be best if she were the one who hated me."

Tanner arches a brow and looks to the side.

"What?" I demand. "What's with that look?"

He reaches up and scratches the side of his jaw. "You're not going to like this but uh..." I frown as Tanner's eyes seem to bounce everywhere but towards me. "I've kinda been hanging out with Lana outside of class, and you know she's friends with Willow, so..."

Had Willow told him? No. He would've said something if he knew.

"So?" I stare at him, waiting.

"I've gotten to know her over the last few weeks, and uh, I don't know, man, that girl doesn't seem like the type to hate anyone. I don't really get why you're being such an ass to her to try and get her to hate you, but maybe you should just drop it. Ignore her, fine. Willow's not the hateful type, though."

"You barely fucking know her," I snarl. "How the hell do you know what *type* she is?"

Tanner shrugs and finally looks back to me, dropping his arms to his sides as he does. "I just have a sense for these things," he replies. "I've got the sense for a lot of things, Ry. Maybe you should remember that." He strides forward and stops just at my side, reaching across my chest and clamping a hand down on my shoulder. Hard. "I'm gonna head back to my dorm before practice," he says. "I forgot something. Don't wait up."

As his hand slips off my shoulder, I turn and watch him stride off. He doesn't look back. Not even once. As he disappears around the side of a building, a drop of rain splashes down on my cheek and then another and another, until it's pouring rain. I'm soaked through to the bone just standing in the middle of the walkway, looking and feeling like a complete and utter prick and idiot.

What the hell is wrong with me?

Nine

WILLOW

"COME ON, YOU'LL have fun," Lana insists.

"You said that last time," I remind her as I flip through the pages of the book in front of me, searching for—there it is! I quickly write down the answer to the question in my notes and then start scanning the next page for more important details that might be on the test.

"That was a bar, but this is a house party," she replies. "And I hear a certain someone won't be attending said party. So, you can feel free to drink and laugh and dance to your heart's content."

"Why is it that every time you try to convince me to 'have fun,' it's at some dumb party?" I ask.

Lana groans. "They're not dumb, and I'm just trying to get your mind off of you know who."

"Who is he? Voldemort?" I roll my eyes. "You can say his name, Lana. And I told you, I'm over it. You were right—"

"Of course, I was," Lana says, cutting me off as she flips her hair back over one shoulder.

I close my book. "Why do you want to go to this party so bad?" I ask, deciding that changing the subject is the best course of action.

Lana rolls over onto her back on the bed across from me and blows out a breath. "Because Tanner asked me to go, and I ... really like him. He's funny. He's smart. He's jacked as fuck—I went to the gym with him last week, and he took his shirt off—he totally did it on purpose too. I swear, I thought I was going to pass out from dehydration. That's how much I was drooling."

"So, you want to go so you can jump in the jock's pants." I deadpan.

She grins at me and lifts one hand, pinching her thumb and forefinger precariously close together. "Maybe just a little bit."

I slam my book down on my desk. "Denied."

Lana immediately pops into a sitting position and turns towards me, clasping her hands together. "Pleeeassseeeeeee," she begs.

"No."

"Please. Please. Please. Please."

"Lana—"

"Please. Please. Please. Please. Please. Please. Please. Please."

"Lan—"

"*Pleeeeeeaaaaassee,*I'llneveraskforanythingelseeveragainjustthisonceIneedawingwomanandyou—"

"Oh my god!" I shout. "Fine!"

She squeals and jumps off the bed, launching

herself across the room and straight into my arms. "You're the best friend in the entire world. I love you so much!"

"Yeah, yeah."

Almost as quickly as I give in, Lana removes herself from my lap. "I gotta get ready," she says, looking down at me. "You too."

I follow her gaze and double-check that there aren't any holes in the t-shirt I'm wearing before arching a brow up at her. "What's wrong with what I'm wearing?"

She sighs. "It's a party," she repeats. "You should dress up a little."

I shake my head. "Just be happy I'm going," I reply. "A t-shirt and jeans is fine."

She shrugs. "Okay, fine, have it your way." She reaches for her backpack and lifts it up, hefting it over her shoulder as she heads for the door. "I'm gonna skip down to my room and get dressed. I'll be back in an hour or so, and we can head out."

I wave her off and reopen my book. I'm halfway through the remainder of my homework when there's a knock on my door. I check the time on my cell and realize more than an hour has passed, so it's no surprise when the knob turns and Lana walks in looking like she's ready to strut down the runway. How she can go from tomboy to club queen is a mystery to me, but it seems to work for her.

"Ready?" she asks, propping her hip on the doorway and crossing her arms.

"Sure, give me a sec." I dump my homework

stuff on my desk and reach inside for a brush. I run it through my hair twice and rush over to my dresser to touch up my eyeliner before grabbing my wallet and phone and sliding them into my back pockets. "Alrighty, good to go."

She winks my way and then strides back out into the hall. "Let's go then," she says. "Tanner's waiting downstairs."

I nearly falter. "Tanner?" I repeat.

Lana pauses at the top of the staircase and looks back. "Yeah, he's picking us up. Didn't I mention that?" No, she hadn't, but she doesn't wait for an answer as she heads down to the first floor. For some reason, I have the distinct impression that she hadn't mentioned it on purpose.

There's no use thinking about it now, though, so I follow her down to the first floor and then out to the street where a dark SUV waits on the curb. As soon as we step outside, the driver's side door opens, and Tanner's sandy blonde head pops up over the roof of the vehicle.

"Ladies!" Tanner leaves the door and hurries around the front to pop open the passenger side and the rear doors with a dramatic bow. "Your carriage awaits."

Lana giggles, and my head whips around as my jaw drops. "Did you just *giggle*?" I whisper.

She stops immediately and shoots me a look. "No," she replies quickly, her cheeks tinting red, and then before I can call her out on such a blatant lie, she hurries forward to meet Tanner at the edge of the sidewalk.

Oh my god, she's in love, I think. That's the only explanation. Lana does not giggle. What could this mean? I mean, I knew Lana and Tanner were getting closer. They'd been hanging out nonstop over the last few weeks, and he's all she seems to talk about. After the fiasco with Harley, I can't imagine that Lana would be so ready and willing to jump right into another relationship unless ... I eye the two of them from where I stand.

Lana laughs at something Tanner says and reaches out to push against his chest. The exact same thing she always does when she's flirting. Yup. She definitely likes him. It's not just a sex thing. If it were, she'd be a lot more obvious. That combined with the blush on her cheeks and the smile that can't seem to go down, makes it obvious. My best friend is in love ... with Ryan's best friend. I release a sigh. I should be happy for her—and I am—but this will likely only complicate things. I cross my arms over my chest as I consider my options. Is there a way for me to get out of this? Lana said she needed a wing woman, but she doesn't need me if she's already got Tanner.

"Will!" Lana's shout draws my attention. She waves me over. "What are you doing? Hurry up. We gotta get there to get a good parking spot!"

And just like that, I have my answer. There's no getting out of this.

THE 'HOUSE PARTY' Lana mentioned is actually at a house on the outskirts of campus. By the time we arrive, though, there are no legitimate parking spots left, so we're left with one of two choices—pulling up and blocking the people already in the driveway or finding a spot down the street. We go with the second option and end up hiking it back to the house.

"Pool room is through there," Tanner says as we walk in through the front door. "Kitchen is back there, but most people are out on the back lawn." He turns to me and winks. "They've got a pool if you wanna go skinny dipping."

"Do you live here?" I ask.

He shrugs. "Nope, I just spend a lot of time here. Bowser's got the best game console setup on campus. There's an entire room upstairs dedicated to it."

I hum in the back of my throat and glance around. Despite Lana's insistence that Ryan wouldn't be here, it still doesn't feel right to me. I almost feel like he could pop up at any moment and what's even more unsettling though, is the fact that I'm not sure if I'd be upset or happy if he did.

"Hey, I've gotta run to the bathroom real quick," Lana announces suddenly.

"Do you need me to—" I begin, but she just waves me off.

"Nah, I'll be right back. Keep Tanner company and grab me a drink, will you?"

She's got a real knack for not letting me answer.

Especially tonight because before I know it, I'm left standing in the foyer of a strange house with loud music next to a practical stranger.

Tanner laughs. "Come on, Willow Tree," he says. "Let's go get that drink she ordered—you know what she likes, right?"

"Willow Tree?" I repeat, confused even as I follow him down the hallway and towards a more brightly lit area.

He looks back. "Your name's Willow, right? Think of it as a nickname."

We step into what looks to be an industrial-sized kitchen. Although it's a bit dated with discolored cabinets and older appliances, it's large enough for several people to gather around an island at the very center and play beer pong.

"Striker!" A big guy with a massive beard calls out. The man comes over and slaps Tanner on the back. "Been a while, glad you could come. Is Anderson coming too?"

It's a bit odd to remember that Anderson used to be my last name too ... until the McRaes adopted me. Now, I'm grateful for my new last name. Everything can be just as Ryan wants it. We can pretend not to know each other, and he can forget I was ever in his life ... that I was ever related to him. It's for the best.

"Nah, he's being a moody bitch lately," Tanner replies with a grin. "Don't worry about him. He's probs off sulking or some shit."

"Girl problems?" the big guy asks.

My whole body stiffens as Tanner looks back at me. "You could say that," he hedges.

"Alright, well, I gotta get back to the game, but if you get a chance—head upstairs later—I want a rematch in the game room."

Tanner laughs and shakes his head. "Sure thing, brother."

I watch as the big guy moves back to the group of friends he'd left and then shift my eyes to Tanner. "You seem to know Ryan pretty well," I comment.

"Does it seem that way?" he asks. "I wonder..."

Tanner and I move towards the opposite counter, away from the island as he snatches a red solo cup from a stack and then proceeds to make a jack and coke. "What about you?" he asks a moment later.

"What about me?" I reply.

"How long have you known Ryan?"

I press my lips together. I don't know how much this guy knows, and I'm not even sure if Ryan would even want him to know. "A while," I hedge.

Tanner stops pouring and chuckles.

"What?" I ask.

He finishes making the drink, dropping a few ice cubes in it for good measure before pushing the cup towards me. "You're just a lot like him," he says. "That's all."

I don't know what to say, so I do the only thing I can think of. I lift the cup to my lips and take a long, deep swallow. The carbonation of the soda hits my tongue a split second before the alcohol, and I wince as the fiery combination slides down my throat.

"Nothing to say to that?" Tanner scans me from head to toe. *Where the hell is Lana?* I think. "Why am I not surprised?"

"Do you have a problem with me?" I ask.

Tanner turns around and props his hip against the countertop before folding his arms over his chest. "No problem," he assures me. "I've just got a wicked curiosity."

Curiosity isn't necessarily a bad thing, but if Tanner finds out about my relationship with Ryan ... and what I said to him six years ago, it could definitely pose a problem. I turn away from him and continue to sip my drink.

"Nothing is going on between Ryan and me," I say honestly. "And there never will be."

"Hmmm. What makes you say that?"

I shoot him a look over the rim of my cup. "Because it's the truth."

Tanner reaches up and smoothes a hand over the side of his face. "I wouldn't be so sure about that," he says. "I am Ryan's friend, after all, and his teammate. I see a lot of him every day. That guy's hiding something big, and I have a feeling you're at the center of it, Willow Tree."

"I can assure you I'm not." I deadpan.

"Still..." His gaze scans the room, and he seems to come to some conclusion. "Do you have your phone on you?" he asks suddenly.

I frown at him. "Yeah, why?"

"Let me see it for a moment." I glare at him, but he just laughs. "I'm not going to do anything weird, I promise." He lifts one hand away from his chest in some sort of strange motion. "Scout's honor."

I debate for several long seconds, and with a sigh, I finally set my cup down and pull out my phone, handing it over. "What are you planning?" I ask as he flips through my phone, his finger sliding across the screen at lightning speed. "Just giving you a number you might need later."

"You're giving me your number?" I scowl. "I thought you were interested in Lana. I'm not—"

He shoves my cell back into my face, cutting me off. "I'm not interested in you, Willow Tree, so don't go all Mama Bear on me. I'm definitely interested in your friend—she's a funny chick."

I take the phone from him and put it back in my pocket, all the while giving him my best stink eye. "I don't trust you," I finally say.

That, however, only serves to make him laugh again. "If you knew how many times someone told me that..." He shakes his head and wipes a finger under his left eye as if he's wiping away tears. Funny. I don't see anything. What a faker. But his grin, at least, is genuine. "Don't worry. I meant what I said about Lana. I do like her." As if speaking of the devil has brought her back into existence, Lana appears at the doorway to the kitchen looking fresh-faced and smiling. She spots us from across the room, and Tanner turns to start making her drink. However, just before she reaches us, my spine straightens as Tanner leans over and whispers one last thing in my ear. "And I never said anything about giving you *my* number, Willow Tree."

Ten

WILLOW

WHEN RYAN LEFT, I used to dream about him all the time. I would cry myself to sleep in the Carson home until they grew tired of me, and I was sent to live with a different family. I'd never been more grateful to be kicked out of a place in my life. Living in that house without Ryan had been hell, and I'd suffered it only because I'd blamed myself. I deserved to be miserable.

It'd been my fault that he'd done what he did. Ryan had beat up Connor Carson because he'd known exactly what that would do—get him away from me. But he wouldn't have felt like he had to if I hadn't told him the truth.

For months after he went to juvie, though, I'd still dreamed of him. I dreamed that he would come back to take me away. That he loved me in the same way that I loved him. Then, as the months had gone by and my circumstances changed, I'd been forced to move on. I thought I'd moved on from those silly, childish dreams as well. My dreams of Ryan had disappeared, allowing me to pretend that I was normal. I was so good at pretending that I was just like everyone else, I'd somehow managed to be adopted even as a teenager about to age out of the system.

Now, it's different. Ryan's here. Close enough that I can see him in person, even if it's from a distance. So, when I open my eyes, and I see him standing right before me once more, I know the dreams have returned. Instead of yelling at me and telling me how disgusting I am, he smiles at me and holds out his hand. What else am I supposed to do other than take it?

"Will..." Even his voice sounds real in my dream. I tilt my face up. I want this. I want him—so bad, it's like a damn drug in my blood, and he's the only antidote. My eyes slide shut, but that's not the end of the dream. Oh no, of course not. At least here, in my mind, I can have everything I want. I can have what I desire, what I crave so bad it fucking hurts—even if it's the most forbidden of fruit.

Ryan's mouth closes over mine, and even though none of this is real—he isn't real—it's a shock to my system. His tongue delves inside and twines with mine. His hand clamps around my waist and back, pulling me hard against him until I can feel his arousal against the lower curve of my stomach. His cock, hard and pulsing, is right there, pressing against me.

I reach up of my own volition and grip his shirt

tight in my fists, kissing this fake Ryan back with everything I have. All of my pain and all of my helplessness that I've felt since the day he left me. I kiss him like this will be the last thing I do on this Earth, and if it is, well, that's okay. All I've ever wanted was for Ryan to be happy. I don't have to be if he's okay. I can just fade into the background and pretend that I'm not as morally corrupt as I actually am.

Sometimes, I wish I had never been born. No life would've been easier and preferable to a life where he's so close and yet so far away. This distance between us is debilitating. Tears slip down my cheeks as I continue to kiss the Ryan in my dream. As if he can feel them, as if I've drawn up some sort of emotion in this pseudo-stand in, the fake Ryan pulls back and looks down at me as I open my eyes.

"What's wrong?" he asks, his brow furrowing. He even looks like Ryan when he's concerned. Man, I'm good. It must be because I've studied Ryan's face that I'm able to recreate him so perfectly in this dream. Wherever I go, whatever I do, Ryan is always here. He's inside of me, even if he doesn't want to be. "Why are you crying?"

I hiccup out a laugh. "I don't want to tell you," I don't want to ruin this moment no matter how fabricated it is.

"Then what do you want?" he asks.

"I want you to kiss me again," I tell him. "I want you to kiss me and I don't want you to ever stop."

Ryan's eyes soften. "I think I can do that," he says and leans down again. This time, as his lips find mine, his hands move to my waist. He lifts me up and deposits me back on a clouded mattress. The world goes hazy at the edges. The details of my dream narrowing down to one point—him and me. It's perfect in every way, even if it is fictitious.

I sigh and lean into Ryan's touch as he strips away my clothes, starting with my shirt and then my pants. Somehow, his clothes seem to dissolve away without any effort on my part. That's just the way of dreams, I suppose. It gives me the pleasure of feeling Ryan's hands on my skin, of feeling him full of desire for me as I take away the remaining barriers that keep us apart, but for me, there's none of that effort. I can finally have him just as he is.

In here, Ryan doesn't shy away from the devious acts—he slides down my body, his eyes meeting mine as he places one hand on each of my thighs and pushes them apart. He spreads me open, revealing me to his gaze. It's funny. Even in a dream, I get embarrassed because as he bares me to his gaze, I can feel my skin get hot, and I can't quite seem to meet his eyes.

"You're so pretty like this, Will," he says quietly. "Your pussy all flowered open for me. Tell me something..."

My chest pumps up and down. "W-what?" I stutter.

"Do you want me to put you in my mouth?" he asks. "I won't do it unless you ask."

I'm so bad, I think. Terrible. Horrible. Disgusting. Wicked. I am all of those things and worse because even with a flaming hot face and tears in my eyes and knowing how wrong this is, I grip the covers beneath me and nod my head.

He grins. "Then hold on, Will," he says. "Because I'm going to devour you." And he does.

Ryan's mouth touches my pussy, and his tongue licks through my wetness, clearing a path straight to my clit. He circles the bud, making me cry out, before sucking it into his mouth. I writhe against the sheets, trapped between him and the bed. It's not enough. It's too much. I feel a crescendo rising, something on the ledge, waiting for me to take the plunge.

I'm scared. Frightened of this place because it's not reality, but I want it to be so bad. This is everything I've ever wanted. I'm panting and squirming against the bed as Ryan moves down, thrusting his tongue into my opening and retracting it while his fingers move up, replacing his mouth over my clit. When he pinches that sensitive nub, there's no going back for me. I feel a gush of wetness escape me as a blinding, white light assails my eyes.

I cry out, my back bowing on the bed as my orgasm overtakes me, and then there's no more.

My alarm clock goes off and my eyes open. The Ryan that I dreamed of is gone ... nothing but a figment of my imagination ... just as he always was. I turn over and bury my face into my pillow and let the tears soak into it as the cushion muffles the worst of my sobs.

TANNER GAVE ME Ryan's number. What other number would he have? He seems the mischievous type, setting things in motion just to see how they'll turn out. Right now, I can't determine if that's advantageous for me or a hindrance. I stare at the name on my screen for the hundredth time since the Friday night party. Do I delete it? Or just ... leave it be? What if I need it? What if, maybe, our paths change? Perhaps I can just learn to love Ryan from afar. If he meets someone else ... if he falls in love ... I can just go back to being his sister.

Though I don't speak the words aloud, they burn in my throat. Venomous creatures are the lies we tell ourselves. I grit my teeth and turn my phone over, shoving it back into my purse as Professor Bradley walks into the classroom. It's useless to think of stupid things that will never happen.

"Hey," Lana whispers as Professor Bradley begins to write something on the board, "are you okay?"

I shake my head and point to the front. "Pay attention," I tell her, adding a wink at the end, hoping she'll think I'm teasing her when in fact, I'm just trying to hide it. No, I'm not okay.

I'm fucked up. Ryan's been so close for so many weeks now, and all I want to do is see him. I close my eyes and can't help but think about the stupid dream I had. When I reopen them, nothing in the room has changed. My whole world is being rocked upside down—Ryan is here at Trinity. It's been six years, and ... *nothing* has changed. He still hates me, and I'm forced to pretend like we hardly know each other.

No matter how much anger he throws my way, no matter how cruel his words are, I can't seem to help myself. I'm a liar to try and believe anything else. I still love him.

Class ends, and Professor Bradley orders us to hand in our completed work on the last reading section. I'm one of the last people in line to turn in my papers—not because I'm deliberately trying to avoid Lana, I know that's not going to happen. I just can't seem to keep myself from attempting to postpone her inquisition. The second I step out into the hallway, she pounces.

"Hey, what's going on with you lately?" she asks, shouldering her bag as she pushes away from where she'd been leaning against the wall. On the way to the staircase, we bypass Amalia—the same girl who'd been so into the reading on the first day. I don't think anything of her, however, until she turns her head and makes eye contact with me. For some reason, a scowl overtakes her expression and she jerks her head away from me and returns her focus to her friends. Weird.

"Will?" Lana nudges me, grabbing my attention once more.

"What?" I glance up at her frowning face.

"You're acting weird," she states. "Is it about Ryan again?"

Even just the sound of his name sends something pulsing through me. I really shouldn't be feeling the way I do. I shake my head. "Of course not," I say. It's like the lies are slipping easier and easier off my tongue the more I voice them. Soon enough, I'll only have to part my lips and an ocean of lies will come pouring out. "I'm fine."

Lana presses her lips together as we push out of the building, and the bright sunlight hits us in the face. She winces, putting her hand up to block it out momentarily as she grows used to it. "Listen," she begins, "I've been thinking. I know you've been having some issues with him being back in your life—and with the fact that he's been a major fucking douche—but have you thought about going to see the counseling services at Trinity?"

"Counseling services?" I repeat. "Is that like therapy or something?"

She nods, lowering her arm as we cross the street. "Yeah, sorta. You know I have to work with the health and counseling department because of my major—and well ... anyone who wants to be a therapist has to go through therapy too. I think you should give it a try. They're super nice, and everything you say is confidential—it's patient policy. Maybe they could help you."

I can't help but chuckle a little. "Am I really that bad?" I ask.

Lana shakes her head. "No, of course not. You know I'm always happy to listen to anything you need to talk about. But the fact is, I'm not a professional yet." She winces. "I just … I feel like I'm failing you in the friendship department. I want to make sure you're okay."

We stroll towards the end of the sidewalk and stop at the next crosswalk when I release a sigh. "You're not failing me," I tell her. "What's going on with me is my problem, and you can't fix everything—though, I know you'll try." I give her a small smile. "I appreciate how worried you are about me, but I need to figure things out myself. I'll give it some thought."

"That's all I can ask for," she says.

It's not, but she won't ask for anything more. Lana's a good friend and she won't push for more until I'm ready. I just don't know if I'll ever be ready to admit my deepest, darkest, most deviant of desires to anyone. Not even her.

Eleven

RYAN

ADDICTIONS ARE MAD, crazy things. Just one taste is enough to drive them to the brink of insanity. I'm starting to wonder, though, if *not* tasting the very thing I'm addicted to is doing even worse things to my mind.

I've never forgotten Willow. I've never even wanted to. Not once. I can't count the number of times I'd palmed my cock in the darkness of some cramped bottom bunk bedroom to thoughts of her. But the distance in between left me both lost in want and "cured" at the same time. I'm not sure how it's possible, but I tricked myself into believing I was immune to her charms, yet these last few weeks have proven that to be utter horse shit. I'm more obsessed with her now than I have ever been in my life.

I've become a stalker.

I know her schedule. I know which dorm she's in and what her room number is. I've even gone so far as to chat up a few of her classmates—making sure to stay as far away from Lana Coleman as possible. Something tells me that Willow's friend is not someone that I can manipulate easily. At first, I started tracking her just to figure out if she was talking about me despite her promise. Then, when it was clear she was staying silent, I'd excused my obsessive tendencies by telling myself I needed information on her to figure out how to make her hate me.

Rumors? Pranks? Hate mail? What can I do to ensure that the next time Willow and I meet, she doesn't look at me with those big, doe brown eyes of hers?

I pump the weights in my fists, and sweat drips down the side of my face. It's not enough.

"Whoa, there, man, you tryna shred your fucking biceps, or are you prepping for an all you can pump jack-a-thon?" Tanner's voice penetrates my skull with about as much subtlety as a bull in a fucking china shop.

I stop pumping the weights and even go so far as to drop them to the floor at my feet before standing straight and stretching my back. "Tell me something, Striker," I say, bending. "Do you ever actually fucking think about the shit that comes out of your mouth, or does it just come out like word vomit?"

"The latter," he says with no remorse or hesitation. Instead, the dipshit just smiles at me. "So, what is it? Perhaps a pretty little brunette you've been thinking about lately?"

I glare. "You're beggin' to get your ass beat," I warn him.

Tanner's amusement sharpens. "Any time, any place, my man." He strides up to me and claps me on the back, as I lift up once more and finish my stretches. "You ready to grab something to eat?" he asks.

I grumble out a reply, grab my sweat rag from the nearest rack, and flip it over my shoulder as I follow him towards the locker rooms. When I first arrived at Trinity, I expected it to be just like all the places before. From juvie to a group home for boys, I have lived surrounded by other guys ever since I was kicked out of the Carson home. Locker room shit talk and the nasty scent of sweat and dirt had become a welcoming smell that meant I was home, but not here.

Here at Trinity, I'm not a snot-nosed brat with a smart mouth and a penchant for violence. Here at Trinity, I'm labeled as a "Football God." Hell, sports are the only thing I've ever been good at. Will was always good at academics. I almost hadn't believed the scout when I'd initially been offered the scholarship, even when it became clear the old bastard was serious, I'd expected the facilities of this place to be low-tier. It was a welcome surprise to find out that wasn't the case. Now, I've grown used to it. The smell of clean, fresh soap. The bright lights that never flicker or go out, and stay out for days because there aren't enough funds to replace the bulbs. There's even a fridge in the assistant coach's office always full of water and a drawer with energy bars.

Compared to what I was used to, Trinity is a lot like heaven. It's hard to believe that one little girl can make this place hell with her mere presence.

"You'll never guess who I saw the other day," Tanner says suddenly, his hand coming down on my shoulder as I stop at my locker. I shrug him off and strip my shirt over my head, shoving it into my gym bag.

I grab my clean towel. "Don't care," I say, pushing past him.

He chuckles as I escape to the showers, finding an empty stall and cranking the hot water on before stripping the rest of my clothes off and stepping under the spray. Just as I'm relaxing under the scalding warmth, something bangs nearby, and the shower right next to mine turns on. I don't need to turn and look over the half-wall that separates the stalls to know who it is.

"I don't know why you keep fighting it, man," Tanner says, proving my assumption correct. He just won't let this shit go. "She seems like a nice girl."

I slam my hand against the plastic half wall so hard, it rattles and shakes. Tanner goes silent, and I turn my head in his direction. "Stop bringing her up," I snarl. "Say her name one more goddamn time, and I'll break your fucking jaw." And if he even thinks about looking her way for anything more than taunting material for me, I'll break a lot more than that—but I keep that thought to myself. He doesn't need to know how insane I am just yet.

Tanner, however, doesn't do anything more than arch a brow in my direction. His lips quirk into a smile and he keeps his eyes on me even as he reaches for one of the bottles stacked in the corner of the shower. He squirts some shampoo onto his hand before lathering it through his hair. "I never said her name," he points out.

Shit. He's got a point. A scowl overtakes me. "I know who you're talking about."

He turns and rinses, that grin of his never leaving his lips. "I could've been talking about Lana for all you know," he replies. "I've been seeing her regularly, you know. Going to a party here and there..." He pauses and then continues. "We invited that cute friend of hers too."

My fingers move up and curve over the top of the wall, and I squeeze until I can't feel the blood pumping through them anymore, giving him a look of death. Tanner doesn't even seem fazed. Then, with careful movements, I unclench my hand from the plastic and turn back around to finish my shower in silence.

I cut off the spray of water, snatch my towel from the hook on the end, and wrap it around my waist before grabbing my dirty clothes from the floor outside the stall. I don't say a damn word to Tanner as I walk out. By the time he comes into the locker room, I'm already in a fresh pair of shorts and pulling a t-shirt over my head.

"Ry—" I slam my locker shut, cutting him off, and sling my gym bag over my arm, making a beeline for the exit. I don't look at or talk to anyone as I pass through—not even the coach as he pops in and heads for his office in the back. I'm grateful to this place and these men—they dragged me out of the gutter after high school and gave me a chance. An opportunity that I, otherwise, wouldn't have. But no matter how good-natured Tanner thinks his teasing is, all he does is remind me of *why* I can't have what I want most in this world. If he knew—shit, if anyone knew the thoughts I have for Willow ... they wouldn't look at me like a football god anymore. They wouldn't be able to look at me and see someone who could hold his own; they'd look at me and see an immoral monster.

The truth of the matter is: Willow isn't the fucked up one. I am.

Twelve

WILLOW

I LOVE WORKING the closing shift at the library, especially on weekends. It's empty, quiet, and peaceful. I can study to my heart's content and not have to worry or think about anything since all of the daily tasks for desk attendants are usually done by five p.m.

Tonight, unfortunately, is a different matter. There's a ginormous stack of books that need to be returned to the shelves, a long line of students wanting to check out study materials, and a cloud of gloom hanging over me. There's really no explanation for it except for the fact that I have the worst luck, and my coworker is a bitch who likes to show up for her shifts at least an hour late, if she even shows up at all.

My literature textbook hangs open on the opposite side of the circulation desk, untouched, as I hurry through the computer to help the students in front of me check out. The faster I work, though, the longer the line seems to become. I'm finally down to the last person in line to check out books when Roquelle finally shows up. Sunglasses over her eyes even though it's already dark outside and a bag over her shoulder as she slides behind the desk.

As soon as my last student is checked out, I slam my textbook closed and glare at her. I open my mouth to say something—maybe to demand where the hell she's been or why she's late, but just as quickly as the bubble of anger fills, it bursts and dissipates as well. Like it or not, I have to work with this girl. Her tardiness will be noted when she clocks in, and hopefully, Mrs. Maes will say something to her. So, instead of unleashing my irritation, I suck it back and take a breath.

"I'm gonna take these down to the basement floor to return them to their shelves," I say, striding over to the already overflowing handcart and pushing it out from behind the desk. I don't give her a chance to say anything back. I'm almost positive anything she says will only reignite my ire. I do note, however, the scowl she sends my way as another student moves up to check out and I head straight for the elevators.

The second the doors are closed, and I'm alone as I descend to the basement. I close my eyes and lean my head back. There's a pounding headache starting in my temples, and I know it's not all Roquelle's fault. It's Ryan's and my own. I can't help it. I haven't been this close to him in years. Everywhere I go, he seems to be there, and whether he realizes my presence or not, I can't stop myself from watching him even when I subbed in for one of the girls in my hall last week. I had no clue he'd be in the class she TA-ed for.

A groan emits from my throat as the elevator comes to a clunky and awkward stop and the doors slide open. I'm fucking hopeless and I know it. Ryan has done nothing but make it clear that he's not interested in me. He wants nothing to do with me, and as far as he's concerned, the only thing that would make him happy would be me disappearing off the face of the earth.

I push the cart out of the elevator and onto the bottom floor. As soon as I step out, I notice something that had been missing on the first floor. Silence. Absolute, blessed silence. It's not a surprise since most of the books on this floor are for the advanced courses, and a majority of them aren't allowed to be checked out. Regardless, I'm thankful for the reprieve.

The cart's wheels squeak loudly against the tiled floors as I roll it towards the very end and turn down the last aisle. I shiver as cold air washes over the bare skin of my legs. *Note to self*, I think, *wear pants when shelving books in the basement.* My hand grips a worn spine and deposits it into its correct place on the shelf, pushing the books on either side a little bit down to make room. It's a mindless task. Something easy that allows my thoughts to wander as I do it.

Of all the places on Earth for me to end up—why did it have to be the same school as Ryan?

Six years had passed, and I'd done so fucking well. At least, I'd pretended to be doing well. I've never forgotten him like he told me to. Not once. But I'd moved on. I'd gotten adopted by a kind, older couple, and then I lost them just as quickly. I'd dated. I'd gotten a scholarship to first school and now Trinity.

What is the universe trying to tell me? Are Ryan and I destined to just circle each other like two broken planets?

"Willow?" I nearly jump at the sound of my own name. I look up and frown at the guy standing at the end of the aisle with a bright smile on his face. He looks familiar, but I can't quite place him. "Hey!" The guy lifts an arm in greeting and then starts down the aisle, walking straight towards me. "Your friend said you'd probably be down here."

"My friend?" He's so tall that I have to tilt my head back as he approaches.

"Yeah." He smiles again—a full-on, megawatt, all-American dream smile. "The chick at the desk," he clarifies.

Resist the scowl, Will, I remind myself. *You're at work. Act professional.* Telling myself that, though, doesn't make it any easier, and when I flash him a smile, it feels just as brittle as it is fake.

"Oh, you mean Roquelle," I reply. "She's my coworker. Did you need something from me?"

He shifts and his smile dims just the slightest bit. Perhaps he realizes I don't remember who he is. "Actually, uh, no, not exactly. It's just … I don't know if you remember, but we met at the bar off campus a few weeks ago, and you told me you worked here—maybe it's weird that I came by..."

A lightbulb goes off in my head. "Oh, right," I say quickly. "I remember. Your name is Jordan, right?"

The smile shifts back to its original megawatt form. "Yeah, that's right," he says, nodding. "I actually just stopped by to pick up some study materials for my class, and I remembered that you worked here, so I thought I'd ask if you were around, and here you are."

"Right." I laugh awkwardly. "Here I am."

His head bobs up and down, causing the shaggy blonde hair at the top of his scalp to sway in time with the movement. "Yeah, anyway, I was uh ... wondering if you were free sometime on Thursday next week. After classes, of course."

"Free?" I shift my gaze to the side when I catch movement behind one of the shelves—the shadow of someone passing by. My ears perk up, but it's hard to hear anything as Jordan starts talking again.

"Yeah, there's this new Thai place that opened up in downtown Trinity, and I was wondering if you wanted to go with me to check it out. Like on a date or something?"

At the word 'date,' my attention shoots immediately back to Jordan. I blink up at him, confused. "You're asking me out on a date?" I repeat.

He grins at me and moves forward. My eyes

widen as I'm suddenly pinned between the cart, shelves, and his massive body. I've been in this position once before—only that time it'd been with Ryan. For some reason, this doesn't feel anything like that. Chills skate down my spine as discomfort wraps around my throat. I put a hand out against his chest and push.

"Um, let me think about it. I'm not sure what my schedule's like," I say quickly.

"Well, my schedule's open," Jordan continues, resting one hand against the shelves above me as he remains smiling. "So, whenever you're available, I can make myself available. Who knows, maybe if it all goes well, I can take you to one of my brother's parties. Have you ever been to a party on Greek Row before? They can get pretty *wild*."

My heart starts to jackhammer inside of my chest. "I don't know if I like *wild*," I state.

He laughs. "Don't knock it 'til you try it."

What the hell is he doing? I push harder against his chest, but he doesn't seem to feel it. Or if he does, he doesn't react. "I have to—"

"Hey, what the fuck do you think you're doing down here?" Fear, relief, and horror flood me all at once. Fear because I worry that this situation has been misconstrued. Relief because Jordan finally backs off, and I feel like I can breathe again. And horror because I recognize that tone and voice. My head turns as if on a spike towards the end of the aisle, and a pair of hard, angry brown eyes glare directly back at me.

"Anderson?" Jordan leverages away from me and smiles towards our intruder.

Ryan's glare shifts to him. "Do I fucking know you?" he barks.

Jordan wavers for a moment and then shakes his head. "Nah, I um, I'm on the basketball team, but I'm a football fan too. We ran a few sports camps together last summer. I'm just a fan."

"Yeah, well, you're also a student," Ryan replies. "Maybe you should grab your materials and get out of here. I can't study with all your fucking flirting." My face grows hot at that comment.

"W-we weren't—" I start before Jordan cuts me off.

"Ah, shit, sorry 'bout that man. Didn't realize anyone else was down here." He scrubs the back of his head in an 'aw shucks' kinda way. "I'll, uh, get going then." Jordan turns back to me and gives me a sly grin. "I'll see you next Thursday, Will? Roquelle's got my number, you can get it from her. Just give me a call."

With that, Jordan strides down the aisle, clapping Ryan on the shoulder as he goes, and disappears around the side. Ryan and I stand there for several more moments, silence echoing around us until the bang of the doors leading to the staircase echo from somewhere far away.

I don't know what to do with Ryan's gaze so focused on me. So, I do the only thing I can think of—I turn away and work on putting the books on the shelves. It isn't until I don't hear his footsteps leaving that I realize he's still there. Then...

"Thursday?" Ryan's voice filters down the aisle towards me, full of some emotion that makes the word come out raspy.

I pause in the process of lifting a book to a higher shelf and instead allow my arm to fall back down to my side, the spine gripped in my fist. "I'm not going on a date with him," I say quietly. Not that he cares, but it feels necessary to tell him. There's absolutely no way I'll be going to Roquelle to get that guy's number.

His sneakers squeak against the tile, and with each footstep, my spine grows stiffer and stiffer. His breath is hot as it rolls over the back of my neck. Just moments ago, I had been caged in this exact spot by someone entirely different. When Jordan had done it, I'd wanted nothing more than to get out and get away. Now that Ryan's here, my only thought is on keeping as still as possible. Why? Because Ryan is like a wild animal, easily frightened. Maybe if I stay still, he will too.

That's so fucked up, I realize. He hates me, but I want him to stick around? I'm a masochist through and through. I'm obsessed, and I know it. It's wrong, and I know it. I *know* a lot of things, but knowing them doesn't make my desires lessen. In fact, there's an opposite effect. For some reason, the power of the forbidden is like a drug to me. Wanting something I can't have only makes me want it even more.

"So, you go on dates now, huh?" Ryan's words

are sharp—like he's trying to shove knives between my ribs.

"Not really," I say. "I mean, I've been on a few, but I won't be going out with Jordan."

"Why not?" The question is so surprising coming from his lips that it actually makes me shift.

I turn to look back at him, meeting that dangerous gaze of his. "Why?" I repeat. "Because I don't want to. Do I need another reason?"

He hums low in his throat and the sound does something to me. It sends a pulsing sensation straight to my pussy, causing my thighs to clench together. "Maybe you're just saying that because I'm the one asking," he challenges.

I turn to face him and bring up the book in my hand to act as a barrier between us. "Why are you doing this?" I shoot back.

"Doing what?" he asks.

"Asking me personal questions?" I frown at him. "You were the one who said you wanted to pretend like we didn't know each other. You were the one who demanded that I stay away from you but everywhere I seem to go, there you are." I inhale sharply. It's not true. It's just wishful thinking, but something doesn't stop me from saying it. Perhaps because I know how angry it'll make him, and an angry Ryan is better than an indifferent one. "Maybe you don't want to admit that you can't help but be around me," I say. "Maybe you actually feel something for me too, Ryan."

There's a moment of absolute silence. His

expression goes slack from shock as if he can't believe that I—little Willow who couldn't do anything without her brother around—actually grew a fucking backbone.

In a flash, though, his hand is on my throat. The book in my grasp drops from my fingers and clatters to the floor at our feet as he shoves me back against the shelves hard. They dig into my spine as he squeezes, and my fingers reach up, locking onto his wrist.

"You think I *like* you?" he growls. "Man, you really are far more delusional than I thought."

I close my eyes for a brief moment, knowing he's right. I expected this answer, but it still hurts. "I never said—" I try, only to be cut off by him once again.

"Oh, don't fucking back out on me now, Will," he says coldly. "You seem to think I give a shit what you have to say."

"I'm just—"

"Shut"—his hand contracts around my throat, not tight enough to hurt, but almost as if he wants to hold me here. To keep me from leaving or running away even as the next words out of his mouth are harsh and mean—"the fuck up, Will." A gasp leaves my lips as he leans down into my face, his fierce eyes coming close until they're all I can see. "You mean nothing to me," he states. Another blade straight to my chest. My lips part, but nothing escapes. "You're just an obsessed girl with a schoolyard crush. We may be twins, but that is a product of birth. An accident. A mistake. Just like you and your pathetic love for me."

Each word cuts me to the core. Sharp. Hard. Unforgiving. My eyes begin to water. *No!* I scream at myself. *Don't be fucking weak. Suck them back. Don't let him see you cry.*

Ryan's free hand falls on my shoulder, a heavy weight, as his face turns contemplative and his eyes grow distant. "Maybe I should show you just how crazy you are," he says.

I don't have a chance to ask him what he means because he finally releases my throat. I cough and tilt my head back as Ryan stands above me, hovering like some sort of dark god.

"Yes," he says, sounding a little unhinged. "I think I should show you exactly how fucked up you really are."

And then his mouth descends upon mine.

Thirteen

WILLOW

KISSING ME. RYAN is kissing me! My mind riots at the sudden feel of his warm lips on mine. It's like I've walked into the most beautiful dream and the worst nightmare all at once. Like touching fire and being consumed by it.

I can't say I never wanted this because that would be a lie. I have wanted this—for ages. For years, but I'd always known the desire to kiss him was too forbidden ever to come true. Yet, here we are.

My heart races inside of my chest, a wild, untamable thing. I blink against Ryan's kiss, but he's still there. *This is really happening.* I should stop this. I should push him away. He's only doing this to punish me. Even so ... there's no strength in me to act. I can't push him away because I don't want to. Instead, I reach up and sink my fingers into his shirt sleeves, and with every ounce of all of the want and need I've been unable to fulfill for the last six years, I kiss him back.

Once he seems to realize that I'm giving in, that

I won't fight this, Ryan becomes harder, more aggressive. His mouth devours me as he pushes my lips apart and delves inside with his tongue. It's a violent kiss—not romantic in the slightest. Then again, whoever said we were romantic? This kiss suits us. It suits who we are.

Two wicked souls unable to part from one another no matter the distance he has tried to place between us. I'm almost heady from the sense of victory. Though I know I should feel shame, it's hard to when I've wanted Ryan's kiss ever since I was a lovestruck teenager wearing my heart on my sleeve.

When he breaks the kiss at last, and I gasp out a breath, his name leaves my lips. "Ryan..."

He stiffens all over, his body growing rigid against me. I expect him to shove me away. It's what anyone would expect him to do after the way he's treated me, and probably the right thing to do too. But the next words out of his mouth aren't derogatory or accusatory. They're cruel, yes, but they send shivers dancing down my spine.

"Spread your legs, Will." His words are a whispered rasp in the stagnant air. It's wrong. It's amoral. It's everything I want.

I move my legs apart and feel his hand glide down my stomach, past the waistband of my skirt, and further until he reaches the hem. I suck in a breath as his skin brushes against mine, and he begins to move back up with my skirt on the outside and his hand on the inside. My eyes close as his fingers find my panties and push them to the side. There's a moment—of shock or pleasure, I'm not sure—where he pauses as he feels just how wet I am beneath the fabric. My chest pumps up and down, and I squeeze my eyes shut even tighter. Afraid.

Afraid that he'll find me wanting. Afraid that he'll be disgusted—as he'd called my love for him before. Afraid that he will turn away from me again.

My fears are unwarranted, however, because in the next instant, his fingers begin moving over the wetness of my pussy, through my folds and to the bundle of nerves that sits there. His thumb rubs over it and my back arches. My lips part on a cry, but before it can escape, a hand clamps over my mouth.

"Dirty noises from a dirty girl, hmmm?" The gruffness of his voice filters over my ears.

My eyes shoot open and his face fills my line of sight. Only him. Nothing else. His eyes, a slightly lighter brown than my own. His face angles are different from mine. That's normal though from what I understand. We're not really identical, after all. We're fraternal. There's nothing in our faces that resemble each other save for the color of our eyes and hair. He watches me, keeping one hand clamped over my mouth as the hand down below moves again, his finger sliding into the opening of my pussy.

I gasp behind his palm and squirm as he pushes first one digit and then two into me, scissoring them apart until I can feel the burn of my opening stretch the slightest bit.

"You want this, don't you?" he taunts, his tone angry, filled with an almost desperate violence. Even as much as I understand that hate, I can't deny the truth. He takes his hand away. "Answer me," he orders.

"Yes," I whisper. "I want it." My eyes burn with unshed tears—of shame or desire? Maybe both.

His lips twist, his brows furrow, and all I see is pain in the depths of his eyes. An agony so ripe and similar to my own, it makes me wonder if he's cruel to me for some other reason. Maybe it's not disgust. Maybe it's something else. Or is that wishful thinking?

"Then you better come fast before anyone wanders back down here," he says.

It takes me a moment to realize what he means by the time it enters my mind. However, it's too late. Ryan moves to the floor, his knees hitting the stone as his hands push up my skirt and drag my panties down and off my legs. I lift one foot, and he sets it down, pushing it further out so that he can tilt his head back and—

"Oh fuck!" I cry out as his tongue delves into my flesh. He licks first up one side and then down the other before spearing it into me, thrusting and withdrawing that wicked part of his anatomy in rapid succession. My thighs tremble. My hands reach down and grasp at the back of his head, fingers sliding through the dark locks of his hair.

Ryan's mouth devours me. Consumes me.

Drags me up a mountain of pleasure and into the skies. I gasp. I pant. I fall. Down. Down into the depths of a hell that he's created for me.

This is what I've been missing, I realize. This was the thing that I could sense between us. This chemistry is electric. It's an evil thing that sits in my body, tempting him to come closer. When he leaves—because he surely will—this will be what I think about at night. The way his tongue moves over my wet flesh. It's so explicit. Even when I close my eyes, it's like I can feel every single touch in sharpened detail.

I love him. I love this. His mouth on me. The way he moves his fingers back into my channel and thrusts them up as he sucks my clit between his lips and laps the needy bud with attention. No matter how wrong it is, my whole body shakes with the undeniable sensation of an impending orgasm. I'm going to come apart on Ryan's mouth, and I'm going to love every second of it.

No sooner has that thought hit my brain than my orgasm does, indeed, slam into me. My head twists from side to side as I clamp down on his fingers and come apart under his ministrations. I press the back of my fist against my lips to stifle the sounds I can't keep my throat from making.

This is the definition of insanity. The practice of depravity. My thighs tremble more as Ryan's head moves back. He reaches up with wet fingers, removing my grip from his hair. Cold air washes against my bare pussy, and as he stands up, I slip down. My legs can't hold me up anymore, and he refuses to help me.

My legs hit the stone that he had just been kneeling on, and I glance up, confused and … stupidly hopeful. *What does this mean?* But in the time it took for Ryan to make me come, nothing has changed in his expression. His eyes are still as ice-cold as before. Only this time, there's a cruel glint in them and a shine to his lips. I put that shine there. That's me on him. I can't stop the small smile of satisfaction that curls my lips upward.

His hands go to his belt and my eyes follow as he undoes it. Ryan frees himself from his pants and holds what has to be the biggest cock I've ever seen up for me to view. Then again, it's not like I've ever really seen another one. Not in the light of day like this. After Ryan left and he'd gone to juvie, I'd sworn never to forget him. But one year had turned into two, had turned into four, and then here we were six years later. So, yeah, I'd experimented. Perhaps he knew that, but I wondered if he knew that experimentation was all I'd done.

Right now, it doesn't seem like he cares as he palms the back of my head, his fingers locking onto the bun on the top of my head and using it as an anchor. He pulls me forward, my knees scraping against the stone as he shoves my face against his cock. It rubs over my cheeks and jawline as he fists it with his free hand and holds it out.

"Suck it," he commands.

I swallow roughly, fear and concern filling me.

I've only done this once or twice, and both times had been a regret.

My lips part and I gently move my hands up until I cup him at the base of his cock, squeezing lightly and then harder until his muscles stiffen under my grasp. Only then do I lean forward and take him into my mouth.

With my eyes wide open, I stare up at him as I suck him until the head of his cock hits the back of my throat, and his lips drop open on a low, masculine moan. Hesitantly, worried he may not like it, I reach up with my free hand and massage his balls, rolling them against my palm and squeezing until his fingers clench in my hair and his cock jumps on my tongue.

"Stop fucking playing with me, Willow," he growls. "And suck my fucking cock."

And I do. I suck him down until my throat burns with the effort. My eyes water as I cup his balls and twist my tongue against the underside of his shaft. He holds me down, pressing me forward until my nose is almost touching the dark wiry thatch of hair that surrounds the base of his cock. Then he takes his hold on my hair, drawing me away, and letting me gasp for breath before pushing me back down.

He does this over and over again. Fucking my mouth and into my throat until I can't remember a time when I wasn't down here on my knees, servicing him.

FOURTEEN

RYAN

WHAT THE HELL am I doing? I've never wanted to vomit and come at the same time before, but when Willow's knees hit the stone-tiled floor of the library basement, it's the only thing on my mind. When her lips part and she leans forward, I damn near come on the spot. *This is so fucking wrong, so why can't I stop?*

I watch my hand lift as if I'm watching someone else's body move. I can't control myself anymore. She's here. She's in front of me. And she just came all over my mouth and hand. My cock is rock hard. My hand finds the back of her skull, and I jerk her forward, unable to stop the force of my movement. Her face turns automatically to the side as she flinches and the soft side of her cheek touches my shaft, rubbing against it. There, I think, that's it. Her skin is so fucking soft. I grasp my cock by the base and let it fall right on her face, pushing it over her cheeks and down her jaw.

"Suck it," I growl.

If I didn't know Willow as well as I do, I might think her gentle movements are hesitation. There's no hesitation in her eyes, though. They burn with desire for what I'm about to give her. She swallows and reaches up. Her lips part and she cups me right above where my hand is on my cock, her little fingers squeezing and contracting. I release a hiss through my teeth and nearly punch the bookshelf in front of me. My whole mind seems to fog over the second her warm, wet mouth opens, and her tongue rolls over the head of my dick.

I can sense her interest, her curiosity. She stares up at me with those big, innocent doe eyes of hers, and just seeing her watching me turns me on even more. It's like she knows just what buttons to push to make me feel out of control. *Has she done this before?* The thought sends spikes of red hot rage shooting through me.

Just as I'm about to rip her off my dick, she swallows down, and my dick hits the back of her throat. A low moan escapes my lips. Fuck, it's hot. The hottest thing I've ever felt in my life is the way Willow's throat closes around me. Then she closes her tiny fist around my balls squeezing and releasing then rolling them against her soft palm. My hand clenches against her scalp and I can feel her hair grow taut in my fist.

"Stop fucking playing with me, Willow," I warn her, "and suck my fucking cock."

And she does. She sucks me down like a fucking pro. Her mouth works against my shaft, tongue scraping the underside and moving in a consistent rhythm. Stars dance in front of my eyes. I can't fucking take it. I'm gonna fucking come.

I don't let her up. Every time she moves back to take a breath, I squeeze against the back of her skull until her eyes jump back to mine. I glare at her, hateful, angry. Violent. I'm rougher than I should be, but she's too fucking good for this to be her first time, and that pisses me off. Where the hell has she been these last few years? Who the fuck has she been with? Is she still a virgin? Or has she spread those sweet thighs for someone else before me?

All of these thoughts roll around in my mind as her mouth convulses over my cock. One breath. That's all she gets and then I'm gonna finish this. I tighten my fist in her hair and yank her off once, just long enough for her to capture a breath of air, and then I shove her back down over my head. In and out, I thrust my cock past those pretty pink lips of hers until I'm sure they're swollen and bruised. I don't give a shit. This is what she gets for tempting me, for sucking off some other guy because there's no fucking way she's this good on her first try. So, this is her punishment. She's gonna take it rough until I'm fucking done with her.

When I feel my cock jump and my spine straighten, I sink into the back of her throat and I hold still. Both of my hands squeeze the base of her skull, keeping her locked against me. Her little nose is pressed right against the skin above my cock. Her eyes water as they stare up at me. She blinks and tears escape, rolling down her blown cheeks. She makes a little noise in the back of her throat that vibrates across my dick, a sound of discomfort. Is she trying to tell me something? To let her go, perhaps? I smile. No way in hell that's going to happen.

"Swallow, baby," I say just before I come down her throat.

Willow has no choice but to follow my command. Her only other option is to choke. So, she opens that filthy little throat of hers and sucks down my seed like the good girl I know she can be.

I pull myself free from her lips and stare down at her on the floor—her cheeks flushed, her lips bruised—and zip up my pants. She reaches up and touches the corner of her mouth, where a drop of my fluid still sits. When she moves to wipe it on her skirt, I catch her hand and redirect her finger to her mouth.

"I said swallow, Willow," I repeat. "That means all of it."

Her eyes widen in shock as I push her finger past her own lips and then urge her to close them. I pull it free a second later, satisfied to see it cleaned of my cum. Now, it's all sloshing around in that belly of hers. A reminder. Of what she is, and now … of what I am as well.

When I release her, her eyes tilt up towards me. Confusion swirls in those depths of hers. I've got a choice to make now. I stare down at her for several moments, trying to come to terms with my own incredibly fucked up decision that led us here, but perhaps this is the way. Perhaps this is what I can do to break her, to get her to hate me and leave me … forever.

It's selfish and cruel, I know, but one touch won't be enough for me. The feeling of Willow's pussy throbbing against my fingers is like water to the wine of what it would feel like having her pussy pulse around my cock. Knowing she's now carrying a piece of me—my cum—inside of her makes me feel ravenous. I want more. I want to bend her and break her and take her apart piece by fucking piece.

"This changes nothing between us," I say coldly.

Her lips press firmly together and my eyes fix on the small tear in the corner of her mouth. I had decided to be rough with her, but was I too rough? Before I can think of anything else to say, Willow sighs and then starts to stand up.

"Of course it doesn't," she says, sounding disappointed. Even though her unwillingness to meet my eyes again after she gets to her feet makes my chest ache, I force myself to scowl at her. It's not difficult to do, actually, considering the thoughts rolling around in my mind.

"You seem to do well on your knees," I tell her. "Your sucking skills could use work, but you're obviously no beginner." It's a taunt and an accusation—one that hits home if the stiffening of her shoulders is anything to go by.

"Is that all you have to say?" she shoots back, turning away from me. "If so, then you can go now. I have to get back to work."

I glare at her as she picks up some of the books scattered across the floor. I hadn't realized we'd knocked a few loose from the shelves during our … fuck what the hell am I supposed to call it? Accident? Mistake? It was my own fault, what we did here today. My will was too weak. My need for her is too strong.

"It's only going to keep happening." I'm not sure if the words are a warning for her or myself. "The more we're together for any prolonged length of time—this will keep happening. Over and over again."

She pauses in the process of shoving a book back on the shelf but refuses to turn around. My own gaze finds the floor, and I blink at what I see there—her panties, right there out in the open for all to see. The dark strip of fabric was like a blaring sign against the white tile of the floor. And the reason that they're there instead of on their owner's body is that I stripped them off of her right before I shoved my tongue up her delicious cunt. Squeezing my eyes shut tightly, I bend down and snatch them up, shoving them into my pocket and tightening my fist around them, nearly coming undone for a second time when I feel the lingering residue of her wetness against my skin.

Fuck me.

"You should leave," Willow says, her voice

cutting. "We wouldn't want our *prolonged* company to make us do something insane again." Her voice is sharp like it's dancing along the length of a blade. It's more than that; it's already been cut by that blade, by me.

She's hurt and though it makes me a bastard, I'm glad. Maybe this time she'll fucking listen to me. I turn around and leave her be. I head towards the stairs and pause when I see a book on the floor at the end of the aisle. I look back and then step over it. Wherever we go, we wreck the places we're in, she and I. Maybe if she cleans up after our messes enough, she'll get tired of me and realize that she's not the poisonous one. I am.

FIFTEEN

WILLOW

LOVE AND HATE are two sides of the same coin. They are both intense emotions, violent in their passion. And as Professor Bradley waxes poetic about the forbidden nuances of Romeo and Juliet, it dawns on me. This is what Ryan and I are—twins, two sides of the same coin. On my side, there is love, and on his, there is hate.

My hand clenches down on the pen I'm using to follow along on the passage we're reading today, and my ribcage seems to squeeze against the pounding of my heart. Tears burn in the backs of my eyes—not of pain but anger.

Why me? I wonder not for the first time. Why do I have to hurt? Why does Ryan? Why couldn't we have been born apart, as two separate people? Why do I feel like I do, and why the fuck won't it go away?

A giggle from behind me snaps me out of my internal reverie, and I glance back over my shoulder. Two girls sit with their desks practically on top of each other, one textbook split open between them, but their eyes aren't on the passages in front of them. They're on me. I frown as one grins and then whispers something to her friend. The friend's face pops up and turns my way.

It's almost creepy the way they stare at me as if I'm a bug under a microscope. *What the hell is up with that?* I turn back around in my seat, but my concentration is shot to hell. Throughout the rest of the class, I can feel their curious gazes on my back. It's a blessing when the clock ticks past the end of our time, and I breathe a sigh of relief as I begin to pack up.

However, my relief is short-lived because as I slide from my desk, a hand shoots out and stops me. "You're Willow, right?" It's one of the girls from before. I look up, noting that she's at least a good five inches taller than me. Her straight blonde hair is cut in a line around her shoulders, giving her a longer bob.

I blink up at her. "Yeah?" The other friend, who's closer to my height, steps up alongside us. "Can I help you?" I ask.

She grins. "How do you know Ryan Anderson?" the second girl asks.

"What?" I turn my gaze to Lana, but she's distracted at the front, talking to Professor Bradley. I turn back to the girls.

"We asked how you knew Ryan Anderson?" the first girl restates her friend's question. "You know, Trinity's quarterback? We heard you've been hanging out with him lately—"

"Well," the second girl says, cutting her friend off. "We've heard you were seen with him—not so much that you two hang out together. So how do you know him?"

My heart starts to race for an all-new reason. My palms grow damp. "Who said I know him?"

"Why else would you be following him around like a lost puppy dog?" the shorter girl says.

I feel my face drain of emotion and go cold. "I'm done here," I say.

When I try to move past them, the taller of the two doesn't budge. Her cool blue eyes stare down at me. "Just tell us the truth," she presses. "If you don't know him, why are you obsessed with him?"

"Obsessed with him?" I repeat, confused. "I'm not obsessed with him."

The shorter girl laughs. "That's not what we hear."

Irritation boils up within me and I shoot her a hard look. "Why don't you clue me in," I snap, "because I don't know what you've heard. I don't know about you two, but I come here to get an education, not to gossip."

If she's offended by my tone, she doesn't show it. No, instead, she laughs in my face. "Oh, come off it," she says. "Don't play that goody-two-shoes card. There's a rumor going around that—"

"What's going on here?" Lana pops up between us, and just as expected, her hand goes immediately to the tall girl's shoulder and pushes her back until there's enough room for me to step away and hike my bag back up my shoulder.

"We were just telling your friend here that everyone knows about her little obsession with Ryan Anderson," the short girl continues. "It's pretty pathetic. Poor Ryan is a good quarterback, and of course, he's hot. Guys like him have to deal with stalker fangirls all the time; I'm sure you're not the first, Willow."

Lana's eyes widen and shoot to my face. My irritation burns hotter. Before Lana can stop me, I step right up to the girl and glare down my nose at her. "Let me tell you something, bitch." I can feel Lana's shock. I'm not one to curse, and maybe in the past, I'd let Ryan and Lana handle any and all bullies that came my way, but I'm a grown-ass woman now. I don't need anyone to fight my battle for me. "It's none of your fucking business how I know Ryan," I snarl. "But yeah, I do know him. *Personally*." I emphasize the last word. Of course, I know what Lana will take from it—that I know Ryan because of our relation—but this girl will take it as I mean it, that I know Ryan a lot more intimately than she likely ever will. "So whatever rumors you're spreading are completely false."

"Then tell us how you know him," the tall girl intrudes.

I turn my face up and my glare falls on her. "No," I say. One word. One syllable. No fucking room for argument. "You're not worth it." With that, I turn and storm out of the classroom.

"Will!" Lana calls me as she rushes to catch up, but my anger is like a violent storm. I've never been this furious before. Never felt the heat of it quite like this. It's a volcano inside of me, bubbling and boiling and waiting to erupt.

How dare he! I scream internally. He hates me, I get that. He wants me to stay away from him, I get that too. But starting vicious rumors? That's not like him. That's catty and petty and ... "It's fucking bullshit!" I shout as I come to a stop at the crosswalk.

"Whoa." Lana screeches to a halt alongside me, staring at me as if I've grown a second head. "Dude, what was that all about?" she asks.

"That was Ryan," I state. "Trying to prove to me just how much he hates me."

"Are you sure?" she asks. "I mean, rumors happen all the time. Do you really think it was him?"

Who else would it be? No one here even knows me, much less dislikes me enough to spread a shitty rumor like that. I can still feel the anger inside of me as it fills my face.

"We're gonna find out," I state as the light changes to green and I start across the street. It's lunchtime now, and as we head towards the cafeteria, I'm almost positive I'll find Ryan there.

He might not like to approach me, but I don't have the same aversion. I'm going to find that asshole right now and demand to know what he's thinking. Rumors are cheap blows, but rumors can spread as fast as wildfire, and they can destroy a person's reputation. It doesn't make any sense. Wasn't this why he left six years ago, to begin with? So there wouldn't be any rumors about him and me? He didn't want that. So why this? Why now? Does he feel like I've backed him into a corner? Well, it's not true. I haven't done anything to deserve this.

My legs carry me into the cafeteria hall, my feet pounding against the tile. I don't even feel the weight of my bag. All I feel is the anger in my chest. As if sensing my volatile nature, people quickly move out of my way.

"Will, maybe you should rethink..." Lana's words trail off. She's still speaking, but I no longer hear her when I spot Ryan with Tanner across the room. I stomp towards them, my focus narrowing.

Ryan's lips quirk at something his friend says, and he shakes his head before opening his mouth to reply. He doesn't get the chance. "What the hell did I do to you?" I demand, shoving my way between them and staring up at him.

Already, I can feel eyes on us, watching like vultures. Ryan gapes down at me, stunned. Maybe he's surprised that I would actually be upset, especially considering how he treated me the last time we saw each other. Not that I did anything to stop what happened in the library. I was just as much a willing participant as he was. His shock only registers for a moment before returning to that scowl of his that always seems to be directed at me, and only me. "What are you—"

"Cut the crap," I shout, stopping him. "Rumors? You started rumors to get me to stay away from you?" I shake my head. "I told you I'd stay away, Ryan, but this is bullshit."

Ryan's scowl drops away. "What are you talking about?" he demands.

"Like you don't know," I say.

"Would I be fucking asking if I knew?" he replies. "What rumors are you talking about?"

"People are saying she's stalking you," Lana pipes up from the sidelines.

Ryan's gaze flashes to her and then back to me.

"They also say I'm obsessed with you—obviously can't be a stalker without a little bit of obsession." The angry words flow from my lips like water.

"I don't know anything about that," he says, stepping back and frowning. "You've got the wrong guy. If rumors are going around about you, then maybe you need to take a look at your own actions."

Pain spikes in my chest. My eyes burn. "*You're a liar*," I spit.

Lana moves closer and grabs my arm. Her gaze isn't on me, though. It's on Tanner, who stands back and watches the proceedings with a calm, unmoved expression. I'm surprised, really. He seems the type of guy to enjoy watching the drama unfold.

Hot and cold. Back and forth. Whatever this thing with Ryan is ... Lana's right; I just need to stop it. I need to accept the fact that it's not real and it can never be real. Even so, I never believed that he would lie straight to my face like this, and I have to admit, it hurts more than I thought it would.

Ryan doesn't say anything, though, after my accusation. He just stands there, stone-faced and silent. It's only due to Lana's tugging that I finally let myself be drawn away. She shoots a look backward before hurrying to drag me out of the cafeteria, her hand firm the entire time. It isn't until we reach the outside that I let the tears fall, and my hands come up to cover my face.

"Oh, babe..." Lana's palm touches my back, smoothing up and down my spine.

I shake my head. "I can't deal with this anymore," I tell her. "I can't."

"I'll find out who started the rumor," she promises. But I don't think she'll have to. Love and hate—my side of the coin is slowly turning over. It's obvious that Ryan just wants me to hate him, and right now ... he might be getting his wish.

Sixteen

RYAN

YOU'RE A LIAR. Willow's words echo around inside my head days after our encounter at the cafeteria. She's right, but not about the rumors. I've been lying to her long before now.

"What are you doing?" Tanner's voice penetrates my concentration as I finish packing the last of what I'll need for the weekend and zip up my bag.

"What does it look like I'm doing?" I prompt him as I slide the suitcase off the bed and set it on the ground. "I'm heading out for the weekend."

"Oh?" He ambles into my room and then drops down onto the end of my bed before leaning back on both palms. "Where to?"

"Nowhere special," I tell him. "I'm just heading up to Boston to visit an old friend."

"Prison friend?" he asks.

I roll my eyes and reach out, shoving him off my bed. He yelps as his ass lands on the floor and skids half a foot over. "I was never in prison, asshole," I remind him. "It was juvie, and yeah, he is."

"Hmmm." Tanner hums in the back of his throat as he gets off his ass and resettles himself on my bed. I'm half tempted to shove him off again just to be a dick, but I refrain. "Any particular reason you're choosing to go on a trip now?" he prompts. "It wouldn't happen to have anything to do with a certain brunette who seemed quite upset with you earlier this week."

I glare at him. "That's none of your fucking business."

He blinks up at me slowly. "What about football practice?" he asks instead.

"I've already talked to Coach. We don't have a game this weekend, and I'm only gonna be gone for two days."

"Boston's a few hours' plane ride away," he says. "What's so special about this friend? Why can't you talk to me 'bout your girl problems?" He clasps his hand over his heart dramatically. "Truly, I'm hurt. Am I not responsible enough?"

I move across the room and grab my phone charger, unplugging it from the wall and shoving it into my backpack. "Responsibility isn't one of your strong suits for sure," I say. "But no, it's about something else." Something I'd almost forgotten about. A promise that I'd made on behalf of Willow. One she knew nothing about.

Tanner collapses back against my mattress and stares at the ceiling. "Then I guess I have nothing else to say to stop you from going," he sighs. "Don't worry, I'll be the man of the house while you're gone. I'll look after your things, and that includes that scrappy little brunette who you didn't even think could get mad at you. She was actually kinda cute all flushed like that. If Lana hadn't pulled her away, I feel like she might've kneed you in the balls."

The vein in my forehead pulses with annoyance. "Why the fuck am I friends with you again?"

"Good judgment?" Tanner says as he sits up.

I grip the strap of my backpack and sling it over my shoulder before reaching for my suitcase. "Doubtful." I head for the door.

He pops up to follow me. "Then perhaps it's because you know I'll find out about those rumors she was so upset about."

I pause at the top of the stairs and look back. "Anything yet?"

Tanner shoves his hands into his jeans' pockets and leans against the door jamb, a cool smile curving his mouth up. "I'll know more by the time you get back," he promises. "And I meant what I said—I'll look after her while you're away."

There's no use telling him not to, and no point in telling him I don't care. Tanner knows far more than he lets on. That much is obvious. No matter how I've tried to hide it, I'm just not that fucking good when it comes to Willow. "Thanks," I mutter, as I turn back to lift my suitcase in my hand and head down the stairs, feeling his gaze following me the entire way.

BOSTON IS JUST over a four-hour flight from Trinity's little podunk airfield. Four hours of recycled air, mouth breathing, cramped seating bullshit. The second wheels touch the ground, and the exit unlocks; I'm up and out of my seat with bags in hand. It doesn't matter that it still takes another twenty minutes just to unload from the airplane. Being on one makes me feel like I'm back in juvie going into solitary for fighting. The claustrophobic tightness in my chest doesn't lessen until I'm out of the damn winged tin can. Flying fucking sucks, but it's a hell of a lot faster than the drive.

I march through Boston Logan International and cut a path towards the outside, finding a row of taxis, and slip into the backseat of the first one I see, tossing my backpack onto the floorboards before handing over the address of where I need to go. For the next thirty minutes, I listen to the taxi cab driver muttering curses under his breath as he weaves in and out of traffic. We pull up in front of a red-faced brick building in the industrial district with a neon sign over the entrance.

The sign is dull with no illumination, but it's not difficult to read. I'm not incredibly familiar with Boston, but from what I can tell, the industrial district is where many of the old factory buildings and warehouses have been renovated into hippy clubs and bars. This place seems to be no different, complete with its own ridiculous name: Purgatory.

Who the hell wants to party in a place called Purgatory? Purgatory is where I've been for the last several weeks, close enough to Willow to taste her on my tongue and yet so far away.

The memory of her actual taste—her juices running down my chin as I licked her clit and fingered her pussy in the basement of the library pounds through my head. Fuck me. This really isn't the plan to sport a hard-on. I adjust my pants and grab my bag from the floor.

"Hey buddy, you sure this is the place?" the cabby asks.

I toss a couple of twenties up front to cover the fair and include a hefty tip without responding as I grab my bag and pop the back door open, stepping out and letting it click shut behind me. Out of the corner of my eye, I see the driver shake his head, pick up the bills, and then put them away as he reverses out of the parking lot.

There's an obvious entrance to the club, but I bypass that and head around to the side of the building, where I spot exactly what I'm looking for. There are two cars in the side parking lot and an employee entrance. The employee entrance is unlocked, so I push into the interior and let the door clang shut behind me. The second my feet hit the concrete floor, however, something crashes around the corner, and I hear the hard thump of footsteps racing towards me in the distance. An unfamiliar girl pops her fiery redhead around the corner. Her eyebrows shoot up at the sight of me, and then a deep scowl overtakes her face.

"Hey, we're closed," she snaps. "So, turn your ass around and get out."

I lift a hand anyway, ignoring the attitude. "I'm not a member," I reply. "I'm here to see a friend."

She starts to shake her head but pauses when another set of footsteps approach, this time from slightly above. I take several steps towards her and turn in the direction of the new set of footsteps echoing in the large open interior space of the building.

The girl eyes me like I'm a disgusting rodent that just entered her sacred space. "Stone," she starts as a hulking beast of a man comes down the stairs to the side and around the corner dressed in jeans and a loose gray t-shirt.

"Don't worry about it, Josi," he says. "I got it."

She harrumphs and turns to give me the stank eye but doesn't say anything more as she strolls off. Stone looks at me for a long moment, his dark eyes glaring, and I can't fight the smirk that lifts to my lips.

"Long time no see," I comment. "Nice girl you got there."

His face cracks, and he shakes his head. "Who? Josi? Don't mind her. She's just protective of the place—especially during the day and especially when random dudes pop in unannounced."

I arch a brow and the two of us stand there for a moment, across the room with each of us sizing the other up. Kinda reminds me of the first time we met. Almost exactly six years ago in a juvenile detention center.

Finally, Stone cracks a grin and marches forward to clap me on the back. "It's good to see you, Anderson." He slaps my shoulder, nearly making me stumble under the weight of his hit.

I roll my shoulder back and grin. "Please tell me you've been laying off the steroids," I say.

Stone rolls his eyes before lifting one arm and slapping his bicep. "This ain't got nothing to do with drugs, my man," he replies. "It's all muscle."

"Yeah? Your brain still all muscle too, or you got something for me?" I try not to show the hope that sits within my chest, but I'm not sure it comes through.

Stone drops his arms and then glances back, but if he's looking for the chick who was first here, she's long gone by now—the sounds of her moving about somewhere else on the distant lower floor. He sighs, gesturing towards the large staircase to the side where he'd come from. "Come on, let's talk about it in my office."

"Office?" I hum in the back of my throat as I follow him up to the second floor. "Big shot now, I see. Got yourself your own office."

Stone chuckles. "Not really," he says. "Just your average joe."

"Yeah, right..." My voice trails off as I catch a glimpse of what the rest of the building contains as we pass the wall that mainly has everything hidden. A low whistle slips past my lips. "This ain't no regular club," I say, taking in the sights.

Stone grunts a nonresponse. There's no need to respond after all. I always knew what kinda stuff he was into. It doesn't really shock me that he's decided to work in a place like this. The painted gray walls shift colors as we move upward, and as we reach a long hallway, I spot swathes of white and blue as a mural of clouds forms and stretches down the hallway between the doors on either side, each one with a large number painted on its front. Kinda interesting for a place like this. Far prettier than I expected.

At the end of the hallway is another staircase. Stone halts at the bottom and turns back to me. "Offices for monitors are up here," he states, waving his hand for me to go forward.

"Dungeon monitor?" I ask as I reach him. Only then do I see the small corner of his mouth tilt up. I shake my head. "Did you really think it would shock me? You working at a sex club?"

He shrugs. "Wouldn't matter if it did since you probably would have still found me."

"I don't think I ever lost you. We might've fallen out of contact, but it's not like you're in hiding." I head up the staircase and stop, turning back. Stone's arm shoots over my shoulder, pointing to the right door, and I head towards it.

Once we're inside, I take a step to the side and wander around, dropping my bag next to the fold-out chair in front of the dark wood desk that's facing away from the large window behind it. I stop beside the cot in the corner and kick it slightly.

"You living here?"

Stone takes a seat at the desk and shakes his head. "Nah, that's just when it's been a long night, and I gotta catch a quick cat nap."

"If I recall," I say, thinking back to our days in juvie, "cat naps weren't really your thing." If anything, Stone wasn't the type to sleep at all. Even when we'd been roommates, he went to bed after me and was up before me. No matter the day. No matter what had happened.

"What can I say?" Stone shrugs. "Old age has changed me."

I roll my eyes. "You're twenty-three," I snort. "Hardly old."

"Why don't you sit down, and we can talk about why you're really here," Stone suggests, giving me a look.

He's right. I'm just putting off the inevitable, and if he wants to get down to the nitty-gritty, then he doesn't want to make the disappointment last. I shove my hands into my pockets and drop my shoulders.

"You couldn't find anything," I guess.

Stone's lips press into a flat line. He props his elbows on the surface of the desk, steepling his fingers, and dropping his chin against them. "I've gone through every contact I've got, my man," he says. "But all we really have is the date you and your girl were found, and where you were dropped off at. There wasn't much to go on, and the records are shoddy at best." He reaches into his desk and pulls out a very slim manila folder setting it down in front of me before resuming his original position.

I grit my teeth as I reach for the folder and flip it open. I expected this, and yet, the loss still sits in my chest like a violent angry thing. I don't know what I was hoping for. Maybe answers. Maybe some hint as to where Willow and I came from. Deep down, I'd always wondered if maybe these revolting feelings of mine aren't hereditary. If our parents weren't as fucked up as we are. I couldn't care less if they're dead or alive.

"Thanks for looking anyway," I say after a tense moment. The words on the page are all ones I've seen before. They don't say anything except my suspected date of birth, age, race, baby weight. There's a similar page for Willow, but that's it.

"I can keep trying if you really—"

I hold up a hand, cutting him off. "No," I state. "That won't be necessary. Maybe it's better this way."

Stone's face softens, and he drops his arms. "It's normal, you know," he starts, "to want to know your past."

The truth is, though, that my desire to find out who the hell our parents were—and why they'd left two babies in a rural fire station drop off twenty years ago—is potent, it's not nearly as potent as the hope that I'd held that maybe ... they'd be able to give me some answers.

"Yeah, well, the past obviously doesn't want to be uncovered," I say. "They dropped us off like garbage and bounced. I don't know why I care."

Silence descends, and then Stone gets up and rounds the desk before propping himself back against it, crossing his arms over his massive bare chest. "The past ain't important," he says. "It's the future that you should look towards."

The future ... I think. An image of Willow laughing assaults my mind. I want that. I want her laughter. I want her near me every day. Her hand in mine. Her body in my bed. Her heart. Her love.

"Maybe focusing on the present is better," I say instead before turning towards him. I set the folder back down on his desk.

"You can keep that," he says.

I shake my head. "Nah. Shred it. Burn it. Throw it away, I don't really care. It doesn't do me any good now."

"It doesn't change who you are, man," he says.

No, and that's the problem. "Did I tell you I'm playing football at a university now?" I ask, changing the subject.

"Oh ho?" He smirks back at me. "Big shot now, eh? You thinking about going professional?"

I laugh. "Hell fucking no. It's just for the scholarship. I like the sport. I like the workout—don't get me wrong—but there's no way I'm gonna make this a lifetime gig."

"Lucky for both of us, we never made juvie a lifetime gig either," Stone comments. "Or rather prison."

I nod in agreement. "Speaking of," I say, "you still talk to any of the other guys?"

Stone leans his head back. "Couple work in a few clubs I know of. Some are locked up. Only one other guy I know of actually did something—Theo's working up to being a professor now."

"A professor of what?" I snap, shocked. "Anger management?" A memory of a scrappy little curly-haired boy pops into my brain with violence in his brown eyes and blood on his knuckles.

Stone barks out a laugh. "Nah, believe it or not, he's going through a program in upper Illinois right now to be a freaking professor of philosophy."

I shake my head. "That's insane." It really is. I can't imagine some kid from nowheresville out in the boondocks sent to juvie over pickpocketing people at a mall as a professor of philosophy.

Nostalgia tugs at me, and as it does, Stone sighs and pushes up from his desk. "How about I take you out for a drink," he says. "You can tell me about your all-American football dreams coming true, and I'll fill you in on our missing brothers."

I want that, I realize. I was away from Willow for six years, and in that time, this man had become my best friend. Now, things are reversed. I'm back with Willow, and I've been away from the home I'd known when I had nothing—not even her.

"Yeah, man," I say. "I think I'd like that."

SEVENTEEN

WILLOW

THE WEEKEND COMES and goes, and with each passing day, I grow angrier. I'm not used to it. Between the two of us—Ryan and I—I've always been the one with the less volatile emotions. Now, however, that seems to have changed. Everywhere I go—class, the cafeteria, the gym, work—eyes follow me. People whisper behind their hands.

The rumors are getting out of control, and Ryan ignores me every time he sees me, so there's no opportunity to get him to say something and put an end to them. Even girls from my dorm have been stopping by to ask me about them. They know me best. They know me as the girl who keeps to herself, has one friend, and goes nowhere but work and school. Now, all of a sudden, they believe the ridiculous rumors about me stalking Ryan. If only they knew the truth.

I could stop all of these rumors. I could just be open and admit that I'm not stalking Ryan because I'm a love-filled fangirl. I'm so much worse. I'm his fucking sister. I wonder what people would say then. Probably worse things. I'm Ryan's twin, and yet, I don't look at him the way a sibling would. The way I look at him is something far more taboo.

"Hey, how are you holding up?" Lana asks as she meets me outside of her last class of the day.

Clutching my books to my chest, I glare at two girls whispering behind their hands as they pass by. "Like shit," I admit.

I can feel Lana's gaze on my face. "It's not that bad," she tries. My head turns, along with my glare, right on her. I don't say anything. I let my eyes do the talking. She, at least, has the grace to grimace and look away. "Yeah, okay," she corrects. "It's pretty bad."

"This is stupid," I snap as we start walking towards the student union. There's a second food court on the bottom floor—a little more expensive than the cafeteria but with a lot less prying eyes.

"It's like high school bullshit all over again," Lana agrees with a groan.

I shake my head. Even after Ryan left, things weren't this bad in high school. *What the hell was he thinking?*

"Why don't you just tell people that you're his sister?" Lana asks, eyeing me from the side.

It's a good question. There are a multitude of reasons not to and even more to go ahead and say it. If I'm honest with myself, I know why I'm holding back. Back when Ryan and I were in foster care there was no chance for us—no possibility that we could pretend we weren't siblings—but here, no one knows. No one outside of Lana that is. If everyone were to know, then we'd be right back to that place. I must be a fucking masochist. There's no way Ryan wants any sort of relationship with me—familial or otherwise.

But that day at the library still haunts me. It keeps my lips sealed and the flame of hope alive, no matter how wrong I know it all is.

"They've gotten worse," I say instead as we stride down the outdoor stone steps leading to the basement food court. "They're not just saying I'm obsessed with Ryan anymore. Now, they've moved on to calling me a whore and an easy slut. Even if I said something about Ryan being my brother, it wouldn't stop the rumors." I pause, feeling her seeking interest. I don't have to look at her to know she's observing me carefully. "Besides, it's none of their business."

Lana sighs. "Still, telling people would at least solve that one problem."

I reach forward and grasp the handle to the glass door leading inside and pull it open, holding it for her as she passes through first. "I'm not telling these people shit," I sneer, unleashing some of the pent-up anger I've been keeping so well contained. "They just need to mind their own business."

When I look up and catch a guy eyeing me with a knowing smirk as he passes with a bag from one of the restaurants lining the back wall, I don't hold back. I keep my books pressed to my chest with one arm and lift my other, flashing my middle finger, so he gets the hint. I drop my arm when he's out of sight and glance at Lana, noting her raised eyebrows.

"What?" I ask.

"I've just never seen you like this."

"Yeah, well, I've never felt like this either," I grumble as we find a table, and I shove my stuff down in the seat across from hers.

A familiar head of sandy-colored hair pops up over the minuscule crowd and makes its way towards us. I repress a groan. It's not that I don't like Tanner. In fact, I think he's a pretty decent guy, and it's become increasingly obvious that Lana is falling head over heels for him despite the fact that he's Ryan's best friend, and she's not looking for anything serious after her last breakup. But for me, it's because he's Ryan's best friend that I can't help but feel uncomfortable around him.

The second Lana sees him in the crowd, however, I know there's no getting away from him tonight. I wouldn't try—not with the way her eyes light up as he approaches. Have I ever felt that way about anyone other than Ryan? Tanner grins her way and then gives her a quick hug when he stops by the table.

"Hey," he says, lifting a hand my way in greeting. "I thought I saw the two of you come in here. Don't you guys usually hit the cafeteria?"

I grimace, but Lana answers for me. "We're avoiding the crowds," she says, cutting a look my way before returning the bulk of her attention to him.

Tanner's lips tilt down, and he shoots me a regretful but understanding look. "I really am sorry about all of this, Willow Tree," he says, "but for what it's worth, I don't think Ryan started those rumors."

I dive into my bag like it's my last lifeline, searching for my wallet. "I'm gonna go grab a bite to eat," I say quickly, not responding to his comment. "I'll be right back." The second my fingers close around my wallet, I snatch it out of my bag and turn to head for the row of restaurants in the back of the ample open space that makes up the food court. I'm going for the gold as I weave in and around tables like it's an Olympic sport.

If there's anything I don't want to talk about right now, it's Ryan and those stupid rumors.

Consciously aware of the eyes on me, I walk towards the burger place with the shortest line and order a quick meal and drink. Ten minutes later, I stride back towards the seating area and spot Tanner and Lana with their heads together, both seeming very intent in their conversation. That is—until I set my food down and take a seat.

Both of their heads pop up, and Tanner flashes me a bright—and suspicious—smile. I frown at the two of them as I slip my wallet back into my bag.

"Alright," I say with a sigh. "Out with it. What's with the looks?"

Lana winces at my tone, but Tanner either

doesn't notice it or doesn't care because he bulldozes past my apparent reluctance to know whatever the hell they're planning and starts talking.

"We were talking about the game this weekend," he says. "And how you two should come."

I scowl at him, reaching for a fry. I pop it into my mouth, letting the salty, starchy goodness calm me before replying. "That sounds like a fucking awful idea," I finally say.

Tanner doesn't let that deter him. He leans forward, propping his elbows on the table, and grins my way. "No, it's fucking brilliant," he states. "Think about it"—he points at me—"is staying holed up in your dorm room going to make people stop talking?" He doesn't even give me an opportunity to answer him. "No, it's not," he says. "If you lock yourself away, it won't stop people from talking. In fact, doing that is just going to make them talk more."

"And what would going to the football game do?" I ask. *Aside from irritate me.* In an effort to rein my emotions back in, I refrain from saying that last part.

Bolstered by Tanner's start, Lana jumps in. "It'll show them that you're not listening," she says, leaning across the table excitedly. "If you go to the football game, you'll basically be showing that you don't care what people say, and if it looks like you don't care, then it'll make the rumors seem irrelevant."

"Yeah," Tanner agrees with a nod. He reaches across the table and snags a fry from my bag, and points at me with it. It almost seems more insulting that he's stealing my food and using it to scold me. "If you keep doing what you're doing—glaring at everyone who talks about you and storming around, then they're going to think all of the rumors are true."

"They're not!" I yell, slamming my hand down on the table. "That's why I'm so pissed off!"

"But that's not how people think," Tanner replies as he tosses my fry into his mouth and chews and swallows it. "People think that the more you pay attention to those rumors, the more credit they have. If you pretend not to care, they'll start to think it's bogus."

Lana arches a brow his way. "Bogus?" she repeats. "Really?"

Tanner looks at her. "What?"

It's in that moment that I see the truth—the way these two look at each other as Lana informs him just how outdated that phrase is, and Tanner laughs it off before they return their attention to me. They've made up their minds. In their eyes, this is the only way to get me out of my predicament. To be honest, it's not like I'm coming up with any grand schemes of my own. I'm well and truly trapped.

I shove the rest of my fries towards the two of them with a resigned sigh and instead focus on my burger. "Fine," I mutter as I peel back the paper edges of its wrapping. "I'll go to the stupid game this weekend."

"Don't worry," Lana says. "Tanner and I will be there."

"Well, I'll be in the game, so I can't sit with you," Tanner says, taking a handful of fries and shoveling them in his mouth. "But we can meet up afterwards and go to one of the parties if you want."

That's if I last through the whole game.

Saturday nights at Trinity University are sacred. To the regular eye, they're just another weekend night. To a Trinity Warrior, Saturday nights are all about the games and parties. The Trinity University stadium is walkable from the rest of campus. Still, Lana and I choose to hop a ride together in her beat-up Chevy and pull up to the parking lot of the stadium just as twilight hits.

"Grab one of the sweatshirts from the back," Lana calls as she rubs her hands together and slips into her own.

I follow her instructions and then round the car to meet her at the tailgate. "Is that yours?" I ask, eyeing the red and black hoodie she's wearing.

A light blush spreads across her cheeks. "It's Tanner's," she admits.

"If you're wearing his hoodie, does that mean you guys are official now?" I ask as we head towards the ticket gates.

"I don't know about that," she admits. "But he's made it clear he's interested."

I wait for her to say more, but when she doesn't, I can guess why. "You like him," I state. "As more than a rebound."

She groans. "It's stupid of me," she says.

"You know what they say," I tease. "Your soulmate comes for you when you're not looking."

"Couldn't he have waited until I went through a hoe phase?" Lana mutters.

There's a beat of silence, and the two of us glance at one another right before we burst out laughing. We don't stop until we're at the back of the ticket line. I can tell we're already starting to draw attention, and it's not all because we're laughing like two maniacs, but honestly, the amusement makes me not care.

Maybe Tanner and Lana are right. Maybe if I just pretend like everyone's stares and whispers don't bother me, they'll get the fuck over it. And although sooner rather than later would be my preference, I'm not too picky. Eventually, these vultures will find someone else to gossip about.

I hand Lana the cash for my ticket when I spot a concessions stand. "I'll grab some snacks and soda," I offer, "you grab my ticket and meet me in the checkout line."

She waves me off, and I hurry over, scanning the crowd for any sign of familiar faces. I doubt Tanner or Ryan will be out and about—not when they're probably getting ready for the game. The smell of burnt popcorn and sweat permeates the air, reminding me of the high school football games I'd attended for Ryan. Those had been significantly less crowded than these.

As I reach the front of the line, I feel an itch at the back of my head, like someone is specifically staring at me or perhaps trying to get my attention. I turn and glance back as the concessions stand attendant asks for my order, but I don't find anyone watching me. Shrugging it off, I chalk it up to the multitude of eyes I've had on me all week, and order one large popcorn and two medium-sized light sodas.

Just as the popcorn is finished, Lana approaches and snags the drinks from my hands, freeing them up to take the giant tub the girl hands me. "Jesus, Will," Lana says, eyeing the thing. "Did you skip dinner or something?"

"I'm sharing with you," I remind her.

She shakes her head, walking around the concessions towards the open entrances leading into the bleachers. Loud chanting reaches my ears, and bright lights hit my eyes as we go from the dim lighting of the inner stadium building to the outside arena. I blink away the little black and white circles dancing in front of my eyes.

Lana lets out a slow whistle. "Damn, looks like the whole school showed up for this game." Anxiety creeps up my throat. She glances my way when she steps forward, yet I don't follow her. "Hey?" She reaches out and touches my shoulder.

"Are you okay?"

I want to tell her, 'no, I'm not.' I want to beg her to let me go back to my dorm and do precisely what she and Tanner told me not to—hole up and hide away. There are so many people here, and I'm sure almost all of them have heard the shitty stuff everyone is saying about me. Two weeks ago, I was no one. I was invisible. Unimportant. But Ryan is a star here, and with my name now attached to his—that sanctuary of invisibility is all but evaporated.

"Will?" Lana's voice cuts through the nervous fog of my mind as she grasps me by both of my shoulders.

I can't let myself be pulled in by the fear, I tell myself. I can't turn back now. "Let's just find a spot and camp out for the night," I tell her through a clogged throat. "I can do this—I just need to stay in one place."

She eyes me but then slowly nods. "Okay," she says. "No problem. Come on. Let's go up top. There will probably be less people up there."

Thankful for her understanding, I let her lead the way and follow her up a metal staircase to the side of several rows of bleacher seats. Looking at them and feeling the slight chill in the air, I'm glad I decided to go with the ripped jeans I've got on rather than the plaid skirt I'd been wearing earlier—the same one I'd been wearing when I'd been with Ryan in the basement library now that I'm thinking about it.

My mind spirals from there, and I find myself

following Lana out of instinct rather than conscious effort. My thighs clench at the memory of Ryan on his knees in front of me, his hands up around my hips and thighs, his fingers between the folds of my pussy. I bite down on my lower lip and nearly trip over my own two feet as Lana slides down a seat and guides me to another end.

However, just before we take our seats, a high-pitched, not at all unfamiliar voice pipes up. "Well, well, well, look who it is." I stiffen just as Lana's back goes ramrod straight.

About two rows down is a familiar head of platinum blonde hair. Harley Pavlov, Lana's ex-girlfriend, flips a strand of hair off her shoulder and eyes the two of us like we're bugs under a microscope. "Are you two on a date?" she taunts, directing her attention not to me but to Lana. "Not surprising."

Lana rips our drinks back up from where she'd set them down and starts to march off. "We're not sitting here," she snaps to me.

I take the chance to glare down the rows at Harley's mousy face. What Lana had seen in her, I'll never know. She's got small features, which might've looked attractive had it not been for the fact that the rest of her is ample and built. She's got pretty hair, but it's wasted on someone so catty and rude.

"Wait, Lana!" Harley calls, laughing as the girl next to her stares me. "Maybe you should stay away from that *friend* of yours"—I don't miss the emphasis she puts on the word 'friend'—"I heard she's been stalking one of the football players."

Lana freezes, and I nearly run straight into her back. Before I can tell her it's not worth it, she turns and glares down the bleachers. "Why don't you shut your dirty whore mouth, Harley," Lana spits. "You've got no room to talk about Willow. You're a fucking cheater and a bad lay. And for your information, I'm not here with her on a date—though she'd be a hell of a better choice than you—I'm here to support my new boyfriend. Maybe you've heard of him? His name is Tanner Striker."

I don't have the chance to marvel over the sudden announcement before I'm already enjoying the sight of Harley's face going slack and her jaw dropping. "You're dating a football player?" she sputters.

Lana arches a brow. "Well, can you blame me?" she replies. "I needed a break from cheating sluts."

"Oh, like he won't cheat on you." Harley rolls her eyes. "He's a jock, Lana. Grow up. Not everyone can be monogamous."

"Lots of people can be monogamous, Harley," Lana replies. "Just not you. Enjoy the STDs."

"Yeah, well, at least my friend isn't an obsessed psycho!" Harley's scream follows us as Lana marches away, and I follow.

Lana is shaking by the time we get to our new seating several paces away from Harley and her friend. She slams down our drinks with effort and then plops down on the hard metal. "God, I wish I'd hit that bitch," she growls.

"Don't worry about it," I tell her, smiling. "She's not worth it."

Lana sighs and then picks up a drink. "Yeah, but it would've felt good," she mutters. She stares at her straw as I settle in and pop a handful of popcorn into my mouth. "For what it's worth, I'm sorry about what she said—bringing up those stupid rumors."

I wave a hand her way. "I don't give a fuck what Harley thinks," I say truthfully. "What I'm more interested in is if you're going to tell Tanner about your sudden decision to make him your boyfriend?"

Lana groans and sets her cup back down to cover her face with both hands. "Is there any way I can convince you not to tell him I said that?"

"And miss the reaction he'll give me?" I ask. "Absolutely not,"

"What about bribery?" she suggests.

"You couldn't pay me enough to miss out on this drama," I inform her.

She groans again, louder this time. "You're a horrible friend."

I laugh. "I'm your best friend, and you know it."

"I'll just explain the situation," Lana says suddenly. "He'll get that I was just trying to put Harley in her place. He'll go along with it if I ask him to. It doesn't have to mean anything."

I couldn't stop the eyeroll that overcomes me even if I wanted to. "Why don't you just accept it instead?" I ask. "It's not like it'll hurt anything. He seems to be into you, and you seem to be into him.

Other than his friends"—it's hard not to make that dig at the relationship he has with Ryan—"he's a nice guy."

"He is. It's just..." Lana's voice comes out croaky, and even though I can feel the eyes on me and hear the whispers, all of that disappears in the face of my friend's struggle. She pulls her face out of her hands and looks up at me. "He keeps his distance, and that makes me want to get closer. It's like he's hiding something, but I'm not sure if that's not my insecurities. I'm afraid I'm going to end up at the same place I was when Harley and I broke up," she admits. "What if we label what we have, and then we end up destroying it that much faster?"

I twist my lips from side to side. "Well, I can't exactly say I'm the kind of person to give you love advice," I say, "but there's no happiness without risk." My thoughts slip back to Ryan. Wondering if the risk I took had been worth it myself.

"So you think I should chance it?" Lana asks.

I inhale and then release a breath. "You've got two options," I say. "One, you don't ever consider the possibility of being more with him." It was once an option I'd considered myself. One that had made me curl up into a ball and cry myself to sleep countless nights before I'd opened myself up for a new type of pain. "Or two..." I swallow. "You go towards the unknown." It was exactly what I had done. Except, for her, this is probably the better choice. "The unknown could be rejection—which is what you'd be doing if you choose option one—

or it could make you happy." I look up and meet Lana's eyes. "I'd go with the choice that has the higher chances of happiness if I were you," I say.

Lana stares at me for a long moment. "You know, Will," she says, "sometimes, you surprise me."

I smile at her and pop another handful of popcorn in my mouth before offering her the bucket. She takes it willingly and hands me my drink as the two of us sit back and look across the stadium.

Unlike Ryan and me, Lana and Tanner don't have the same restrictions and obstacles. They have a chance at true happiness. I'd once thought I could overcome anything as long as Ryan was with me. The truth, however, is far crueler than fiction. In books and movies, maybe we could've been. There would've been some crazy twist of fate that would've made our love okay.

Instead, all we have are the taboos of the forbidden fruit. One bite, and we'll both end up somewhere near the pits of hell. What scares me most of all about that, though, is the fact that I still think I'd be willing to take that risk if he was too.

EIGHTEEN

RYAN

IT'S EASY TO get lost in one's own thoughts. Easy to lose track of the place around you. And it was easy to forget all of the shit I have to deal with at Trinity while I'd been away. Two days, I'd been gone, but the second I'd returned, I was forced to face it all over again. For the last week, I'd been steadily avoiding every place I thought Willow might be as I'd tried to figure out what to do about this new development.

Tanner, for a change, had been helpful. I'd been skipping meals at the cafeteria for several days in a row until he'd mentioned that Will had moved to eating in the food court in the student union. It didn't take a genius to figure out why. The student union usually had less of a crowd than the cafeteria. Willow had never really been too comfortable in the limelight anyway. This new development has to be hell for her.

Guilt eats away at me. I know she thinks I'm the one who started this, but what bothers me most is that I'm not, and I can't seem to pinpoint where it's coming from. Forty-eight hours of my absence had done nothing for the wild rumors now spreading about her. Should I have denied it immediately, or was it better to remain silent?

I wanted Willow to hate me enough to avoid me, maybe even to change schools, but now that it looks like that might be a possibility, my heart keeps hammering inside my chest with constant anxiety. I just got her back. After six fucking long years, I've finally got an opportunity to see her again, even if it's only on the sidelines.

Without warning, a wet towel launches across the locker room and slaps into my face. For a split moment, I feel like the universe is telling me to fuck myself because I started this shit, and I need to stop wavering on my decision. It's not, though. It's just Tanner. Like a bubble has been popped, all of the noises I've been drowning out rush right back to me. Guys slamming lockers closed as they rush to get ready for the big game. The other conversations. The sinks in the back of the locker room running. I didn't realize how fucking loud it was until it was right there.

Tanner stands over me decked out in his football gear, his helmet in hand as he arches one eyebrow at me. "The fuck are you thinking about so hard, man?" he asks.

I wave him away. "Nothing."

"Thinking about a certain girl?" he asks.

I shoot him a stern look, but there's no

amusement on his face. No taunting. Just plain curiosity. I don't have it in me to lie anymore. I sigh. "Don't ask if you already know," I say.

Surprisingly, Tanner doesn't press the issue. Instead, he sets his helmet on the bench next to mine and takes a seat. "Level with me," he says, propping his elbows on his knees. "You didn't start those rumors, right?"

I grit my teeth. "Like fuck I did," I snarl.

"Don't get defensive." Tanner's voice is calm. His eyes level. "You've been trying to drive her away since you ran into her. It's a valid question."

"I didn't start those fucking rumors about her stalking me or being a psycho or a whore. Willow's not a fucking whore."

Tanner nods. "No, she's not. She's a nice girl."

I cut a look his way. "How would you know?"

He doesn't hesitate to meet my gaze. The fucker must have a death wish because he doesn't even flinch. I've beaten down guys twice my size in juvie. Hell, in a fight between Stone and me, I'd come out on top at least fifty percent of the time, and that guy had been built like a brick shithouse. Big and indestructible. I'm just too angry half of the time to quit.

"I'm going to be straight with you, Ryan," Tanner finally says. "Whatever you've got going on with you, you need to knock it the fuck off."

I gape at him. "You don't know what you're fucking talking about," I snap.

"Then tell me," he challenges, arching that

goddamn brow of his. I swear it's one of his quirks, and every time he does it, he somehow manages to manifest this look of both amusement and superiority. "You're right, I don't know. So, you tell me. Tell me why I'm wrong to protect my friend when I can see someone trying so desperately to hurt her."

"I'm not..." My words fail me as I stare at him.

"You are," Tanner says when I can't seem to keep going. "You're fucking hurting her, and even though you're my friend, Ryan, you gotta tell me why. What the hell did that girl do to you to make you hate her so much?"

I'm hyper-aware that we're not alone. Though it seems like no one is paying us any attention as the rest of the team gets ready for the game, I can't take that chance that someone might be. I stand up and turn. "Come on," I say, and head towards the hallway.

I don't look back to see if he's following me. If he wants to know, and I know he does, then he will. That's just the kind of guy he is. My hand hits the door's lever, and I push out into the massive, open hallway. I can hear the sounds of screaming fans already. Someone runs past with their arms ladened with foam fingers. I keep going. Passing through until I reach the exact place I'm looking for: a storage room.

I check the door and find it unlocked, then I glance back, catching a glimpse of Tanner as he jogs to catch up with me. He frowns as I hold open the door and step back, gesturing for him to go first.

"This is some shady shit, my man," he comments. "If you're angry enough to off me, can we do it somewhere else—perhaps after the game?" He gives me a slightly amused smile.

"You want to know why I avoid Willow, don't you?"

He drops the smile and steps through the doorway. I follow behind him and let the door close behind us even as I reach out and flip the light on. The fluorescent bulbs buzz to life, illuminating the two of us and the baskets of extra footballs, padding, and other supplies in vaguely yellow lighting. We're alone. Just him and me and the demons I'm ready to unleash.

I've only ever told one other person of my feelings for Willow, and Stone is hours away, likely getting ready to open up that sex club of his for the night. "I love her." The words escape me, and with them comes a rush of relief. Almost like admitting the truth aloud is enough to lift a massive weight off of my shoulders. It's only temporary, I know. The second I step back out of this room, I go back to being just the guy that torments her and makes her life a living hell, all to protect her from this very thing.

"You love her?" Tanner repeats. The look of shock on his face isn't surprising. No man who claims to love a woman would treat her the way that I do.

It's toxic, the way I treat her. It's wrong. It's

cruel. And yet ... it's better than being away from her, dreaming of her every night, wondering where she is and if she's safe, or if she's happy. A better man might be able to let her go. A better man would have done anything and everything to get away from her and give her the chance to live an ordinary life. I'd tried to be that better man when I was younger. Now, all that was once good inside of me has dried up. I've been away from her for too long, and I can't seem to do it again. Yet, being near her is also turning me into a ruthless asshole. Just a few weeks ago, I'd pushed her to her knees and shoved my cock into the back of her throat. I'd felt just what I'd dreamed about for years, and it had been worse than anything I could've imagined. It'd been hot enough to light me on fire and burn me from the inside out, and I would be lying if I said I didn't dream of doing it all again. Feeling Willow's lush lips wrapped around my cock, sucking the cum from my balls as I cupped her face and looked into her gorgeous brown eyes.

"Yeah," I say. "I fucking love her. I want to fall asleep with her in my arms and wake up with her. I want to break the fingers of any man who so much as touches her. I want to tie her to me in every way possible."

Tanner shakes his head. "Dude, she's—"

"I'm not done," I say.

His eyes widen, but he takes a step back and gestures as if telling me to keep going.

My hands clench into fists at my sides. "I want

her," I reiterate. "But I can't have her."

He frowns. "What do you mean? I'm pretty sure she likes you too. She wouldn't put up with half of the shit you throw her way if she didn't."

"Will—" I stop and swallow. My palms feel sweaty. I unfold them and wipe them against my pants. My throat locks on the words as if my own body is fighting them, fighting against fate, but I push them out regardless. "Willow is my sister," I finally say. "She's my twin."

Tanner stares at me, his lips parted and his brows drawn low over his eyes. When I expect disgust or horror, there is none. It's not hidden, it's just not there. He continues to stare at me, his eyes communicating one thing—he thinks I've lost my ever-loving mind.

"Are you on drugs?" he finally asks.

My jaw drops. "What?" Of all the things that I thought he would say, that was not it.

"Seriously?" he demands. "If you're roided up or taking something else, you need to tell me. We can't let you play if you're—"

I punch his shoulder hard enough that he lets out a breath of air and is jerked backwards. "I'm not on fucking drugs, you dick!"

"Well, that's the only explanation I can think of for that load of shit you just told me," he says.

"It's true," I grunt.

Tanner shakes his head and turns away from me, shoving a hand through the top of his hair. He just as quickly turns back. "You're sure?" he asks.

"Willow and you—I mean, you two don't even look alike."

"We're fraternal," I said. "Obviously."

Tanner still doesn't look convinced. I never thought I'd be in this situation right now—revealing the biggest skeleton in my closet and my best friend not believing me. It's fucking surreal. It's probably God torturing me for all of the sins I'm so ready to commit if it means being near Willow.

"How do you know?" Tanner asks.

"We were dropped off together as infants," I start to tell him. It's not information he can't find out if he honestly tried. It was easy enough for Stone to find for me. "You know those drop-offs some old fire stations have due to the old safe-haven laws?" I ask. He nods but continues looking at me like I've suddenly grown two heads. It's starting to get on my nerves. "Well," I snap, "the two of us were found wrapped up together and deposited in one of those twenty or so years ago. We were only a few months old, but whoever documented us probably had us checked out. Think about it, Tanner. We're the same fucking age. We both have brown hair and brown eyes."

"Shit, man, lots of people have brown hair and brown eyes. Those are common traits," Tanner says immediately. "It doesn't mean you're related."

Is he just trying to torment me? I wonder. *Doesn't he have any idea how I wish it weren't true?*

"Tanner." I take a slow and steady breath

through my nose and exhale it through my mouth. "It's true—I'm in love with Willow, and you're right. She does like me. More than that, she loves me the same."

"Then why don't—"

"Because I want her to be happy," I say abruptly. "I want her to be fucking normal, okay? If we try and people find out the truth, what the fuck do you think they're going to say?" I ask. "If you think the rumors that are flying around about her now are bad, wait until that happens. She and I can never fucking be together. It's wrong, and god, I can't believe I'm saying this, but you fucking know it is." Now, it's my turn to stare at him like he's lost his mind.

Tanner paces across the room, back and forth, shaking his head. "No, no, this doesn't make any sense. You're not—" He cuts himself off. I don't know what the fuck he's talking about, but as I hear the rumbling of the crowd somewhere in the stadium and the Coach yelling, I know our time is up.

"We have to go," I say, turning and reaching for the door.

Before I can touch it, however, Tanner's hand lands on my arm. He turns me around and slams me back against the door, getting up in my face. His expression is dark, his eyes serious. "Okay. Say I believe you," he snaps.

"There is no believe or don't believe," I say. "It just is."

"Whatever." He growls in frustration. That's something I can understand, but his reaction isn't. What the hell is going on with him? "The fact is—you can't fucking continue to treat her like this. Regardless of whether or not you think she's your sister."

"She is."

Tanner pulls one hand away from the door and punches it. Hard. I freeze on the spot. I've been in some sketchy situations. I've gotten my ass jumped and beat, but right now, I feel as though I'm facing a wild animal. Someone on the verge of snapping, and I have no fucking idea why.

"Tanner?"

"You want her," he states. It's not a question, he and I both know that. "She wants you." Now, it's like he's no longer talking to me, but more to himself. He looks contemplative. His eyes jump back and forth yet they don't seem to be focusing on anything. "I'll figure it out," he says before pulling away.

"Figure what out?" I demand.

Coach's voice sounds just outside of the storage room. "Just..." Tanner grits his teeth and then shakes his head again. "Give me some time," he says. "I promise I'll explain, but I can't … not now. Not yet."

Just as I'm about to force him back and say fuck it to his 'not yet, not now' bullshit, the door to the storage room jiggles, and we both jerk back as it flies open. Coach stands there, huffing and puffing. He glares at the two of us.

I open my mouth, ready with a bullshit excuse, but he just holds up a hand. "I don't care," he growls before I can get a word out. He reaches for the two of us, grabbing ahold of our jerseys and yanking us out of the room. "I don't care—what you do in your private time is your business, but this is team time now, assholes." He pushes us forward towards the back of our teammates, who've all collected out into the outer hallway awaiting their introduction to the field. "Get your asses in line. We're about to go onto the field."

"Wait!" I say. "We're not—"

He doesn't give me a chance to say anything. Instead, he drops our jerseys and storms towards the front, leaving me gaping after him. Tanner claps me on the shoulder, and I look up to see that he's returned to his usual self, the façade of amusement back on his face. It's a striking contrast to the earlier dark looks and dangerous vibe that was rolling off of him in waves. I feel myself stiffen under the weight of his palm.

"Well, buddy," he says with a laugh. "Looks like Coach has no problem with us being closer than your average friend."

I stare at him in a mixture of shock, dawning realization, and horror.

Fuck. Me.

Nineteen

WILLOW

I'M NOT QUITE sure what it is about football games that seem to draw all sorts of crazy people together. Trinity Warrior fans litter the bleachers. Despite the chill in the air, some of the guys are shirtless, with their entire fronts and backs painted in red and white to show just how much they support their school. I mean, I do too, but damn—not enough to stain the dorm showers later.

"Look, they're coming out now!" Lana stands up and claps excitedly, and I follow suit. I clap along with the rest of the crowd as my eyes search through the sea of red and white jerseys running out of one of the entrances down below. There are so many, and we're so far up that it's hard to read each player's name on the backs.

The second my eyes land on number 22, however, I know. 22 was the same number Ryan had played in high school. Maybe we'd been apart for years, but I knew without a shadow of a doubt that he would've wanted to keep that number. He always believed that it would bring him good luck.

"That's Tanner," Lana says, pointing out number 43 right next to Ryan.

As if he senses our eyes, Tanner's head turns and tilts up. He scans the crowd until he lands on us, and then he grins and waves. Next to him, Ryan's head jerks around. Even from where I'm standing, I can see the surprise on his face—Did Tanner not tell him we were coming? Then he turns and says something to Tanner, and from the tenseness of his shoulders, I can only guess what it's about.

The team finishes lining up, and Lana and I retake our seats. I rub my hands together and reach for the popcorn as the kick-off starts. Ryan moves into place behind the center of his defensive teammates with Tanner towards the end of the row. A whistle blows, signaling the beginning of the game.

For several plays, Lana and I watch in near silence. The only thing disrupting our quiet viewing are the times when we pause to snack or check our phones. Mine beeps, and I glance down, frowning as an unknown number pops up. I ignore it and put my phone away, only to look up when a whistle blows again.

"What's going on?" I ask as my attention shoots towards the field. There's a circle of guys surrounding another, and for a brief moment, I panic. Then it sets in that the jerseys are black and gold—it's the other team, not ours, and not Ryan.

"Some guy got hit too hard, I think," Lana says with a shrug.

I glance her way, eyeing her as she appears to focus a little too hard on the game in front of us. "Are you okay?"

"Hmmm?" she responds, and then without looking at me, she nods. "Yeah, of course. Why?"

I arch a brow. "Because you're extremely quiet," I point out. "You'd usually be up and screaming by now. You're not exactly the type to sit through a game in silence."

Lana winces and then shoots me a quick look. "If you could not be so observant about my habits, that'd be great," she says with more than a hint of snark.

I laugh. "You wouldn't love me nearly as much."

She sighs. "You got that right," she agrees readily, and then, because she knows I'm not going to let it go, she turns towards me. "I'm just thinking about Tanner—and what I said earlier."

"To Harley?" I ask.

"Yeah." She sucks her bottom lip between her teeth and bites down, worrying about it. "It's just..." Lana's face grows pained. "I mean, I *do* like him, and you're right about the whole taking a chance on the path that might make me happy bit."

When she doesn't immediately go on, I lean forward. "But?" I supply.

She groans. "But like I said before, he's also a little odd at times."

"Odd how?" I ask.

"Well..." She drifts off, her eyes darting to the field and then back to me. "Tanner's usually so easy going, but he gets these phone calls every once in a while, and after each one, he seems to get really tense. I know you weren't really comfortable hanging out with him initially—because of Ryan—but he was actually really excited to get to know you."

"Me?" I repeat. "Why?"

"He said it was because you were my friend, and he wanted to know my friends, but I think he's trying to hook you and Ryan up." My heart nearly stops in my chest. If that's true, then that can only mean one thing—Ryan hasn't told him. Because there's no way, Tanner would try to get Ryan and me together if he knew the truth. Pain hits me square in the chest, gripping claw-like fingers around my heart and squeezing until I want to sink onto the bleachers and curl up into a ball.

As if sensing my sudden inner turmoil, Lana's hand lands on my leg and squeezes. "That's impossible, and I want to tell him why, but it's your secret to tell, so I haven't said anything. I promise I won't. Not until you give me the okay."

"Thank you," I say tightly. "I appreciate that." I pat her hand and then refocus my attention on her. "What about the phone calls?" I ask gently, switching the subject back.

She huffs. "They kinda throw me off," she admits, looking away.

"Why do they throw you off?" I ask. "Maybe they're from his family. Not everyone is on good terms with their family, you know."

"Yeah, no, I know that," Lana agrees. "But after each call, he gets really pensive for a few minutes. He seems to get texts a lot and always appears like he's checking something on his phone. When I've asked him about it, he changes the subject. Doesn't even give me an excuse or tell me who it was, just switches the subject and puts his phone away."

"Everyone's entitled to their secrets," I remind her. "You don't need to know everything he does."

"No, you're right, and it's not like I have to know. I'm just worried … what if it's someone else?"

"Do you think it's someone else?" I prompt.

Lana pulls her hand away from my leg and sinks her face into both of her palms. "I don't know," she mumbles miserably through her fingers. "But I can't stand the thought that it *could* be."

I reach up and rub my hand up her back. "Tanner's not Harley," I remind her gently. "Why don't you just ask him if he's interested in someone else? The best thing to do in relationships is communicate." Even as the words leave my lips, they feel like the height of hypocrisy. What right do I have to tell her how to act in her relationships when mine is ... far from normal and far from communicative.

If anything, Ryan and I have kept to ourselves too much, and telling him the truth all those years ago had ruined any chances of us having a future together—as lovers or as siblings.

"You're right." Lana sits up suddenly, disrupting me from my internal thoughts. She turns her eyes towards the field. "I just need to ask him."

My hand falls away from her back, and I smile at the determined look that enters her eyes. "You should," I agree.

She clenches one hand into a fist and brings it down on her leg. "I'm going to. Right now. Tonight."

My eyes widen and flash between her and the field. "Uh..." I grab her arm when she means to stand up. "Maybe you can wait until halftime," I say quickly. "Tanner's a little busy right now, and I doubt he could give you any answers like this."

Lana blinks and looks back at me. Her lips pop open, and she jerks her head back and forth from where Tanner sprints across the green football field, tackling a guy from the opposing team to my face. Finally, she collapses back against the bleachers under us. "Yeah," she says. "You're right." She shakes her head. "Sorry, I just got so caught up—I wanted..." She drifts off, scrubbing a hand down her face as I release her arm.

I laugh and shake my head. "No worries," I assure her. "I get it, but let's just wait until halftime then, if you want, I'll walk down there with you."

Lana gives me a gentle smile and reaches for my hand, taking it in hers. "You're the best."

I squeeze her fingers, rubbing them with mine

as a wind whips through the crowd. The two of us return our attention to the game and watch as the numbers on either side of the board climb.

HALFTIME COMES AND I follow Lana down the bleachers. While she heads for the front rows just behind the benches to try and catch Tanner before the rest of the players head back to the locker room, I head off to dump our now empty cups and popcorn bucket. I cut a quick look back and spot Tanner approaching the front row, heading straight for her with a smile on his face as she waves him over.

I could go back out there, but I want to give Lana time to ask him what she needs to, so I head for the bathrooms instead. A full cup of soda has my bladder screaming for relief, but I'm only in the stall for a few seconds when the door to the girl's bathroom bangs open again.

The other stall doors remain unopened, however, and instead, the sound of heels click over the broken floor tiles as loud, feminine voices echo up to the ceiling. *Who wears heels to a football game?* I wonder with a grimace. I stare down at my scuffed converse and shake my head as I finish my business and then start to get up.

"Can you fucking believe that bitch is here?" I freeze at the familiar voice.

"Ugh, I know, right? Like it isn't bad enough that she stalks him during the week, she has to come to his games too?"

"She's so obsessed with Ryan that it's pathetic. I don't know why he doesn't just get a restraining order and be done with it."

I know these voices. Faces flash through my mind until I come across the ones that match the voices talking on the other side of the stall door. They're the girls from my class, the same girls who'd first told me about the rumors—or rather who'd first ridiculed me to my face. Anger has my hands squeezing into fists.

"Someone needs to teach that girl a lesson."

"You're telling me. I heard that she's been seen hanging out with Tanner Striker lately. Do you think she's switching obsessions?"

They cackle like villains straight out of a stupid teenage bully show. I reach back and flush the toilet, letting them know someone's in here right before the door to my stall swings open. I don't look at them as I stomp to the sinks, wash my hands, and then slap the dryer to get it working.

"Oh, well, speak of the devil." My back stiffens, but I shouldn't be shocked. I don't know why I am. I'd half expected them to ignore my presence even though they'd just been so blatantly talking about me, but perhaps they feel righteous in talking shit right to my face. I turn slowly and lift my eyes to glare at the shorter one. Then, I look down. Of course, she would be the one wearing heels.

"Careful, Megan," the tall one says. "She might decide she likes girls better—after all, I hear her bestie doesn't discriminate." My face goes hot with rage. Before I even know what I'm doing, I take a step forward, and my fist is swinging through the air.

My knuckles collide with the tall girl's face first, and when the shorter one—Megan—screeches in disbelief, I turn and backhand her as well. "Oh my god!" They collapse together, scrambling as they try to get away from me.

I've never hit anyone before, much less two girls back to back, but I can feel my body welling with rage as I take a step towards them. "Talk shit all you want about me," I snap, pointing at them. "My relationship with Ryan Anderson isn't yours or anyone fucking else's business." I'm practically vibrating with emotion now. My hand starts to shake, so I drop it and just stand there, staring at the two of them. "But if you try to say shit about Lana, I won't hesitate to knock you down a fucking peg or two, got it?"

"You're fucking crazy!" the taller girl screams.

I scoff and shake my head as I take a step past them. I stop just before I hit the door. "Then you should know better than to mess with me," I toss back over my shoulder as I push out of the bathroom and take a breath of fresh air.

Unlike the girls I left behind in the bathroom, no one bothers me as I make my way back out towards the arena. In fact, no one seems to be paying attention to me at all, which is a refreshing change from the rest of this past week. For the moment, at least, I've gone back to being invisible, and as I stop just inside the entrance and gaze out over the green field marked with white lines, I take the opportunity to scan it.

I catch sight of Ryan with his head bent towards another player as they seem to discuss something. However, whatever is being said must be frustrating because after a moment of the other guy talking, Ryan shakes his head and says something before turning and stalking away. He's a good player, always has been, but tonight something is off. He's not playing like he used to back in high school. He's not playing like someone who'd won a sports scholarship at all. His body might be on that field, but his head certainly isn't.

"Will!" I look up at Lana's voice and realize she's standing not too far away, half bent over the railing that separates the front row of bleachers from the football field, and Tanner is still with her. He lifts a hand and gestures me forward. I head towards them.

"Hey, Tanner," I say in greeting as I approach them. "Aren't you supposed to be in the locker room?" Have they been out here talking this entire time? No other players are hanging about that I can see.

"Hey, Willow Tree." He gives me a megawatt smile, the shadow of a dimple appearing above the corner of his mouth. "Coach, let me hang back. I know the drill and I'll run back in a few minutes to get caught up, but I wanted to see ya before I went."

"Tanner says there's going to be a few parties going on after the game," Lana says excitedly.

I groan. "You guys got me to the game. Do you really think I'm going to want to go to a party after this week?" I ask.

Tanner shrugs. "Yeah, why not?" he counters. "You've had a stressful week. Come with us. Have fun. Dance. Drink. Blow off some steam. It can't hurt, I promise." He gives me a wink.

I cross my arms over my chest. "How do I know this isn't a trick?"

Tanner's eyes widen comically and he lifts both hands in mock surrender. "Trick?" he repeats the word, emphasizing it with a tone that sounds both amused and offended. "I would never trick you, Willow Tree. I'm a man of honor."

"That's a load of bullshit," I say with a laugh, shaking my head.

"Come on, Will," Lana wheedles, capturing my attention again. "You should go. We'll both be there, and it'll get your mind off of all the shit going on with school as well as ..." She drifts off, but it doesn't take a genius to fill in the gaps.

I've never been a big drinker, but maybe alcohol would numb me enough not to feel so hurt after the week of hell that I've been through. The rumors flying around and Ryan's presence have definitely taken their toll. I can almost hear Ryan standing next to me now, though, as he would've done had I not been stupid enough to tell him the truth all those years ago, had I not driven him away.

He would have been just as protective as he always was. Drinking at a college party? It was dangerous, and he wouldn't want me to go. That, more than either Lana or Tanner's cajoling pleas, makes the decision for me. Ryan might think I'm innocent and in need of a keeper. He might think I have no business going to a party, but fuck him. He gave up the right to influence my decisions a long time ago.

I straighten and face Tanner once more. "Okay fine," I say. "If you guys are going, just be aware, though—I'm actually gonna drink this time. It really has been a stressful week." I frown when I notice the girls from class coming out of the entrance not far from where we're standing. I scowl their way. "A mega stressful week," I amend coolly before turning back to Lana and Tanner. "I want alcohol and I want to forget about it."

Lana brightens and claps her hands together. "This is gonna be so awesome!" she squeals. "I can't wait."

"Striker!" someone yells, calling for Tanner.

"Welp, that's my cue, ladies." Tanner takes a step back from the railing and then tips an invisible hat before he turns and jogs over to the rest of the team.

I turn to Lana. "Did you get to talk to him?" I ask.

She nods. "Sorta," she admits. "We're gonna talk more at the party, but he assured me that he's not seeing anyone right now. I think …" She takes a breath, and the smile she flashes me is brighter than I've ever seen on her. "I think this is really gonna work out."

I slip an arm around her shoulders and pull her into a half hug. "I'm sure it will," I say. If anyone deserves happiness, it's my friend.

TWENTY

WILLOW

DESPITE RYAN'S UNUSUAL distraction, the game ends with a landslide win at 34-10. Fans cheer in the bleachers. Bright red and white strips of paper fly around as a few guys in nothing, but paint and shorts release handheld confetti cannons. Lana and I laugh at their antics as we descend from our upper seats and head for the exit.

Once we reach the crush in the stadium's hallways, I grab her hand to lead her to the side, and we skim around the large collection of people as they chat and move along at a snail's pace. We don't stop until we hit the glass doors and make our way out into the parking lot.

"Wow, I can't believe they turned it around like that in the second half," Lana says, panting as we stop at the edge of the sidewalk, and she puts her hands on her knees.

"Are you okay?" I ask, concerned.

She waves a hand my way. "Totally fine, it's just you've got longer legs, and it's harder to keep up."

I roll my eyes. "It wasn't that bad."

"Willow!" I look up at the sound of my name being called. A familiar face peeks above the crowd, shaggy blonde hair and a bright smile. I rack my brain to remember his name. Thankfully, by the time he reaches where Lana and I are standing, I've got it.

"Hey, Jordan," I say in greeting.

He seems to brighten, and I'm glad I remembered his name this time. He turns to Lana. "Who's this?"

"Oh." I glance at Lana, who seems to be eyeing Jordan with casual politeness. "Lana, this is Jordan—I don't know if you remember, but we met him at—"

"The bar, right?" Lana holds her hand out. "It's been a while."

Jordan leans forward and takes her hand. "Yeah, it's good to meet you—again."

"You too." Lana releases his hand and takes a step back. "What brings you over here?"

"I was actually coming to see if Willow was going to one of the after-parties." He turns towards me.

"Uh, yeah," I say, gesturing to Lana. "Just a party with a few friends."

He brightens immediately. "Do you need a lift?" Jordan reaches into his jean's pocket, pulls out a pair of car keys, and shakes them meaningfully. Then he pauses and glances at Lana. "I mean, both of you are welcome if you need a ride, but I just thought I'd ... God, I sound like an ass, don't I?"

I laugh as he drops his arm. "No, of course not," I say quickly.

Lana's gaze burns into the side of my face. "Actually, yeah," Lana says. "Will could use a ride. She rode with me to the game, but my car's gonna be full. I gotta wait on a few more friends—so if you two want to go ahead..." She lets her words drift off as my head snaps around.

"What are you talking about?" I demand, widening my eyes.

She blinks back at me. Slowly. *Oh, this bitch. She's doing this on purpose.* "Well, Tanner texted me and asked if we could carpool," she says easily. I narrow my gaze on her. I can't tell if this is a lie or just an excuse to get me in a car alone with a hot guy—aka Jordan.

"You have four seats," I point out.

She arches a brow at me. "But a lot of crap. It'll be crowded, and it's not like we're not all going to the same place."

"We don't know that," I say quickly, flipping on Jordan. "What party did you say you were going to?"

He scratches the back of his head as he glances between the two of us. "I didn't say actually," he replies. "But it's the big house on the edge of Camden drive. It's not far from campus."

"That's Chase Meyer's place," Lana pipes up. "That's the place we're going." She claps her hands together. "Great, if you could drive Willow, we'd really appreciate it."

"Lana," I growl her way and reach out, snagging her arm. I look to Jordan. "Can you just give us two seconds?" I don't give him a chance to answer before I'm already dragging Lana a few feet away and spinning her away from him. "What are you doing?" I demand.

Lana looks up at me. "What does it look like I'm doing?" she asks. "I'm finding you a ride."

"You are my ride," I point out.

"Well, about that—" she starts, only to be interrupted a moment later.

"Lana!" Our heads pop up at the sound of Tanner's voice reaching over the noise of the students still milling about outside of the stadium. My lips part as I see that he's not alone.

"What..." I glance back at her.

She winces. "I wasn't lying when I said Tanner texted me and asked to carpool," she says quickly. "I just didn't know how to tell you that Ryan's riding with me too. When Jordan offered a ride—I thought—"

I hold up a hand, stopping her. "I know what you thought," I say. She thought I'd want to avoid being in a car with Ryan and no doubt being stuck in the backseat, inches from the man that left me craving his touch.

"Are you mad?" she asks.

I shake my head. "No, I'm not mad," I tell her. "You're right. I'll ride with Jordan. He's *nice*." Or rather, he's better than being stuck in a car with Ryan right now.

"He's more than nice," Lana says. "He's hot as fuck, and he's totally into you. Why don't you take this chance to get to know him? Maybe being around another guy—one who's nice to you"—she stares at me with meaning. What she means is, one who's also not my fucking twin brother—"will help you see that there's more to life than Ryan."

I'm already half-turned away from her, preparing to move back towards Jordan, but I pause at those words and look back at her, stunned that she actually said it aloud. "I know there's more to life than Ryan," I snap.

Her head jerks back at my tone, and she frowns. "I just meant—"

"It's fine," I cut her off, irritated as I pull away. "I'll take Jordan up on his offer. I'll meet up with you at the party."

"Wait, Will!"

I don't wait, though. I turn and start towards where Jordan's waiting with his feet on the black pavement just over the lip of the sidewalk with his hands in his pockets. Lana's gaze isn't the only one I can feel boring a hole in the back of my head now. There's another, even more intense, one. I ignore both of them.

"Everything okay?" Jordan asks.

"Yeah," I lie. "But she's right. I didn't realize she'd offered Tanner and his friend a ride. Is your offer still good?" I can't even bring myself to say

Ryan's name right now.

"Of course." Jordan smiles down at me, and I wish more than anything that I could be attracted to him. Lana's right. He's good-looking. Tall. Nice. Everything that I should want. The only thing he's missing is the one thing that I actually want: He's not Ryan Anderson.

Twenty-One

RYAN

I WATCH WILL walk away with that asshole from the library. I will her to turn around and look at me, but she never does. Will's little friend steps in front of my field of vision, but just looking at her, I can tell her smile is fake. She doesn't like me.

"We ready to go?" she says brightly.

Don't do it, I tell myself. It's better if I just keep my mouth shut and not ask, but in the next moment, my conscience is thrown out the window with a firm *fuck that.* "Where is she going?" I demand, glaring down at the chick before me.

"Who?" The chick—Lana, I remind myself—blinks up at me. Does she think I'm fucking stupid?

I glare at her. "You damn well know who," I grit out. "Where the hell is Willow going, and who the fuck is that guy?"

Lana puts a finger to her chin and tilts her head while arching a brow. "I don't know that it's any of your business," she says steadily, and I have to admit, she's got some serious lady balls to be able to look me in the face and deny me the information I want.

I take a step towards her as fury rises, but before I can say anything more, Tanner steps in the way and puts a restraining hand on my shoulder. "Actually," Tanner says, "I think maybe it'd be a better idea if we go separately after all."

"If you need a ride, Tanner," Lana replies. "You're always welcome. Ryan can go home, though. He seems a little stiff."

I reach up and cup Tanner's wrist above where he's got ahold of my shoulder. "Keep a leash on your bitch, Striker," I growl.

Tanner's hand grows firm, and his head snaps to me. "I respect you, Ryan," he says slowly, calmly, "but call her a bitch again, and we'll have a problem."

"We've already got one," I sneer, shoving him off of me and taking a step away. "Take her up on her offer, though. Hope the pussy is worth it."

I don't give him a chance to say anything else as I turn and walk away, my blood boiling in my veins. I haven't been this fucking angry in ... a long damn time. Despite the beating I just took on the field and the fact that my muscles are bunched up tighter than a nun's pussy, I want nothing more than to pound my fist into some asshole's face—preferably the little shithead that had practically skipped off with Willow.

Does he think that giving her one ride will open the door? No. He's got no chance. She doesn't want him. She'll never want a guy like him. *I'm* the one she wants.

I freeze as I reach my car. *What the hell did I just think? I'm the one she wants?* No. I already decided a long time ago that I wouldn't do this to her. But even as I remind myself, I can't help but recognize the cruel jealousy that whips through me and curls around my throat strangling me.

Placing one hand on the top of my car door, I squeeze my fingers into a fist. Willow is not mine. She can never be mine. Closing my eyes as I repeat those words like a mantra in my head helps ... but only for a moment.

Memories flash before my mind. Will on her knees with her mouth open, my cock hitting the back of her throat as she swallows around me and her eyes watering with the effort it takes her to suck me off. She was so fucking beautiful like that. Like some sort of sacrificial maiden on her knees for her king.

I wanted more than that one stolen moment. It'd been dangerous to take her like that. The library was a public place, and though we'd been hidden, there'd still been a risk, but perhaps ... I'd wanted that risk. Maybe I wanted people to find out so there'd be no going back. Who knew about our true relationship but Tanner? And he didn't seem to think I was serious. Maybe I could have her. Even if for only a moment—what I wouldn't give to have her for more than a single night.

I'd burn in hell for eternity just for all of her.

Twenty-Two

WILLOW

I'M A FUCKING idiot, but right now, I can't seem to care. Jordan seems all too happy to cart me to the party house, and by the time we arrive, it appears that the celebrations are already in full swing. People litter the front lawn of what looks like a three-story ranch-style house. The wrap-around porch features nearly half a dozen chairs and other patio furniture, and almost all of it is taken.

We get out of the car, and Jordan escorts me up the front steps, avoiding the several empty beer bottles scattered about. Jordan reaches the door and opens it ahead of me. The second he does, a loud cheer erupts, and one of the painted guys from the game comes running down the front hallway with a giant jug of amber liquid with the nozzle spewing back and forth.

I gasp as he passes by, splashing my front with the stuff. Reaching down, I lift my shirt and wrinkle my nose. Thankfully, it's just more beer, but damn I didn't expect to already smell like an alcoholic before even having one drink.

"Fuck!" Jordan's usually bright demeanor shifts as he too gets splashed with the stuff. He turns and shoves the painted guy out onto the porch and slams the door closed behind us. "What an asshole."

My eyes widen at his sudden shift, but when he glances down, the dark expression on his face fades. A strange sense of déjà vu overcomes me. He'd been similar at the bar the first time I'd met him. "Sorry," he says. "I just really like this shirt."

"Uh … no problem."

"Do you wanna get a drink?" he offers, gesturing towards the hallway where I can see more people milling about. Hard thumping music drifts towards us from speakers somewhere in the house.

A drink at least will distract me from Lana's absence. "Yeah, sure," I say. "Let's go."

I let Jordan lead me towards the kitchen. Without checking with anyone, he goes directly to the fridge, withdraws a bottle, and then moves to the side.

"You seem pretty comfortable here," I comment casually.

He pauses and throws a smile my way over his shoulder, but it doesn't reach his eyes. I carefully keep an eye on him. "Yeah, my buddies live here, so I'm over here all the time."

Jordan leaves the unopened beer on the counter and reaches for a red solo cup from a stack next to a keg. He presses some sort of lever and out spews the same type of liquid in the painted guy's jug. A loud screeching laugh jerks my attention away, as a couple of girls who look like they're dressed for the club stumble into the kitchen and head straight for the refrigerator. I move out of the way as they rummage through it, one of them pulling out a large pitcher of orange liquid.

The redhead of the bunch stops and looks at me, narrowing her eyes as if in deep concentration. Then, "Oh my gosh!" she squeals. "You're Willow McRae!"

I blink in astonishment. "I'm sorry?"

Great, Will. Apologizing for being yourself. A real winner, you are. It's no wonder Lana is your only friend.

I shake my head, clearing away those annoying thoughts, and try again. "I mean, yeah. I am. Do I know you?"

The redhead laughs. "Oh no, of course, you don't. We're not even in the same department, but I've heard about you. You're like famous all over the school."

I stiffen, realizing she can only mean the rumors that have been circling since last weekend. "Hey, Will, here's your drink." Jordan holds out the red solo cup, and I snatch it from his grip, tipping it back and draining half of it in one go. If I'm going to survive the rest of the night, I'm going to need a hell of a lot of liquid courage. I'm so not cut out for the college social scene.

"*Molly*," one of the redheaded girl's friends whines, "stop playing with the stalker girl and come get your drink."

I guess the redhead—Molly, since I must be the stalker girl—rolls her eyes. "For the record," she says, "I don't think you're a stalker—don't mind Bridget, she's a fucking bitch half the time and high the rest."

"Fuck you," the girl, who I assume is Bridget, replies.

"Sure, as long as we sixty-nine," Molly shoots back before facing me again. I stare at her in confusion. Did she just ... offer to sixty-nine her friend? The one she also just called a bitch?

"Thanks," I say awkwardly. "About not believing I'm a stalker."

She laughs at what I can only assume is a bewildered expression on my face. "Stalkers don't usually get caught, and I've seen you around—if anything, it seems like you avoid Ryan Anderson. I mean, he's hot and all, but he's no Henry Cavill, you know?"

She's chattering away a million miles a minute, and I can feel Jordan growing antsy at my side. I cut a glance his way and notice that he's already pulled the top off of his beer and is guzzling it down. His expression looks both bored and irritated. What is *wrong* with him? I wonder with annoyance. He's the one who offered to bring me here, and Lana was right—he was totally acting like he was interested in me up until right fucking now. Now, he just seems like he'd rather be anywhere else but here.

Molly must notice, too, because she leans

around me. "Hey, Jordan, if you wanna head off, I can take care of Willow here."

Jordan glances at me and then gives Molly a tight smile before running his hand down my back and around my hip, pulling me closer. "Nope," he says. "I'm fine right where I'm at."

He might be, but I am suddenly very much *not*. Until Lana, Tanner, and Ryan arrive, however, Jordan's pretty much the only person I even kind of vaguely know here. So, I don't say anything. Instead, I do the only thing I can think of. I tip my solo cup back and drain the rest in one go before holding it out for him.

"Can you refill it for me?" I ask with a sweet look.

He smirks down at me and reaches for it. "Sure, sweetness." He takes it from me, and I'm relieved to feel his hand disappear as he moves back to the keg.

"Anyway, as I was saying," Molly starts, but before she can even get any further, one of her friends reaches over and drags her closer.

"Bitch, I know you freaking heard me," her friend says. "You never said how much you wanted." She holds up a separate solo cup and smacks Molly in the face with it.

"Ugh. Just fill it up to the rim of the lines," Molly mutters, shoving her back. "You're such an ass sometimes, Jill."

"Only when I need to be," the third girl, Jill, shoots back as she starts to pour. Behind her, the brunette, Bridget, seems quite content to sway to the music and sip from her own cup.

"Hey, I got an idea!" Bridget pops off the wall and marches towards where I stand next to Molly. "We're gonna play some games in the living room. Are you guys down?"

Jordan returns to my side and hands me my drink. This time, thankfully, he keeps his hands to himself. "What kind?" he asks, his tone curious.

"Spin the bottle, truth or dare, we got a few joints if you're interested," she replies, seeming to have completely forgotten about her earlier 'stalker girl' comment. Then again, when she'd said it, she didn't seem all that concerned with it. The term had just slipped from her lips like the only thing she could think of—and considering she was comfortable with calling the girls who seemed to be her friends insulting names, maybe it hadn't been a big deal to her. They aren't trying to exclude me, at least. Maybe it wouldn't hurt to join them for a while.

I look up at Jordan. "I'd like to play, if you're cool with it," I say.

"Sure, why not."

"Awesome," Molly looks back at her friend and smiles. "Let's head in."

Jordan and I follow the three of them as they sway and sing along to the lyrics pouring from the invisible speakers. Already, I'm feeling a gentle fuzz in my mind. I definitely drank that first cup way too fast.

I half expect the living room to be decked out in sports gear befitting a college bachelor pad, but instead, it's actually fairly neat. There are a bunch of guys and girls scattered about the room. Some are chatting on the couches, and others are making out on the loveseat. In the center of it all is a collection of about ten guys and girls spread out in a circle, each with their own drinks in hand. Jordan and I find a spot next to the girls and take a seat.

As they start discussing what game we're going to play, I set my drink down and push it slightly behind a side table that's shoved against the wall at my back before subtly withdrawing my phone from my pocket. I check my messages, seeing that there's one from an unknown number, but I quickly delete it and move down to the new one I've got from Lana.

Lana: Hey, gonna be a lil late. Tanner needed to run by his place for something. Call him if you need something, my phone's gonna die soon.

I press my lips together and type a quick response back.

Willow: K. I don't wanna stay long so I might leave when y'all get here. I can come back and get y'all if you let me borrow your car.

"Will?" I jerk my head up at the sound of my name and shove my phone back into my pocket.

I plaster a smile on my face. "What's up?"

"We're gonna play truth or dare," Molly says. "Are you good with that?"

"Yeah." I reach for my drink and tip it back, sipping slowly.

The game begins. Starting with Molly and as it moves from her to a guy across from her, I realize that they're playing based on whoever answered or was dared last rather than in any sort of clock type order. It's almost a relief since the majority of these games are people focused on pranking and daring their friends, and I hardly know these people to begin with.

Several long minutes go by, and I laugh as some of the guys are dared to do stupid break dances that almost end up with a few girls across the space getting kicked in the head. A girl runs to the kitchen and comes back with shots, passing them out to the ones who refuse dares. While I wasn't paying attention to their house rules, it seems that even though you can get out of a dare by saying truth—truth speakers still need to take a shot.

"Willow!" Someone finally says. I look up and note that Bridget is smiling at me. "Truth or dare?"

"Truth," I say automatically.

"Is it true that you're in love with Ryan Anderson?"

I stiffen. The room seems to go silent, and I feel a massive hole open in my chest, threatening to suck me in and swallow me up. I scowl. "Dare," I grit in return.

"Hey, you can't—"

"Shut. Up. Bridget." Thankfully, Molly reaches over and slaps her friend's arm. "She can change it if you're gonna ask stupid fucking questions."

Bridget huffs and glares at me, then suddenly—as if a lightbulb has popped off in her drunken brain—she glances between me and Jordan and grins. "Fine," she says. "I dare you and Jordan to kiss."

I blanch. "I don't think—"

"You have to do it since you refused the truth," she snaps, cutting me off. "You can't break the rules a second time."

"It's okay, Will, you don't have to—" I reach over and touch Jordan's arm, stopping him.

"It's fine," I say. "She's right. I don't want to ruin the game." But this will be the last fucking time I play, I decide silently.

His eyes brighten and he reaches for me too quickly. I jerk back and feel the cup I had pushed back towards the table, at the bottom of my spine. "Shit, stop!" I put a hand to his chest and reach back, grabbing it, thankful that it hadn't tipped over. Maybe it'd been a stupid idea to put it so close to the entertainment center where all the TV wiring was. I push it towards the middle of the group where several others have placed their cups and then turn towards Jordan.

"Okay," I say, giving him a wan smile. "Let's do this."

Jordan gives me a small smile and leans

forward. I'm viscerally aware that all eyes are on us. Too fucking aware. So much so that when Jordan moves a hand to my face and cups my cheek, I don't expect it. I nearly jump out of my skin at the feel of his fingers grazing my jaw as he smooths his hand around the side of my face, and then suddenly, he's all I see.

His lips land on mine, sloppy and startling. Not knowing what else to do, I hold still as Jordan adjusts his hand on my face, lowering it to my neck and then collarbone. He tilts his head and then moves his mouth over mine, gently pecking, but with each one, his lips part and his tongue creeps out, licking over the seam of my mouth. I squeeze my eyes shut, not wanting to watch everyone around us stare while he tries to pry apart my lips with his tongue.

Ten. Nine. Eight. I count backwards from ten in my head, hating every second that I feel stuck here. For some reason, however, each second feels a million years long. Maybe it's because I don't really want to be sitting here, kissing Jordan. *Seven. Six. Five.* I jump when the hand on my collarbone moves down even further, nearly touching my boob. *Four. Three. Two.* Fuck. Fuck. Fuck. I don't know if I can keep this up. My head starts pounding as the last number jumps in front of my mind's eye. Just as I'm ready to pull away and call an end to this stupid dare, Jordan jerks forward, latching on to me with both hands now—one on either arm—and shoves his tongue into the cavern of my mouth. My eyes pop open, and I struggle for a moment as he deepens the kiss, groaning for good measure.

My body doesn't seem to be working, though. A strange fog clouds over my mind as I put both of my palms on his chest and push weakly. His tongue coils around mine, and I nearly gag, but he doesn't seem to notice. In fact, he takes it a step further. One of his hands moves towards my boob and squeezes.

"Enough!" I finally manage to pull myself away, panting and staring wildly at him as I cross my arms over my chest. "The dare's over. This is done." Jordan's eyes open far slower than my own, and when they do, they're totally and completely centered on me.

It's at that moment that I realize something. I don't want to fucking be here. I only agreed to come here because Lana and Tanner were coming. I was going to get drunk with my friends—with people I trusted. I don't know these people, though. I hardly know Jordan, and now I'm realizing how stupid and petty it was to jump in a car with a guy I barely know just to stay away from Ryan.

"I think I'm—" I'm halfway through turning back towards the group and telling them that I'm done playing when I catch sight of Bridget, holding up a phone with her camera pointed at me. She laughs and clicks something on it.

"And that's a wrap!" she says with a giggle. "Thanks, everyone, for your cooperation."

"What?" I blink at her.

Bridget rolls her eyes. "We just wanted to see if

you would do it," she says. "Jordan bet Mike that he could get you to kiss him before the night was over." She gestures with her phone to one of the guys sitting across from Molly. He's scowling as he reaches into the back pocket of his ripped jeans and starts pulling out his wallet.

I stare at him in confusion. *Why the hell would he and Jordan bet anything on me?*

"This is fucking cheating," Mike snaps as he unfolds his wallet and pulls out a twenty, flinging it at Jordan. My eyes follow the movement, staring at the crisp green bill that Jordan picks up and waves to Bridget.

"I'll get your half later," he says, making my stomach drop. "Thanks for the assist."

Thanks for the assist. My mind repeats the words in my head. *Thanks for the assist.* Like he's thanking a teammate for passing him the ball, but instead of the ball, she merely set him up to make a fool out of me.

As my confusion clears to make way for outrage, my rationality stops working. I see my hand reaching for my cup in the center with the rest of them before my mind even registers that it's me picking it up. And as I do register that fact, it's already hovering over Jordan's head as I tip it over and dump what remains of the contents all over his face and shirt.

"What the fuck!" Jordan jumps off the floor and yanks his shirt out from his chest, where it's already starting to stick to him. That's right, I recall belatedly. He said he liked that shirt—enough that he'd been pissed at painted guy earlier for nearly spraying him with beer. Now, he's covered in it. That's karma for you, though. Dick.

I quickly stand and shove him back before turning and storming through the ring of people still sitting around in a circle. Everyone hoots in laughter as Jordan starts cursing up a storm. "Dumb bitch!" he shouts.

I don't listen. I don't care. I shove by Bridget as she laughs and waves her phone. "Don't worry, stalker girl!" she calls out. "We'll let Ryan know that you've moved on."

Fury flares hot in my chest, but worse than that is the humiliation. My face burns with it as I stumble through the house and nearly fall into the doorway. *What the hell is wrong with me?* I think as I struggle back onto the path I'm trying to take.

I shake my head, trying to clear away the sudden fog that seems to have overtaken me. I push myself into the hallway and continue until something smacks into my shoulder, and I look up to see Jordan storming towards me from the other end of the hall. I turn back towards the front door, not even caring what he just threw my way.

The crinkle of plastic under his heavy footsteps tells me that it was probably one of the solo cups from the living room. If it had anything in it, though, I didn't feel it. In fact, as each second goes by, I feel like there is less and less feeling in the rest of my body.

Where the fuck is Lana?

"Hey!" Jordan's suddenly in front of me, anger radiating off him as he slams a palm down on the wall in front of me. "This is a three hundred dollar fucking shirt," he snaps.

I glare up at him. "So?"

He pushes me back against the wall. "So, what the fuck are you going to do about ruining it?" he demands.

"Absolutely fucking nothing, asshole." My hand meets his shoulder, but there's no force behind the shove I try to give him. "Get off of me."

"Oh, hell no, you little bitch," Jordan grits out. "I didn't fucking act all nice to you just so you could throw beer on me and walk the fuck away."

A swell of warning rises within me as a sudden epiphany hits me in the gut. I'm not safe here. Jordan's eyes are dark, angry, and maybe it's stupid just now to realize that he's not only stronger than me, but it doesn't look like anyone else is coming after us. There's literally no one in this hallway, and I don't feel I should be here anymore.

I try to work over all of the reasons I could be feeling the way I do. What had I eaten earlier? Am I getting sick? Is it because I drank my first beer too fast ... the first beer ... I look up at Jordan. "Did you put something in my drink?" The words pop out of my mouth before I can stop them.

For a moment, just a split second, the anger in his eyes morphs into something worse—fear. He reaches into his pocket quickly, and something clatters onto the floor. My eyes go to the little metal container, like the type that holds mints, and I realize as the top pops open those aren't fucking mints.

"Open your fucking mouth," he growls.

"What—" Jordan's fingers pry my lips apart as his free hand grips my chin, holding me in place.

Panic claws its way up my throat as I feel one of those fucking pills touch my tongue and as soon as it does, it immediately starts to dissolve. I recoil from Jordan's hands, fighting him with everything I've got—not that it's much at all. In fact, everything I've got is pretty fucking pathetic. I'm weak, and every hit I deliver—a smack to his side, a punch to his bicep—feels like it does nothing. Nothing!

"That's it," Jordan says quickly as he forces my mouth shut and starts to massage my throat. I hold the pill still on my tongue, trying not to let it work its way to the back of my throat. "Fucking swallow it, bitch," he mutters. "Just swallow it, and you won't have to remember anything else for the rest of the night."

His words register in my mind, even as he holds my mouth shut, keeping me from spitting out the bitter pill. I realize this must be the second pill he's given me tonight. My question had made him panic because he realized I figured it out. One pill was dangerous enough, but who the hell knows what two will do. Tears creep into my eyes and slide down my cheeks as I try to shake my head.

Why? I wonder. *Why is he doing this to me?*

"Swallow!" he hisses, and when I shake my head again, a look of determination enters his eyes. He clamps a palm over my mouth, holding my jaw shut, and reaches up to pinch my flaring nostrils closed.

No, no, no, no, no. No air escapes the pinch of his fingers, and I can't open my mouth. I'm choking. And as if my body is seeking what he's preventing, I automatically swallow. The second I do, he releases me and takes a step back. My legs collapse, and I shove my fingers directly into my mouth, reaching for the back of my throat until my gag reflex kicks in and I puke all over the floor.

"Shit!" Jordan jumps away from me.

Now he's got a beer-stained shirt and puke-stained shoes. It's a two for one.

Twenty-Three

WILLOW

JORDAN REACHES DOWN and fists a handful of my hair, yanking several strands out as he yanks me back up to my feet. "You know what," he snarls at me. "I'm gonna fuck you and maybe have Bridget video it. Maybe we'll sell it, and you can pay me back for my shirt—and the shoes."

He doesn't give me a moment to reply before we're on the move. My feet trip, but he doesn't seem to give a fuck as he leads me around the corner and through an open doorway. My knees hit the floor once more as he shoves me inside and slams the door closed. I hear something lock, and my heart nearly stops in my chest.

I look up, and in the dim lighting from the window, I see we're in a bedroom and there's a bathroom directly across from where I'm at. I take a breath. Two seconds, maybe three max, before he catches me. I have to make it.

I shove up onto my feet and nearly fall, but something in me must realize the type of danger I'm in because I don't hear Jordan's curse until my hand latches onto the knob of the bathroom door. I half fall, half throw myself inside the bathroom and slam the door, reaching up and flipping the lock just as Jordan's body hits the wood on the other side and mine collapses onto the cold tile.

Thankfully, the house we're in is older—the wood is solid. The door remains shut and unbroken.

"Get out here, you little cunt!" Jordan's fist pounds the door.

Tears burn at my eyelids. Pushing up from the floor, I take a step back and then another and another until my spine hits the wall, and I slowly slide down until my ass hits the tile again. I feel panic creep up my throat, wrapping ice-cold tendrils of fear around my neck and squeezing until I can't breathe.

My phone, I think. I still have my phone.

I fumble for my back pocket, and I've never wanted to cry more in my entire life than when I feel the hard rectangle that will no doubt save my fucking life tonight. My vision is blurry as I turn the screen on. There aren't any new messages from Lana, but I click on her icon and call her right away.

Pressing the phone to my ear as I wait for her to pick up, I flinch when Jordan rains another barrage of punches against the bathroom door.

"Hey, it's Lana, just leave me a message, and I'll get back to you." I yank my phone away and look down at the screen. *There's no way. Not now. Lana wouldn't send me to voicemail.* I hit the call button once more and reach up with my hand, biting down on a finger to repress a sob. It catches in my throat and swells until I feel like I'm fucking choking.

Lana doesn't answer. I try Tanner. I've never called him before, but I have his number. I dial it once, but that, too, goes straight to voicemail. Tears leak out over my cheeks, sliding down my jawline and dripping onto my collarbone.

Outside, in the bedroom, I hear Jordan cursing up a storm. Something breaks, and then he punches the door again. I'm starting to get used to it, and that bothers me more than anything else. "You're gonna have to come out of there sometime, stalker girl," Jordan taunts from the other side. "If you're not out in the next ten minutes to face the fucking music..." He pauses, and I hold my breath, waiting for what he'll say next. He jiggles the doorknob, and I find myself staring at it in the darkness, afraid to see the lock turn back. "Ten minutes," he repeats. "Or I'm gonna find a fucking crowbar, bitch."

With that, I hear him storm away, but I'm still not safe. The headache from earlier is now a raging typhoon inside my skull, pounding against the walls of my mind and making me wish someone would take a sledgehammer to my brain just to make the pain stop. It's hard to concentrate, but I force myself to anyway. My throat grows drier and drier with each second that passes. My chest aches. Something hot crawls up my spine.

Who else? Who else can I ...

My hand stills as my finger hover over a familiar name. He's at the top of the list. Why? Probably because I've pulled him up so many times just to stare at his name. All because I miss him. He used to be my savior, my everything. Even growing up with nothing, moving from one place to another with our stuff packed in black trash bags, I'd always had him. I want him. I feel things for him that I know I shouldn't. It's wrong. It's debased. It's disgusting—just as he'd told me.

But it can't be denied any longer. I don't want to call him, but I can't stay here. I need someone. I *need* him.

I don't know how to get out of here. If I walk out there now, there's no doubt Jordan will be on me—that's if I can even manage to walk a straight line. With how numb my legs feel, that's a solid no. My vision blurs. I hate myself for getting into this situation. I should've never gotten in Jordan's damn car.

And as I sit here, in the dark of some bachelor pad bathroom with a would-be maybe rapist on the other side with two fucking personalities—because yeah, I'd kinda seen that he was a bit off. Too friendly. That first night at the bar, he'd been pushing the drinks, offering to buy me shot after shot, and each time I'd turned him down had resulted in a look of irritation, but he'd never pressed.

No, not until tonight. Not until he had me exactly where he wanted me.

What the hell was I thinking? Was I going to prove to Ryan that I didn't need him? Stupid. So fucking stupid. This is a train wreck of a situation, and I have no one but myself to blame.

My eyes fall to my cell phone screen once more. My battery is running low, and I can feel my vision and thoughts fading. I'm tired ... so fucking tired. My arm is trembling as I lift the phone closer to my face so I can see it better. Everything is blurry. I don't have the luxury of waiting or trying someone else. I need to do this now. Fuck the consequences. Ryan might hate me, but he wouldn't ... God, I pray he doesn't leave me here all alone. Not with Jordan.

With trembling fingers, I hit the call button. *Please pick up,* I beg the universe. *Please pick up.*

I'll never ask for anything again, I swear. *I just need someone ... no, I need Ryan. I need Ryan to save me.*

The phone rings for so long that my heart feels like it'll beat right out of my chest. I want him. I need him. *Please, Ryan. Please pick up the phone.*

"This better be fucking good," Ryan's voice comes over the line loud and irritated. "I don't know who the fuck gave you this number, but I'm—"

"Ryan," I whimper his name, thankful—so fucking thankful he answered.

A pause. "Willow?"

He doesn't sound angry anymore. That's good, right? A loud bang ricochets against the bathroom door behind me. "Willow, I'm waiting! You've got five more minutes!" Jordan yells. "And let me tell you something, when those minutes are up ... you're gonna wish you'd just been a good little girl and stayed where I put you."

Vomit clogs my throat, and I clamp a hand over my mouth, almost like I'm a child. I don't know why, but there's a part of my brain that says maybe ... just maybe if I stay still and quiet—play dead—he'll go away. But this isn't the wild, and Jordan isn't some dumb animal. He's a man—an angry, violent, two-faced asshole with far more nefarious intentions than any creature from the animal kingdom.

"Did Tanner give you this number?" Ryan asks. "That motherfucker."

My back hits the toilet seat as I scramble further away from the door. I crumple inward on myself, squeezing into a tight, protective ball, and pressing the phone as close to my ear as possible. I feel hot tears descend down my cheeks. "Ryan..." I hiccup. "Ryan, I'm sorry. I'm so sorry, but *please*, I-I—"

More banging on the bathroom door. The sound ricochets in my ears. I can't hold back the sob anymore.

"Will?" Ryan's voice drops from demanding irritation to something that I haven't heard from him in a long time. For a moment, he sounds almost ... concerned. "Why do you sound like that?"

"I-I need—" I can't seem to get the words out. "Ryan, I'm sorry. I-I—" My voice is messy, the words are slurred, and I know they're probably barely understandable. Embarrassment arches up over me.

The pounding ceases then something else in the room breaks, glass from the sound of it. I wonder if he even knows whose room we're in. If they even care that he's in here destroying their shit.

"Willow, what's going on?" Ryan's voice is like a boon, reminding me that I'm not alone. I just need to get it out. I need to tell him.

"Ryan, I need you to come get me," I say quickly. "I need you to ... come get me. *Please*."

I squeeze my eyes shut, but once I do, they don't seem to want to open again. I sag back into the place between the toilet and bathtub. The floor under me tilts, but I don't open my eyes. Heat races across my skin, blazing a path that's hotter than Hades, and I can't even care about it. All I care about is that Ryan can hear me.

Silence and then ... "Where are you?" he demands. Relief pours through me.

"The party house," I say, and now, I'm starting to hear my words slur. Maybe they have been for a while, but it's hard to hear when the only thing pounding in my ears is the racing of my heartbeat.

It sounds as though he's rushing. I hear keys jingling on the other end, and his next words are breathless. "Where are you in the house?" he demands.

"I-in the bathroom," I reply. "In one of the bed ... the bedrooms. Ryan ... there's a guy." My head slumps to the side with the phone caught between my shoulder and ear. It's too heavy to hold up anymore. "H-he tried. He tried to—I stopped. Locked the door." The words aren't coming out in full sentences anymore.

"If he touches you, I'll rip his goddamn dick off and shove it down his throat." Ryan's threat makes me huff out a short chuckle, but even that feels like it consumes too much energy.

There was something else I needed to tell him. What was it? I rack my brain before it comes back to me.

"Ryan," I jerk against the cold porcelain toilet, reaching up and fumbling with the phone. "I took—he gave me—pills. He, I don't know what they are."

Even as drugged up as I know I am right now, and with fog rolling into my mind, I can hear the vibration of his anger through the silence on the other end. "I'm on my way," he says. "Whatever you do, do not leave that fucking bathroom. I'm coming, Will."

God, I hope so, I think. Because the next thing I know, the world tilts and disappears into a gray fog.

Twenty-Four

RYAN

MY BLOOD IS fucking boiling. I dial Tanner's fucking cell for what feels like the hundredth time, and finally—fucking finally—he answers. "Dude, what is—"

"Why the fuck aren't you with Willow?" I demand the second he picks up.

There's a moment of confused, stunned silence, and then he responds. "What are you talking about? You knew we were going to meet her at the party. We're heading over there now. I had to stop by my place to grab my car charger—both my phone and Lana's were dying."

My fingers squeeze the steering wheel until the plastic creaks under the pressure. Logically, I know I shouldn't be as angry as I am. This isn't Tanner's fault, but goddamn it, he hadn't heard her voice. Will never fucking sounds like that—stuttering, shaky, *frightened*. My heart picks up the pace as I speed through the streets.

"Well, something's fucking wrong. Where's the

fucking party you were going to?" I bark. "I need an address." Right now, I'm just flying down the streets surrounding the campus, searching for a house on a corner that looks like it's having a party. I haven't come across one yet, and I grow more and more frustrated with each passing second.

Willow is out there, and she needs me.

"What's wrong with her?"

I blow past a stop sign and screech around another corner and punch the fucking steering wheel when once again, I see no house in sight that screams 'party here, motherfuckers.' "Give. Me. The. Address." I spit out each word, violence singing in my veins.

"It's the frat house on 25th Street and Camden," Tanner says. "We're literally on our way there now."

I glance at the street I pass and turn the wheel, fishtailing the back of my vehicle as I spin a u-turn and press down on the gas. "I'm closer," I snap. I'm just about to punch the end call button when something else occurs to me. Willow had said something about a guy—was it the guy she'd left with? I'd recognized him from that day in the library. He was always hanging around her, smiling her way, checking her out. I already know if I find what I think I'm about to, the chances of me getting arrested tonight are high as fuck. "Tanner." I squeeze his name out through gritted teeth.

"Turn here," I hear him mutter, his voice quieter, which means he's not talking to me but probably the girl he's with. "What do you need?" he asks, his voice growing louder once more.

"I need you to take care of shit," I say, feeling ice in my veins and rage in my chest. "If he fucking hurt her, I don't know if I'll be able to fucking stop from killing him. If I lose control, I need you to take care of her."

There's a quiet moment on the other end, but Tanner gives me the answer I need. The only thing I've ever asked from him. "I've got your back, man," he says, and with that, I end the call and press the pedal to the floor.

Less than five minutes later, I'm screeching up to the frat house Tanner directed me to. My car shudders to a halt just in front of the driveway, cutting across the back of two cars hanging out into the street. I don't even think about parking properly. There's no time for that.

I leave the keys in the ignition and am out of the car before it's even fully shoved into park. If anyone wants to steal it tonight, they can go for it. The only thing on my mind right now is Willow.

Beer cans litter the front yard, and a half-naked guy painted in our school's colors is passed out next to a folding lawn chair cuddling an empty jug. I storm the front steps, ignoring the calls and hand waves from a few of the still coherent party-goers on the porch as I shove into the house.

Bedroom. She'd said. Somewhere nearby. The first floor. Music thrums throughout the house, and I'm panicked as I start searching. Throwing open closed doors and charging through the place until I dimly hear a crash to my right and turn, following the sound.

"Man, you gotta calm down," I hear some guy saying. "She's probably passed out in there. How much did you give her?"

"She was fucking asking for it," I hear another guy say. I round the corner and find a bedroom in pieces. Neither of them seem to notice my entrance.

"Yeah, well, Ricky isn't gonna like the fact that you trashed his room. He said you could borrow it if you wanted to get laid, not to fucking ransack the place because she locked herself in the bathroom."

On silent feet, I move further into the room and then close the door. My chest heaves up and down while my hands ball into fists. My sights are set on the taller of the two standing before a door across the room. Jordan fucking Hagen is about to get his face bashed in because I have no doubt that the girl these two are talking about is Willow—my fucking Willow—behind that bathroom door.

"Just get me a goddamn crowbar, so I can—"

I take one step further into the room and a second, and as he lifts his head, I launch myself at him. He doesn't even see me coming. My fist crashes into his face, and I relish in the feel of split skin under my knuckles. The first hit is all it takes to unleash the beast inside of me. One hit turns into two and then three, and then I start to lose count as the fucker roars and tries to fight back, but there's no fighting this. There's no fighting me. I clamp my hands around his throat and squeeze until his legs kick out from beneath me as he scrambles to break my hold. His face turns a bright tomato red, then blue and purple.

I do finally release him, but only so I can send one fist crashing down against his face once, twice, three more times. Blood flies and a few drops slap my cheek. I don't care. I can't feel a damn thing. Only the rage pouring through me.

Vaguely, I hear yelling behind me. I recognize that we're far enough away from the source of the music that I should be hearing clearly, but I don't think it's the music or anything other than rage clogging my eardrums right now. Everything focuses on the piece of shit in front of me. At least, until the running of footsteps outside in the hallway invades, and the door bursts open. Despite it all, however, I don't stop, even when the guy beneath me collapses and goes limp.

Fuck him. He thinks he can do whatever the fuck he wants? He thinks he can hurt my girl? Mine. She's fucking mine.

"—an! Ryan! Fuck! Goddamn it! Stop!" Someone's hands land on my shoulders, and when I don't react, those same hands become arms, circling my throat and lifting me up and off the bastard. I reach up, locking my bloodied fingers on the guy's forearm, and then I bend over, launching the asshole through the air right over my fucking head.

Tanner grunts as he lands on top of the fucker I'd just knocked out cold. There are screaming and panicked voices in the room, but I don't care. I step over the two of them and move towards the door. I try the knob, but of course, it's locked.

Smart girl. But that won't stop me now.

I back up. "Will, if you can hear me, baby, I need you to stay away from the door." I wait for a moment, but when there's no answer, I suck in a breath and step back. I lift my foot, and one solid fucking kick shatters the side of the door frame as the door slams inward. Wood splinters and rains down against the tiled floor inside. I storm into the room, my heart pounding, and my body practically vibrating. When I see her, curled up in a ball, slumped over between the toilet and the bathtub, I almost turn my ass right around and go back to beat the asshole who did this to her some more. But I can't. She needs me now more than he needs to die.

"Will..." I crouch down in front of her, reaching for her.

Sweat clings to her brow and slides down the side of her face as I cup her cheek and smooth a strand of her dark hair out of the way. My voice must rouse her because she hadn't reacted to the door breaking, but now her eyes crack open—the warm brown irises dull and unfocused.

"Ryan?" she practically whimpers out my name when she sees it's me. Tears form in her squinting eyes and slide down her already stained cheeks. Black lines mark the paths they've already taken, and a new wave of fury overcomes me. I pull my hands away and ball them into fists. I can't lose it now.

Gently, I move my arm around her back and then beneath her legs, lifting her into my arms as she lands against my chest with a plop.

"Oh, my god." I turn at the sound of that familiar feminine voice.

Lana stands in the bathroom doorway, her eyes locked on Willow as she slumps against my chest. Shock covers her face, and I know if Willow were conscious, she'd want to reassure her friend, but I don't have the patience for that. Instead, I merely shoulder her out of the way as I reenter the room to find the second guy who'd been here talking to Jordan, trying to rouse him and Tanner alongside both of them.

Tanner takes one look at Willow in my arms, and his face goes cold.

"I've called the cops motherfucker," the guy on the floor with his friend snaps. "You're so fucking dead."

"No," Tanner answers for me, turning back to them. "He's not." He points to the door but speaks to me. "Get her out of here, Anderson." He never uses my last name—not unless he's fucking with me or … he's pissed, which he is right now. Just like me. "I'll deal with this."

I don't question it. As much as I want to kill the bastard that started this, Willow is more important than anything right now. I pause just before I hit the door. "If I see his face again," I warn Tanner, "I'll kill him."

"Don't worry," Tanner replies. "You won't."

"Wait!" Lana says, but I cut a look to Tanner as I head for the door, and he gives me a nod as he steps in front of her, stopping her from following me. "What the hell are you doing? Let me see her!" I ignore Lana—not caring that she's Will's best friend. At this moment, I need her to myself. I need to reassure myself that she's okay, and I need to be the first thing she sees when she opens her eyes again.

As I carry her from the house and outside, Willow remains limp in my grasp. She doesn't even open her eyes when I strap her into the front seat of my car, and as I drive away, two cop cars speed past with their red and blue lights flashing.

I held back tonight, but as I glance over at Willow and her tear-stained face, I wish I hadn't. I wish I'd done more than beat that bastard unconscious. I wish I'd fucking murdered him.

Twenty-Five

WILLOW

THE WORLD IS swimming in front of me. I feel like I'm floating, swaying down a long lazy river like the kind in the waterparks I never got to go to as a kid because no foster family ever wanted to take the temporary kids. No one wants to spend money on the kids who'll only be around for a few short months. It's kinda nice. It's warm and I feel safe.

I've only ever felt this safe when we were younger, and Ryan would crawl in my bed and whisper secrets to me as he stroked my hair after a nightmare. Stupid secrets—like which of the other kids were stealing money from our foster parents or who stole a pack of gum from the corner mart store. I didn't really care about the secrets, but Ryan would say them and then tease me, telling me how good I was because I wasn't like them or anyone else. How I was so much nicer, and how he wished I'd always stay that way.

There were many reasons why I fell in love

with Ryan. It didn't just start one day, but it blossomed over the years. My love hadn't been so quick to form and easy to burn out like that. No, there's a reason I can still feel it flame inside of my chest despite all the shit he's done to me.

Despite the anger, the cruelty, the rumors, the torment—I love him because I know the real him. I know this isn't him.

The real Ryan Anderson is someone who holds his sister's hand when she's scared. He promises to fight all her monsters for her, to protect her, and make her happy. Even half asleep and floating along this lazy river of numbness, I feel tears prick at my closed eyelids. The truth hits me like a ton of bricks.

I miss him. I miss Ryan. I miss the way we used to be. I miss him holding me after nightmares. I miss feeling like there was someone else in this godforsaken world that cared about whether I lived or died. Without him, everything fucking hurts. It feels like I'm crawling through life on the ground, scraping my knees, cutting my palms to shreds, and nothing is worth it. This pain is too much, and there's no reward. No light at the end of my tunnel.

Only darkness.

It's too much.

When I was a kid, so many foster families took us in out of a sense of obligation, of duty. Not to us, though. Never to us. To some unknown god. As if they needed to rack up as much good credit here on Earth as they could just in case they needed some extras to help them out when they finally got to those big pearly gates in the sky.

They'd forced Ryan and I both to attend numerous church services. We'd been baptized. We'd been relegated to the 'special children' in Sunday school. The ones who didn't have a mom or dad, but a nameless, faceless guardian that always eventually had an excuse to send us to someone else. Ryan was too argumentative, or I was cold and unwilling to talk to them.

Everyone says the babies always get adopted first, but not us. It was as if everyone had already known that we were born bad—no, not we, but me. I was born bad, and I fucked up everything for Ryan. I was the reason he never got adopted because he'd never wanted to leave me behind. I was the reason he got sent to juvie because he felt like he had no choice. He had to get away from me because I was wicked. The things I want ... they're wicked.

A sob works its way up my chest and unleashes. Why? It's not fair. I didn't mean—I never meant for this to happen. If God created us, if He created me, then why did He make me this way? I sob again and realize that it's not just in my dream, I'm sobbing in real life too. Big, heaving wails that wrack my chest and make me feel like my rib cage is breaking.

"Willow." I hear someone's voice from far away, and damn me if it doesn't sound like him—like Ryan. "Willow, please, baby. Please stop crying."

I wish I could. For him, I'd do anything, but I can't do this. Not because I don't want to, but because my body won't let me. Once the gates have been opened, the tears pour forth, and they just continue to stream down my face unbidden.

I'm broken. Shattered. Beyond redemption.

Maybe it's the stupid assholes from the party. Maybe it's Jordan. Maybe it's the drugs. My body doesn't seem to care whose fault it is; all it knows is that we've been holding it in for so long there's no more room. All of the emotion I kept bottled up for years, refusing to let it out—to any foster parent, to the McRaes, as kind as they'd been, even to Lana, my best friend—it comes rolling down my face in the form of big fat tears.

"Please don't cry, Will. Goddamn it, I hate when you cry." Ryan's voice sounds tortured, like the very thought of me crying hurts him.

The real Ryan would feel that way, wouldn't he? The real Ryan was my hero. He was strong and capable, and no matter how wrong it is to think this, he was so goddamn sexy. Even in high school, he'd been built big. Strong. Masculine. Tight abs and broad shoulders that could block out the sun.

"Everything's alright. Everything's gonna be alright." Warm arms encircle me and drag me against a wide, firm chest. Smooth sheets brush my skin. My *bare* skin. That's when I realize that this isn't a dream. The bubble I'm floating in pops, and as it does, my eyes crack open, and I tilt my head back to see that the voice speaking to me is none other than the one person I have to finally admit I can't be without. No matter how hard I try to be good, I'll keep coming back to him because without him, I feel empty. Without him, I'm as good as dead—a living corpse.

The world around the face hovering over mine is hazy, but I see him. I see his dark brown hair as it hangs down over his forehead, the strong bridge of his nose jutting out from his face. The chiseled underside of his jawline. How can someone be so perfect and beautiful—as if he was crafted to suit my every desire—yet be as untouchable as a dream? It's not fucking fair.

The tears only come harder. "I'm sorry," I find myself blubbering. "I'm so"—I hiccup—"sorry." Apologizing is the least I can do. It's not enough, and it never will be, but that doesn't mean I shouldn't still say it. If it weren't for me, none of this would've happened. Not juvie, not Jordan, not even his cruelty.

God, what must Ryan think of himself? I pushed him to be hateful, ruthless ... worse than he's ever been to anyone else. All to me. The one person he always promised to protect. Maybe he's right. Maybe I am poison.

"What?" Ryan's hands touch my hair, brush the strands back, away from my face and over my shoulder as he rocks me back and forth. "Why are you sorry?"

We're seated on a bed, with his legs spread wide enough that my body can fit between them. I'm no longer wearing the clothes I was in earlier. Instead, I've been stripped and redressed in an oversized jersey. Thankfully, however, I can feel my underwear—so I know I'm not bare beneath it. Who knows what I'd do if I was bare? It's obvious, I'm not good at resisting him.

It's almost as if the universe is torturing me, punishing me for what I feel by giving me what I crave most. The cruel Ryan is gone and in his place is the Ryan I've been praying would return to me for years. His face is full of nothing but concern. His hands are gentle, which only makes me cry harder as I turn and bury my face in his chest.

"I ruined everything," I confess through broken sobs. "I wish I had just kept my mouth shut. If I had, then you wouldn't have … we wouldn't be … I'm sorry, Ryan. Please forgive me. I'll stop. I'll let you go. I won't ever..." Even if it kills me, and it probably will, I'll let him go. If that's what he wants, I'll stand back and … I'll let him be normal. I'll never approach him again. I'll switch schools. I'll disappear.

"What are you talking about?" Ryan demands.

I look up at him through waterlogged eyes. Is he really going to make me say it? Is he really going to force me to voice my sins? I guess I was wrong, then. He's still as cruel as before, only this time he's worse—because this time, it's like he doesn't realize what he's doing to me—kindly holding me, stroking my hair, comforting me, and then asking me to bare my twisted soul to him.

"I love you." I force the words out, hiccupping just after they escape.

There's a pause, and then, "Will..."

I shake my head and reach up, awkwardly fumbling to push my hands over his mouth to stop him from saying anything more. "Stop," I tell him, forcing my voice to remain even. It's hard. Possibly one of the hardest things I've ever done—even more so than the first time I did this. Because my first confession had been filled with butterflies, with hope. I'd seen the way Ryan looked at me, mistaking that for romantic interest. I thought ... if we were twins then it only made sense he'd feel what I was feeling.

We'd never really experienced any of those supernatural things other twins did. There was no sixth sense. No mind reading. We'd just been two people as close as they could be. Despite that, Ryan had felt like the Yin to my Yang. The light to my dark. My other half.

Everything. Ryan was and always will be my everything.

"Will, I know—" Ryan tries to mumble around my hands, but I press down harder.

"No, you don't know," I insist. "I love you. I've loved you for six years—no, longer than that." I look up at him, beseeching him with my eyes, willing him to see the truth. "I've loved you for my whole life, Ryan," I confess. "And no matter what you do, no matter what happens—you can bully me, you can rip me to shreds, break my heart into a million pieces, and I'm still going to love you until the day I die." I catch my breath, feeling something swelling within. "You were right," I whisper the admission. Beneath my hands, his lips turn down.

"What are you talking about?"

My hands fall away from his face, landing between us, palms against his chest. "I am poison," I say. "I know this—my love for you is wrong—and I tried, I wanted..." It's hard to say it out loud. "I knew all along that what I want can never be, but I wanted you to love me anyway. It was selfish and wrong. I'm sorry. Everything that's happened, it's all my—"

Ryan cups a palm over my mouth, stopping my rambling tirade, in the same manner, I had him. My head tips back and I sniff hard. His eyes meet mine, and unlike the past, I can't seem to read them this time. He takes in a shuddering breath, and it rumbles against his chest and me when he releases it. "Will, there's something I need to tell you."

This is it. This is the moment I've prepared myself for. I don't want to look him in the eyes when he rejects me a second time, but I can't seem to pull myself away from his penetrating stare.

People say eyes are windows to the soul, and if that's true, then Ryan's is a tortured one. There's nothing but torment and pain and regret in his irises. It hurts to see. It makes me want to comfort him, but that, too, would be cruel of me and I've already done enough.

"Will, I tried," he whispers, his voice quiet,

breathy in the darkened room we're in. I never asked, but I can only assume it's his. It smells like him. Everything around me smells like him. It's like he did it on purpose because now his scent is invading me, driving out all rational thought as he leans forward and presses his lips first to my forehead and then down on the tip of my nose.

He pulls away briefly, and I blink in confusion. What is he doing? This is the strangest rejection I've ever heard of.

"Will..." His hands tighten against my back and pull me in closer. "I tried to stay away from you," he says. "I wanted you to have a normal life. I'm so sorry ... but I can't do it anymore."

"What?"

He closes his eyes, and when they reopen, there's a fire burning in the dark brown depths. "I love you too, Will," he says. "I've always loved you, and I always will."

I bite down on my lower lip as a fresh wave of tears assails me. Even now, he's trying to be kind. I shake my head. "I know you do," I reply, "but it's not the same. It's not like—"

"It is how you love me," he says, cutting me off. "I love you so fucking much, too much. Willow, I want to bind you to me in every way possible." He yanks me against his chest until there's no room left between us until I can feel the very physical proof of his words. "This is what you do to me, Will. It was never just you, it was both of us."

I don't have enough time to consciously

understand the gravity of his words—the reality of his confession—because as soon as they're free, his head descends and his mouth takes mine in an all-consuming kiss that burns away everything else. His kiss drives out all of our demons and leaves nothing but pleasure behind, and for someone who's been lost in the dark for far too long, it's like a breath of fresh air that I can't help but inhale.

So, inhale it I do.

Twenty-Six

RYAN

I'M GOING TO hell in a sinking boat. I'm going to burn for the rest of my days—in life and death. And right now, I've decided that I really don't give a shit. I'll let the flames consume me as long as it's *only* me. I'll take her sins and eat them and let them sit in my belly until the Devil comes to rip them free. I'll do whatever I have to because she's worth it. She's worth every bit of the agony I know is coming my way.

There's no fucking way I can stop this now that it's happening. My hands reach for her and she doesn't resist me. No, not my Will. She meets me in the middle and lets me take what I want. I push her lips apart and delve inside, kissing her like she's the last thing I'll be able to have before the world ends and who the hell fucking knows, she just might be. I hope so.

I've tried for so long to stay away from her, and that left me with nothing but internal scars I'm not sure I'll ever heal from. So, now I'm going to do what I've always wanted. I'm going to give her the kiss I've been waiting to give her for ages. Not one filled with jealousy. Not one filled with hate, but one that is filled with all of the lingering feelings I've been burying for too fucking long now.

I burrow my tongue in Willow's mouth and stroke it against hers, and even as I do, I find myself flipping her around and pressing her back down against my sheets. Egyptian cotton. God, I've never been more grateful in my life for being such a priss when it comes to sheets. All those years in juvie made me appreciate the finer things, and now, I'm glad that she's here so I can give it to her too.

Willow moans as I leave her mouth and trail my kisses downward. Over the hollow of her throat and towards her collarbone. I lick along the edge before sucking a piece of her skin until the pale surface turns red. My hands skim her hips, pushing upward and past the jersey I'd changed her into right after she'd puked her guts out in my car.

The reminder has me pausing. "Will." I jerk up and over her, hovering as panic takes place. Her eyes open lazily, and she stares up at me with a hungry expression through slits. "Will, I don't want you to regret—"

"I'm not going to regret this," she interrupts, reaching for me. "Please, Ryan. I don't want to stop. Please don't stop."

I'm weak—so fucking weak when it comes to this girl. My girl. It's been hours since I grabbed her from the party. I'd forced water down her half-conscious throat for half that time and let her sleep the rest. Her words are no longer slurred, and she must have puked up most of whatever that bastard gave her because now, as she latches onto my upper arms, there's nothing about her that spells drugged out and in need of help.

If anyone needs that, though, it's me right now. I need help from myself, from the sins I'm about to commit. And as I lower myself back down over her, I hope no savior comes.

Her skin is perfect beneath my fingers, so smooth and beautiful. I press kiss after kiss along her belly, and with each movement, I push the shirt she's in up a little more before finally just ripping it off and letting it fall away to reveal everything.

There are some bruises on her skin—likely from that fucking asshole. The sight of them sends rage pouring through me as I stroke my thumb over the surface of her skin, but I don't want to focus on that right now. I don't want to show her any more anger. I want to show her love.

"Spread your legs, baby," I whisper, and Will gives me the greatest gift of all time because she does. She opens her legs and lets me sink down between them as my hands find the waistband of her panties. Even in the dark, I can tell the crotch is wet. My sweet, dirty little girl. I run a finger slowly up the center of her and relish in the way her body quivers all over. "Do you want something, Will?" I ask, half taunting.

Amber brown eyes flash as she glares down at

me and undulates her hips. "I want you to take these off of me," she says in response.

Killing me. This girl is fucking killing, but oh, what a way to go.

I kiss her hip and then grab either side of her panties. "As my lady commands," I reply and pull them down and off, backing away until they're free of her feet. But before I throw them over my shoulder, losing them to the cluttered floor of my bedroom, I bring them to my face and press the wet spot to my nose and mouth, inhaling.

"Oh, my god." Willow's scandalized tone is almost funny—no, who the hell am I kidding? It's fucking hilarious.

"There's no god here tonight," I tell her as I pull them away and grin at her before letting them drop to the floor and pressing her back into the mattress as my fingers find the sweet pussy that I've been dying to get inside for years. "Just you and me."

Willow's hand slides into my hair, her nails scraping against my scalp that light up the nerves beneath my skin and send radiating shots of pleasure down my spine. I spread her wider, pushing until her thighs are up and over my shoulders. I'm about to fucking wear this girl like a fucking pair of earmuffs.

The first long lick up her slit has a shudder working through her. The second has her hand clenching against my skull. But as we move onto the third and fourth, she finally starts to relax. I chuckle low in my throat, my breath blowing out against her wet flesh because that was just what I was waiting for.

Without warning, I dive down and shove my tongue as far deep inside of her as I can get, licking her from the inside out as my thumb moves up to the reddened clit at the top of her pussy. Will gasps and her back bows off the bed. Her nails scratch at my scalp, and her thighs tremble, but I'm far from done.

I massage her clit as I dive deep for more. More and more. There'll never be enough of her for me. I suck her towards the back of my throat and swallow, lapping at her like a starving dog.

"Oh, fuck … Ryan. Oh, right there, please …" Willow's curse is like a boon to my ears. Her trembling body is like nirvana. Everything about her is perfect to me—including the orgasm that crashes over her a moment later and floods my mouth with her taste.

Who knew the forbidden fruit would taste exactly like heaven?

Twenty-Seven

WILLOW

One orgasm isn't enough for Ryan. No, he's a perfectionist, and as I come down from my first high of the night, I realize he's quickly aiming to push me right back up that slope. Ryan spreads me open and dives into me like he's looking for a place to drown, like he's looking to swallow me whole. His tongue slides through my slit, first up one side, then down the other, and finally delving into my depths. My muscles contract as pleasure shoots through me.

"You taste so fucking good, Will," he rasps between my legs. I can't believe it. It's like this is a dream, one I never want to wake up from. "So fucking good..." he repeats just before his head lowers, and he laps at me again.

He devours my pussy like a starving man, holding me open with his fingers. I can't hold back the moan that bubbles up out of my throat as my fingers spear through his hair and curl around the dark chocolate locks. My back bows as the stirrings of yet another orgasm flutter in the pit of my stomach.

Spots dance in front of my eyes. "Oh, my god," I whisper. "I think I'm gonna come again."

Ryan chuckles, the sound brushing over my sensitive clit, making me jerk and whimper as another bolt of pleasure shoots through me. He settles me again with a hand on the lower curve of my belly. "You think?" he whispers back, breathing against my wet flesh. "No, baby, I know you are."

Spoken like a man with true confidence, but Ryan isn't all talk. No, he's a man of action as well. He spears into my pussy with two fingers, curling them as his lips descend on my clit, and he sucks it into his mouth. My legs tremble with the effort it takes to hold back my orgasm. I want this dream to last; I want there to be more. I can't bear it if, after he finishes, he just gets up and leaves me. What if he thinks it's a mistake?

Tears leak out of the corners of my eyes and my nails scratch at his scalp. Despite my intentions, my body can't seem to resist his ministrations a second longer. I come apart under his talented fingers and tongue with a low, throaty moan, a gush of liquid flooding me even as he laps it up like it's candy.

And just when I think it's over, just when I think he's going to back away and look at me with that expression of his, one that's always full of guilt and partial hatred—though now I wonder if that's not more for himself than for me—he withdraws from my legs and crawls up over my body to kiss me.

Ryan's tongue thrusts into my mouth, and I open for him automatically, stunned and so incredibly turned on by the taste of my own orgasm on his lips. He kisses me with a barely contained violence, like he wants to prove something.

"Do you have any idea what I want to do to you, Willow Anderson?" he whispers against my lips.

I smile. "It's actually Willow McRae now," I remind him. "I changed my name a few years ago."

He chuckles and shakes his head. "One day, it'll be the same again," he replies, kissing me again before pulling away to reach down and lift the shirt he's wearing up and over his head.

My gaze trails up his chest, over the rigid lines of his abs and up the hollows to the wide, broad shoulders befitting of a football player. Shadows dance across his skin, making him almost appear like a monstrous creature of the dark, but if he is—then we both are.

"Please don't stop this time," I whisper, reaching for him and curling my arms around his neck. "Don't stop until it's done."

"Will..." His hands come around my back, fingers finding the clasp of my bra. He quickly undoes it, and I don't resist as he slides the straps down my arms and completely off, tossing the piece of fabric to the side before returning my arms to their rightful place—around him. "Nothing short of a natural disaster could stop me from taking what I want right now. What I've wanted for fucking years."

"Oh yeah?" I feel breathless, weightless, like nothing could bring me down from the cloud nine I'm surfing on, and I know his next words are only going to lift me higher. "And what's that?" I tilt my head back and arch my back, brushing my breasts against his bare chest until he can feel the scrape of my hardened nipples against his skin. It makes something unfurl inside of me, a demoness waiting to be set free. Something lustful, something ... *more.* "Tell me," I beg him. "What do you want most in this world?"

His nostrils flare and his hands cup my back. Moving down, I yelp as he abruptly shifts, lifting me almost effortlessly until I'm astride his hips. The only thing separating us now from being one is the pair of loose gray sweatpants he's wearing.

"I want all of you," he whispers back. "Every." He kisses my lips. "Single." He kisses my jawline. "Inch." He kisses the hollow of my throat. "Of you."

My lashes flutter. My insides throb. I only have one answer for him, and it's the same as it was six years ago.

"I'm yours, Ryan," I tell him. "I've always been yours."

His head lifts and he moves forward. Our mouths clash like a battle of wills, and I can feel the mattress against my spine as he presses me into the sheets. It smells like him. It feels like him, warm and safe. His arms around me. His tongue in my mouth. It's surreal.

Ryan's hands move over me, his fingers reach

for my breasts, pinching and squeezing my nipples, rolling them until electricity sparks and spirals within me. I arch my head back as I moan and writhe under his attention, but he doesn't stop there. His hands move back to my legs, spreading them open, moving them on either side of his hips.

"I want you, Will, without anything between us," he tells me. "I want to feel you. Every piece of you. Please tell me you're on birth control."

I laugh, but it's more like an exhale than a genuine laugh. "Yes," I tell him. "I am, and you don't need to worry about if I have ... um, anything else. I've never actually..."

Ryan's body goes still over me and his head pulls back. "What?"

I blink up at him, trying to read the mood. Has something changed? "I've never had sex with anyone," I say. "That's what I meant. I was just trying to tell you that I'm clean. You are too, right?"

He nods. "Of course, I wouldn't be doing this if I—" He cuts himself off and shakes his head. "Wait a second, you're serious? You've never had sex? Not in all the years I was gone?"

I shake my head. "I mean, I tried having a boyfriend here and there. I um ... did a few things that I ended up regretting later, but I've never gone ... all the way." Is that sad? I think. Is he disappointed? I mean, I'm twenty-one and still a virgin. It's not unheard of, but it's also ... not super common. Maybe he was expecting me to be more experienced. "Are you upset?"

Ryan breathes deeply through his nose and jerks his head to the side as he hovers over me. "No," he says sharply. "I'm not upset, and for fuck's sake, definitely not with you. I'm angry at myself. I thought—after what happened in the library—I just assumed ... I mean, I did it thinking..."

"Hey." I reach up and cup his face, stopping the disjointed words spilling from his lips. "It's okay. I don't mind. What happened in the library—"

"Was cruel," he cuts me off. "I'm sorry, Will. I'm so fucking sorry about what I did. I know you didn't want that, but I—"

"I did," I say, placing a palm over his mouth and forcing him to look me in the eyes. "I wanted it, Ryan. It was hot. I dreamed about it afterwards. I loved everything you did to me in that basement. It was dirty and defiled and..." I squirm beneath him, rubbing my thighs together. Just thinking about it, remembering it, makes me hot. "I want you to do it again sometime, but right now, I really, really want you to fuck me. I want to go all the way, Ryan, and I want that with you."

His mouth is on me before even giving me a second to wait for his reaction. He thrusts his tongue back into my mouth, our teeth clashing, our bodies writhing together as he reaches down and frees himself from his sweatpants. Ryan reaches for my wrist and brings it forward to the place between his legs, and suddenly, something hot and hard is against the palm of my hand. He feels so smooth, like velvet-covered steel. I can't help but squeeze, eliciting a groan of pleasure from him as he jerks in my grip.

For several long, tense moments I jack him off, running my hand up and down his cock as I feel and explore everything about it from its width to its length. He shudders in my grasp. "Please, fuck, Will. You gotta stop, or this is going to be over before it even gets started," Ryan says.

I smile at that. "I can't help it," I tell him. "You feel so good."

Hands land against my shoulders and push me back abruptly. I gasp as Ryan grabs one of my legs and hooks it over his shoulder, cutting off my careful exploration. "I'm going to feel a hell of a lot fucking better in a few seconds, sweetness. Are you ready for me?"

Is he really asking me that right now? I wonder. "Ryan," I say, "I've been ready for you for six years, and if you don't put your cock inside of me right—*ohmygodfuck*!" Before I can even finish my demand, Ryan reaches down and positions the tip of his cock at my entrance, pushing in, just the smallest of fractions, but it's enough for my entire body to go on high alert.

"I'm sorry, were you saying something, baby?" Ryan's smiling, laughter in his eyes as he gently nudges his hips forward and slides even deeper.

I bite my lower lip until I swear I can taste blood. He's so thick and long, and I've never done this before. Sure, I've fingered myself, brought myself momentary pleasure in the darkness of my own dorm room, but never anything like this. There's a difference between your own hand and someone's—no, not just anyone, Ryan's—body.

"Don't stop. Don't stop. Don't stop," I practically beg as he works himself deeper, stretching me, filling me until there's no place that separates us.

"Not in a million years, Will," Ryan promises just before pulling back slightly and delivering the last thrust that brings him all the way home inside of me. There's a burn of friction, a slight twinge of discomfort, but I'm so wet that it's there and gone in a moment. Despite what people say, there's no real pain. It doesn't hurt. It feels fucking incredible.

I thought there was no place higher than cloud nine? I was dead fucking wrong. Because whatever this is—wherever it is on the universe scale—it's better. So much better.

Ryan waits a few seconds, and I can see the sweat percolating on his brow as if it's costing him everything to keep still, to keep me from hurting. "You can move," I tell him, "please move."

"Are you sure?" he asks, sounding as if he's been running for several miles and is almost out of breath.

I nod. "Yes, I'm sure."

With that, Ryan exhales and then drives into me. His cock withdraws and spears back into my pussy, hard and hot and hitting someplace inside of me that makes me feel like flying. I reach up as my legs fall back to the mattress, hooked over his thighs, and lock my nails into his shoulders.

"More," I pant. "Fuck, Ryan, please. I need more. Give me more."

"You're gonna fucking kill me, baby," Ryan replies, but he does as I ask, and gives me more. All that I could ever want. He powers into me, thrusting, and hitting that spot inside repeatedly. So hard and fast that it's no shock when I come for him for the third time tonight. A few moments later, as I come down from my biggest shock of the night, he stills and grunts as he holds himself inside of me.

Something warm floods my insides, and I bite down on my lip once more as I feel him filling me up with his cum. And when he backs out, moving away, I clench down on my muscles automatically. It's wrong, and I shouldn't want it—birth control isn't one hundred percent, but I like the idea of wearing his mark, of feeling him inside of my belly when I move.

"Hold on," he whispers, leaning forward to brush a kiss over my already bruised lips. "I'll get a washcloth for you." I don't have a chance to say anything as Ryan gets off the bed and pulls his sweatpants back up before heading to the bathroom. I assume he's cleaning himself up in there as well because, after a few minutes, he comes back holding a warm washcloth.

"I'll do it," I say as he spreads my legs and moves down.

"No." My breath catches in my chest as he moves the damp fabric over my swollen pussy. "I got it." He cleans me thoroughly and then tosses the washcloth across the room to what I assume is a laundry basket of some kind, though it's kind of hard to tell in the dark.

Ryan crawls back onto the bed with me and pulls me into his arms before pressing a kiss to my forehead. *This is it. This is everything I ever wanted, and everything I never thought I would have.*

Minutes go by and I try to fall asleep, but it evades me. I don't know what I'm supposed to do after sex. I've never gotten this far with anyone else, and although a part of me is glad that Ryan was my first, another part of me really wishes I had some sort of experience so I wouldn't feel like I have to pretend to sleep against his chest as I listen to him breathing.

"These sheets are going to catch fire with all those thoughts running through your head," Ryan says, amusement lightening his tone.

I sigh. "I'm just wondering about what happens now," I tell him truthfully.

"Well," he says, "now, we're supposed to be falling asleep so that tomorrow, you can wake up and go to the police station and file a report against that fucking bastard who drugged you tonight—"

"No, I don't want to talk about him," I say, cutting him off.

Ryan tenses, but doesn't move. "You have to do something about him, Will. If you won't, I will."

I glance up. "What would you do?"

He doesn't look at me. "You don't want to

know."

I blink and reach for him, cupping his face as I force him to meet my eyes. "Yes, I do," I insist. "I want to know."

"Will..." His hand lifts and touches mine, the one against his face. "I might look like the boy next door type now. I might play football on a scholarship for Trinity today, but I wasn't that person four years ago. When I went away, I did things. I went to juvie and met people. I'm not a good man."

I shake my head. "I refuse to believe that's true."

"That's because you see the good in everyone."

"No, I don't. I definitely don't see the good in Jordan."

His eyes narrow. "Then go to the police station tomorrow," he orders.

I blow out a breath, lowering my hand. "What is that going to do?" I ask. "Police hardly ever believe girls like me."

"You'll have people to back you up," Ryan says. "I'll go with you. So will your friend; she saw when I went to get you. Tanner will as well. You don't have to do it alone, but you should go."

He's right, and I know he is. How many other girls has Jordan drugged? There'd been a whole mint can full of those pills. At the very least, he should be arrested and taken in for questioning for having them, right?

"How are we going to explain you, though?" I

ask. "Why you were there? Why you're with me? Are we going to tell people that you're ... I mean, that we're..." Twins. I don't say it, but I don't need to. He can read the rest in my face when I look back up at him.

"We can just say that I'm your boyfriend," he tells me, shocking me.

"Boyfriend?" I repeat.

He arches a brow and pulls me closer. "You didn't think this was a one-time thing, did you?" he asks. "I meant it when I said I wanted you, Will."

"But we're ... I mean, it's illegal, Ryan. You and me. It's not just illegal, it's ... what are people going to think? We could be kicked out of school. You could lose your scholarship." All of a sudden, the consequences of what we'd just done hit me like a freight train. I sit up and pull away from him. "Oh my god ... what have we done?" Worse, what have I done ... to him?

"Will, calm down. No one even needs to know." Ryan's hands find my arms, and he turns me back to face him. "Your last name is different from mine now. No one knows that we're ... twins." It takes him a moment to say the word, almost as if he doesn't want to admit it. Probably because he doesn't. Neither of us does. "No one knows. I mean, I told Tanner, but he didn't believe me. So, I think if we tell him we're dating, he'll just chalk it up to a prank or something."

"I told Lana," I confess.

"What?"

My chest aches at the look he gives me, full of diminishing hope and a hint of betrayal. "I didn't see this coming, Ryan," I say quickly. "I thought you hated me, and she knew something was up between us. She kept asking, and I just didn't know how not to tell her. She's my best friend."

"Tell her you lied," he says immediately. "Tell her you made it up, that we were high school sweethearts. Tell her we were just foster siblings. Not related."

"I told her we're twins."

Panic makes his eyes go wild as he reaches up and scrubs a hand down the center of his face. "We can fix it," he says. "We can..." He grits his teeth and stares down at his lap for a long moment. The fear on his face and tension in his body only makes me want to take him into my arms and hold him. And we're alone, so there's no reason why I can't.

I close my arms around him and pull him towards me until his face is nestled between my breasts. His arms wrap around my back and squeeze me tight. "I can't lose you again, Will," he whispers.

My heart constricts at his words, at the hope and desperation in them. I stroke his back, run my fingers through his hair and feel his heart beat rapidly against mine. I've never lied to my best friend, but I think a lie would be much better than the truth for the first time in my life. I know Lana, and I know that if she were to ever find out about this, about Ryan and me...

I shake my head, cutting myself off from that

train of thought. There's only one choice in front of me right now, and that's Ryan. I reach down and cup his face, lifting it to meet mine.

"You're not going to lose me," I promise. "We'll figure it out."

"I really am sorry, Will," he says. "For everything I've done. If I could take it back, I would. Just please ... don't leave me."

They're irresistible, those eyes of his. I can't help but lean forward and brush my lips over his, and as I do, I whisper the last but most pure of promises. "Never, Ryan," I say, my mouth over his. "I will never leave you."

Twenty-Eight

WILLOW

SUNLIGHT STREAMS IN through the slatted blinds and hits me right over my eyes, making me moan and roll away as a bolt of intense sharp pain shoots through my head. Warm hands move over my shoulders and down my arm. My naked shoulders. My eyes shoot open and I look behind me.

"Morning, sleepyhead."

I stare at Ryan's smiling face and at the lock of brown hair that curls down and hangs over the top of his forehead. "It wasn't a dream..." I say more to myself than to him.

His smile widens and he leans forward, taking my lips in a kiss. "No," he whispers against my mouth, "it wasn't."

"You're really here." I reach for him, turning completely as I slide my hands around his neck and bring his face back to mine. I kiss him hungrily, wanting more. He tastes like mint and—I freeze and yank my head back, slapping a palm over my mouth. "Oh my god."

Ryan frowns at me. "What's wrong?"

"Did you already brush your teeth?" I demand, but even before he's given me an answer, I'm already on the move, tossing the covers away and reaching for the first thing my eyes land on—a red and white jersey on the floor.

"Yeah, why does—"

"I haven't!" I snap, looking over my shoulder. Heat infuses my face. Oh my god, I probably have morning breath.

And Ryan being Ryan just … laughs. He shakes his head and slumps back into the bed, chuckling to himself. "You're so weird, Will," he says.

"*I'm* the weird one?" I turn and gape at him. "I haven't brushed my teeth, and I was drugged last night, who knows what I—"

"You also puked," he states.

I stiffen, turning back to him in slow, minute increments—like a broken doll trying to twist on its own. "I. Did. *What*?"

He lifts an arm and then lets it fall back to the bed in a very half-hearted, noncommittal gesture. "Don't worry about it," he says. "I managed to get you to drink water after you did, but you also downed half of my mouthwash after mistaking it for water."

"I don't remember that at all," I say, putting a hand to my forehead. I glance back at him. "But you're sure my breath didn't—I mean, when we..."

Ryan chuckles again, the movement making his

stomach clench. My pussy tightens in response, and I'm viscerally aware of the slight twinge between my legs. Muscles that have never been used before, were worked over last night, and that only makes my face flame even hotter.

"You didn't have puke breath if that's what you're worried about," Ryan says. "If you want, though, my bathroom's that way." He motions lazily across his room. "You can use my toothbrush." He slides me another heart-stopping smile. "It's not like we haven't already swapped spit."

We swapped a lot more than that last night, I think, but instead of saying anything, I get off the bed and move across his room. My eyes rove the four-walled unit. It's a new world to me. Growing up, we'd always shared. The only times we hadn't shared a room had been when we had shared with another girl or guy. I've never seen what a purely Ryan room would look like, and it's a new experience for me.

The walls are a bland gray but plastered with sports posters. Clothes litter the floor beneath my feet. The rest is fairly simple. There's one bed with a flat, slatted wood headboard, a trunk at the end of it, and a dresser pressed against the wall between the window and the door to the bathroom.

After my perusal, I move to the bathroom and do as Ryan suggested. I make use of the facilities and then brush my teeth, scrubbing the inside of my mouth as if doing so will erase my feelings of embarrassment before heading back out into the bedroom.

Ryan doesn't look as if he's moved a single inch. In fact, I almost think he's fallen back asleep because as I approach, his eyes remain closed, giving me a rare chance to observe him without his consideration.

Even without shadows falling across him, the lines of his abs are still fairly deep. My fingers itch to touch them. I'm only a half step away from the side of the bed when Ryan's eyes pop open, and his hand shoots out, snagging my wrist and dragging me across the hard length of his body to deposit me right back on the bed as he rolls and pins me with his weight.

A breath escapes me as he comes down and hovers over me. "Hey." It's a simple greeting, but one that was impossible a week ago.

"Hey," I say back, unable to stop the smile that comes to my face.

My heart hammers, and my lips part. A tingle of electricity races through my system as Ryan reaches up and pushes my hair back. "God, I never thought I'd see you like this," he says, his words falling quiet. Almost as if he's afraid to say it too loud, fearful that if the universe realizes its mistake, it'll rip us away from each other once again. But now that I've had this, now that I've had him, I won't let that happen.

"Ryan." My fingers sink into his hair and draw him down, and he comes without resistance. His mouth meets mine with a gentle exploration. Last night had been all about heat and want and desire and everything that we'd been denying ourselves for too long. This is about love, healing, and relishing in the gift we've been given.

Against my thighs and beneath his sweatpants, I feel Ryan's cock jump and nudge against me. I huff out a quick chuckle. "Sorry," Ryan mutters, pulling away, "forgive him. He's always like this in the morning."

"Oh, always, huh?" I blink my eyes open and arch a brow up at him.

"Well, he's always like this when he wakes up with you nearby," he amends.

"Does he need a little help?" I ask as I smooth one hand down his side and then around, tugging gently at the strings of his waistband.

Ryan goes rigid and drops down over me, capturing my hand between our bodies as he groans. "You have no idea how much he wants that," he says.

"Then why don't—"

"But we need to get up," he says, interrupting me. "You're going to the police station today."

Those words douse me in cold water. When Ryan moves back once more, I pull my hand away and push against his shoulder. "You should let me up."

"Will, I didn't say that to upset you," Ryan says quickly.

No, of course, he didn't, but that doesn't erase the fact that he just ripped the nice moment we were having in half and tossed it in my face, reminding me about all that happened the night before. I shake my head and push more insistently against him.

"I need to get dressed," I say. "Do you have my clothes from last night?"

Ryan sighs and finally gets off me. One moment he's on top of me, pressing me down into the mattress, making me feel safe and warm, and the next, he's standing next to the bed and feeling a million miles away. "They were covered in puke," Ryan reminds me. "I tossed them. You can wear my jersey and a pair of my basketball shorts—they've got adjustable strings."

"Okay, do you mind giving me the room to get dressed?" I ask.

Ryan strides over to his dresser and rummages through it for a moment before withdrawing a pair of gray basketball shorts. He tosses them my way as he snatches a plain white cotton t-shirt and yanks it on over his head.

"I'll be in the kitchen," he says. "I've got roommates, but they won't bother you. Come down whenever you're done."

"Okay," I say, but the door's already closing behind him before I'm even done with my answer.

Pressing my lips together, I go ahead and get to work. The night before is a bit fuzzy between the game at the party house and ending up in Ryan's bed, but I know for a fact that I'd been wearing underwear before we'd had sex. A quick search of Ryan's floor uncovers my bra and underwear. I quickly yank Ryan's jersey off before slipping back into them and then pulling on the basketball shorts and jersey once more.

Without shoes, I creep out into the hallway barefoot and find a staircase. I'm halfway down when I hear masculine voices. For a brief moment, panic overwhelms me, but a figure appears at the bottom of the stairs, holding a water bottle and my shoes.

"Hey." Ryan holds the same tennis shoes I'd been wearing the night before. "I did the best I could to get the puke off of them. They might be a little wet, but they're clean."

I smile and finish descending the staircase. "Thanks," I say, taking them. I pause for a moment on the last step and then decide to hell with it. I arch up on my toes and press a quick kiss to his cheek before sitting down and pulling them on. They're damp but not soaked, thankfully. I tie the laces and take the water bottle he holds out for me when I'm done.

"Ready to go?" he asks.

"As ready as I'll ever be," I reply.

"Hey, Anderson." I freeze at the sound of another man's voice and turn to catch sight of a tall, redheaded guy standing in the doorway to what looks like the kitchen with his arms crossed over his chest. "What should I tell Coach?"

"Tell him I'll be late for practice today," Ryan replies.

"Will do."

"Thanks, Johnson." Ryan takes my hand and pulls me up from the stairs. "Come on, Will."

Ryan wraps an arm around my waist and leads me towards the front door. As we pass through, stepping onto the porch and then down the steps, I realize that I just spent the night with Ryan and now someone else knows I did too.

It wouldn't be such a problem if ... Lana didn't know the truth and if I didn't think this would somehow, someway eventually get back to her. Last night, Ryan and I had talked about lying, and I'd meant it. I want to be with him. Now, in the bright light of day, however, reality descends and I know sooner or later, I've got to make the right decision.

"Are you okay?" Ryan's question, though full of genuine concern, feels like the simplest of questions compared to the feelings racing through me.

I shake my head as he pulls into one of the guest parking spots in front of the campus police station and cuts the ignition of his car. "I'm about to go into the police station and report a what ... drugging and attempted rape?" I wince as the last word leaves my lips. It feels wrong even to say.

"Yeah, we are," he says adamantly. "That fucker can't get away with what he tried to do to you."

"Ryan, I don't know, maybe..."

"Don't tell me you were going to let him, Will. I saw you last night. You called me, panicked. You were passed out, locked in the bathroom, and when I got you in my car, you puked—"

"Which you did a great job of cleaning, by the way," I say, glancing around and giving him a small smile.

He frowns at me. "Don't try to change the subject, Will," he says. "Why don't you want to go in there and report what happened?"

I scrub both hands down my face and sigh. "It's not that I don't want him to have consequences, but there are several reasons that someone like me might not want to go in there and report it."

"Like what?" he demands.

I huff out a breath and reach down, unclipping my seatbelt so I can turn and face him fully. "Well, for starters—what if they don't believe me?" I ask.

Before I'm even finished saying the word 'believe', he's already shaking his head. "That's not—"

"That is the way it works," I interrupt him. "Maybe not every time, but they're gonna ask stupid questions. Questions that should have nothing to do with it. How much did I have to drink? What was I wearing? How long have I known him?"

"Those things don't fucking matter," Ryan grits out. "What matters is that the asshole needs to be held accountable for his actions."

"Yeah, and what if I report him and people call

me a liar?" I ask. "What if I report him and get backlash, and he doesn't get any consequences?"

Ryan's features contract, and he turns away, his fingers gripping the steering wheel so hard that the plastic creaks under the pressure. "I won't..." He inhales a breath. "I won't make you go if you don't want to. If you would prefer we take care of this outside of the law..."

"What?" I blink at him and reach for him, cupping his shoulders and forcing him to look at me. "No! Ryan, no, that's not what I mean. I don't want you to take care of things outside of the law." The very idea is preposterous. "Please say you won't do that."

Ryan meets my gaze. "I can't do that," he says. "He fucking hurt you—he touched you, and you were..." His jaw clenches and unclenches, a muscle jumping beneath his skin. "You didn't see you the way I saw you last night, Will," he says, his voice rough and deep. "I don't ever want to see you like that again."

"And you won't," I assure him. My hands move towards his back, and I lean forward, pulling him in for a hug. "I promise. You won't ever see me like that again."

Ryan stiffens against my comfort, but after several seconds, he relaxes and then even brings his arms up and hugs me back. "We're in this together," he whispers as he turns his cheek and presses his lips to the side of my throat. "You and me, Will. Like old times. For all time."

A shudder works through me. "Yeah," I whisper back. "We are."

Just him and me, until hell do we part.

Twenty-Nine

RYAN

I KNOW WHAT Will said, but what she said doesn't necessarily agree with the possessive asshole that's taken over my brain. That guy wants to drag the asshole who assaulted her last night through the streets with a chain wrapped around his neck and attached to the back of my car. So, even though she ultimately decided to report him, she only reports him for drugging her.

It's not enough for me, but I don't say anything. At this point, if I were to reveal my plans to her, she'd do everything in her power to stop me. Not for his sake, of course. Even she's not that magnanimous, but because she knows me. She knows what I'm capable of, and if it gets out—if I get caught, I'll be off the football team and I can kiss my scholarship goodbye.

I don't really give a fuck. Dick stain Jordan can't continue walking around thinking he can get away with hurting her like that. Not because she's my sister, my twin, but because she's mine now. In every way I've wanted her to be, and I protect what's mine.

Well over an hour later, after I've already dropped Will back off at her dorm, I pull up to my place and spot the navy blue truck in the driveway. Tanner pops his door open and gets out, and I meet him up on the front porch, keys in hand.

"Johnson said you were gonna be late to practice," Tanner says. "Not that you'd miss it entirely."

"I was at the station with Will," I state as I unlock the door and push into the rental house. Unlike Tanner, who chose to rent an apartment on the other side of campus, I chose to split this house closer to the stadium with a few of our teammates. Seeing how Tanner is still sweaty and wearing his workout gear, I'm guessing Johnson and Doriset are still at practice. "You duck out early?" I ask, heading for the kitchen.

"Something like that," Tanner says cryptically.

I arch a brow as I move towards the refrigerator and prop it open, reaching inside and snagging a couple of water bottles. I sigh and let the door shut as I toss him one. "Say what you're going to say," I prompt him.

Tanner reaches up and catches the bottle without batting an eye, just like any good athlete would. "What are you planning to do?" he demands.

I don't lie or pretend to misinterpret him. "Teach the bastard a lesson," I say calmly as I crack the bottle open, tip it up, and down a good mouthful.

Tanner arches a brow, but the bottle remains unopened in his fist. "Didn't she report him?" he asks. "I can guarantee that if the basketball Coach catches wind he tried to rape a girl, he'll be off the team."

"Maybe." After what Will said in the car, I'm not entirely sure. Sports are pretty important at Trinity, and from what I know about Jordan Cooper, he's a good player. Too bad he's shitty everywhere else. But there's another problem. "She didn't report him for the almost rape," I tell Tanner.

Tanner's fingers stiffen on the water bottle, and his face darkens. "What the fuck do you mean? She didn't report him?"

I shake my head. "She reported him drugging her but didn't say shit about the almost rape. I'm sure the officers can put two and two together, but unless she comes right out and says it, I doubt they'll add that to their 'investigation' if that's what you can call it. No, at most, he'll get reprimanded and may be benched for a season, but he won't be kicked off."

"Why wouldn't she fucking say something about that?" Tanner demands.

I scrub a hand down my face and set my bottle on the counter. "Probably because she's scared of what people will say about her. She's already got to deal with those nasty, fucking rumors. Something like this will just push her over the edge. I disagreed, but I didn't want to push her. Besides, I'll take care of the asshole myself."

"And how are you planning on doing that?" Tanner inquires, mimicking my movements as he sets his water bottle on the counter as well, leans back, and crosses his arms over his chest.

"If I tell you, are you gonna help?"

Tanner tilts his head at me. "What do you think?" he asks.

"I think you better give me a yes or no answer before I tell you shit that could get me arrested." I deadpan.

Finally, he cracks a smile, but it's not his usual easy-going one. No, this smile is twisted. It's mean. "Yes, I'll help you," he states.

"Good." I pick up my bottle again with a nod. "Because I could use another pair of hands for what I've got planned for Jordan Cooper."

"Does this mean you've worked out your feelings for her then?" Tanner asks. "I mean if you're going all avenging angel for her and shit."

"We're … together," I hedge. "That's it for now."

Tanner's smile softens, and he shakes his head, a chuckle working its way up his chest. "Thank fuck for that, man." He lifts away from the counter and strides towards me. One of his big hands lands on my shoulder. "Glad you're over this whole twin thing—as amusing as that was, a joke can only be taken so far."

"Yeah." My laugh is forced, an imitation of what it should be. "Sorry 'bout that, but can I ask you for another favor while I'm racking up a debt today?"

His smile slips away as he lets his hand fall to the side. "What's up?"

"Can you keep this from her friend for now?" Willow's confession and the fact that she's told Lana the truth—and worse, Lana, unlike Tanner, believes her—runs through my mind. "We don't want anyone to know for now."

It hurts to say those words because they're a lie. I want people to know that Willow is mine. Hell, I want the whole fucking world to know. I want to fuck her again. I want to put a baby in her and watch her belly swell, and even though it's fucked up, I can't find it in myself to care. I want to tie her to me with bonds that are impossible to break. Damn the consequences.

Tanner nods. "Yeah, man, I can do that. Your business is your business. Whenever you're ready for her to know, my little Willow Tree should tell her."

My eyes narrow on him. "Your little Willow Tree?" I repeat coldly.

Tanner laughs and backs up a step, holding his hands up as if placating an angry animal—and a part of me figures that he is because that's what I feel like right now. "Don't worry," he says. "I'm not going after your girl. I'm perfectly happy with mine."

I eye him for a moment longer. "See to it that it

stays that way," I say. "Now, about my plan to deal with Cooper..."

Thirty

WILLOW

"WILL, OH MY god!" I blink, and suddenly I'm assaulted by a rapidly moving mass of a person, or more specifically, Lana. She barrels straight into me, making the door to my dorm room slap open and slam into the wall as she wraps her arms around me and squeezes until the last of my breath escapes my lungs.

"Tight!" I wheeze, reaching out and trying to lightly smack her back to get her to release me. "Too tight! I need air!"

Her hold loosens, and I suck back a breath of relief. Lana moves back and then reaches up, cupping my face in her hands and forcing me to meet her intense gaze. "Where the hell have you been?" she demands. "I've been worried sick. You don't call, you don't write."

"I did call," I remind her. "And I did write—via text."

She narrows her eyes on me. "That text sounded nothing like you," she prompts.

That's probably because it wasn't me, but I don't say as much. After Ryan dropped me off and I showered and changed my clothes, I'd managed to charge my phone and go through it. Before it'd died, it looked like Ryan had sent Lana a "don't worry" message informing her that I was okay and would be staying with him. The reminder nearly makes me melt. It's been so long since sweet Ryan was around that I'd almost forgotten how I ended up falling in love with him in the first place.

"When I saw you at that house, you looked really messed up." Lana's words bring me back to the present.

I blow out a breath and nod. "Yeah, I was pretty messed up," I agree.

"Tanner just said that you had a problem," Lana says. "It has something to do with Jordan, doesn't it? What did he do to you?"

Discomfort shifts through me, though considering the events of the morning—the campus police station and the reports—it's not a new feeling. I step to the side and gesture for her to come the rest of the way inside. Once she's in, I quickly shut the door, flip the lock, and turn around. "I'll tell you what happened," I inform her, "but only if you don't freak out."

Lana pauses, halfway into the process of climbing onto my extra long twin bed. Her head turns, and she narrows her gaze on me. "That sounds like you know I'm going to freak out," she says.

"Yes, I do know."

"Then how can I agree not to freak out if you already know that whatever you're about to tell me is going to make me freak out?"

I blink. "Just ... try not to get too upset then?" I suggest.

She huffs and finishes climbing onto my bed, flipping around and crossing her arms. "Fine," she says. "I'll *try*."

I bite my lip. Even though her words say one thing, her tone says something entirely different. "Lana."

She holds up her hands. "I said I'll try," she repeats. "But I can't make any promises. That's the best I can do."

I sigh, my shoulders drooping. She's right. There's no use in fighting her. "Yes," I finally say. "Jordan did something to me last night. He drugged me."

Lana's jaw drops. "That slimy motherfucker," she seethes.

"But!" I hurry to say before she can climb off the bed and storm off—no doubt to find him and remove any and all chances he'll ever have of siring children. "I've already gone to campus police and reported him."

She still bristles, but her anger seems slightly contained at this news. "That was a good choice," she agrees with a nod before locking onto me with her eyes. "It still doesn't explain, though, where you went."

I walk across the room and prop myself against the bed at her side. "What do you know?" I ask.

"Well..." She puts a finger to her chin. "All I know is that Ryan called Tanner upset, and then we were rushing to get to the party. When we got there, you were unconscious, and Ryan carried you outside."

I can practically picture it from the words she's saying. A part of me wishes I'd been awake for it. The thought that Ryan had ridden in like a white knight and rescued me is still hard to believe—even with the soreness in my thighs and the rough scruff-burn I'm hiding beneath my clothes.

"Well, I'm okay now," I say, sucking back a breath and giving her a bright smile. "Promise."

Lana turns her discerning eye on me. "And Ryan?" she inquires.

My heart stops. "What about him?"

"Are you two ... I mean, have you guys worked out your differences?" she asks. "From the looks of it, he seemed really concerned for you last night. Jordan was knocked out cold when Tanner and I left."

"You didn't take him to the hospital?" I ask. That's definitely something she would have done.

In response, however, Lana gives me a look of pure disgust. "Absolutely not," she says. "I mean, I kinda had an idea that he'd done something wrong, but I didn't know what. Tanner, though, just said to leave him in his own rot because he'd get what was coming to him soon."

"Wow. I can't believe he'd say something like that," I murmur.

"I told you," Lana says. "That boy has secrets. He's got layers to him. One minute, he's all happy-go-lucky, and the next, he's dark Tanner. Boy's got something he's hiding."

"Oh?" I nudge her gently. "And are you planning on being the girl who peels back those layers of his?"

A blush forms across her cheeks and she turns her face away. "Maybe." I laugh, tossing my head back and allowing the feeling to roll through me. Despite the night before, I feel a little freer today like all that nasty shit that went down after the game was another person or another time. Today feels fresh, like a new beginning. Maybe that's because of Ryan.

"Listen, Will." I glance down as Lana reaches for my hand. "I'm really sorry I wasn't able to help you last night—my phone was dying, and so was Tanner's. We had to stop by for his car charger since I didn't have one. By the time we got Ryan's call, I—"

"Hey, no, stop." I grab her hand back and squeeze it. "It's not your fault," I quickly tell her. "None of what happened is the result of anything you did."

"I pressured you to go with him, though," Lana says. Her brows draw together, forming a little scrunched V between them. "I didn't know what kind of person he was, but I know how you've been about Ryan and I just wanted you to, I don't know, form relationships with other guys."

"You meant well," I tell her.

"Yeah, well, it's taught me a lesson," she says with a sigh. "I won't try to pressure you to go after any more guys. Lord knows one screw-up on my part is bad enough."

I roll my eyes. "You're so not a screw-up."

"I so am."

"Are not."

"Are too."

"Do you want to make it up to me?" I prompt.

Lana pulls her hands away. "Ice cream?" she asks.

I grin. "Ice cream," I agree.

The week after the attack and my subsequent surrender to my feelings for Ryan comes and goes. Ryan takes it upon himself to find me after as many classes as he can—though in deference to Lana, skips the ones I share with her. More and more people see us together, and as time goes by, it seems to affect the rumors that have been circulating.

Just like rumors do, they morph and shift until somehow, I'm no longer a stalker but a crazy possessive wannabe girlfriend. Thankfully, Lana doesn't believe them, but if only she knew the things Ryan and I were doing ... I should feel bad about lying to her, but every time Ryan kisses me, I can't help but feel like I'd do anything just to keep it going.

"What are you thinking about, beautiful?" I blink in surprise as Ryan's voice sounds behind where I'm sitting in one of the library's private study booths. A split second later, the feel of his warm mouth touches my skin as he nuzzles against my back and presses a quick kiss to the nape of my neck. I close my eyes as a shudder works through me.

"I *was* working on a class project," I inform him. "Before I was so rudely interrupted."

He chuckles, deep and low, sending signals to my brain that remind me of dark bedrooms and silky sheets. "Mind if I interrupt you some more?" he asks, coming further into the booth until he has me pressed directly against the desk.

"Can I stop you?" I snark back.

Hands wrap around my middle and descend. A gasp rises from me as he pushes his fingers beneath the waistband of my pants and underwear and then wiggles them even further until they're rubbing at a suddenly very wet spot between my legs. "Hmmm." He hums in the back of his throat. "Seems like you don't want to stop me," he replies.

I don't. I really don't. Being with horny Ryan has made all of my teenage fantasies come true. It would be a lie to say that I'm not a little sad that it's obvious he has far more experience than me—which means he's been with far more people—but at the same time, I can't say I'm not reaping the benefits of a man who knows what he's doing.

"That's it, sweetness," Ryan says, pressing his lips to my ear as my hips arch off the chair, and I meet his fingers as he slides the first one into me on the initial thrust and then two on the second. "You're so fucking wet for me, aren't you?"

I barely manage to repress a whimper. "Ryan." I try to keep my voice as even as possible, but I can already tell it's not working. "I work here. We can't do this."

"You're not working right now," he reminds me. His thumb rubs over my clit, making the synapses firing off in my brain short circuit. All I can focus on is the pressure he's exerting between my thighs. "That's it," he urges me on as my hips start to move. His fingers thrust in and out of me as his free hand reaches for the button of my jeans and pops it open to give himself more room. I'm going to cream my panties for him, I just know it.

It's wrong and deviant and oh, fuck me sideways ... it's fucking delicious.

Ryan groans against my ear as I tighten down on his hand and an overwhelming orgasm hits me like a punch to the stomach. I gasp and come all over his hand as my fingers scrape against the top of the desk. I bite down on my lower lip to muffle my moan until I taste blood, and only when I come down from the high of the orgasm he just gave me does Ryan finally pull his fingers free.

"You're so—" I'm half turned back towards Ryan with a firm frown of disapproval on my face when I freeze at the sight of what he's doing. Ryan grins as he sucks the two fingers that I know were inside of me moments before into the back of his mouth.

He groans and reaches down with his free hand, adjusting what I can see is a rock-hard erection behind the zipper of his jeans. "You taste like nirvana, Will," he rasps as he finishes licking the remains of my orgasm off of his fingers.

I'm done. So fucking done. My brain is fried, and I can't think of a damn thing to respond with. He's made me come stupid. Ryan laughs at whatever dumb expression I can feel is covering my face and then reaches down to cup my head and press a kiss to my lips. He doesn't just kiss me, though. He invades me. I shudder as he rolls the juice he just sucked down over my own tongue. Tasting myself on him is an act of delicious defilement, and it seems the further we go down this path, the more wicked I become.

"Wanna go on a date with me?" he asks as he pulls back.

I swallow roughly. "Is that why you sought me out?"

"Y*up*." He pops the last part of his answer in a childish manner that's accompanied by a boyish grin.

I shake my head. "Well, I can't concentrate on studying after an interruption like that," I tell him as I pull away and reach down for the books now scattered beneath the desk, thanks to our antics. I begin pushing them back into my backpack.

"So, is that a yes?" he asks, leaning back against the frame of the booth.

"Depends," I reply. "Where are we going?"

"Do you have any plans for this weekend?" he asks.

I frown. "That sounds like another question and not an answer to mine," I tell him.

"That's because it is. Now, do you have any plans for this weekend?" he repeats.

I sigh. "No, not that I can think of. I just need to finish this project, but most of my shifts have been moved to weekdays." Thanks to me finally telling Ms. Maes about Roquelle's frequent tardiness, she's been put on weekend duty as recompense.

"Great, I'm gonna drive you back to your dorm, and you're gonna pack a bag," Ryan suddenly informs me as he snatches my backpack out of my grip and moves out of the booth.

I gape after him in shock before his words finally penetrate my brain, and I'm forced to hustle to keep up with him. "What do you mean I'm gonna pack a bag?" I demand as we stride down the hallway and head for the stairs leading to the first floor. "Where are we going? I thought you said it was a date?"

"It is," he says.

As we hit the ground floor, I move up to his other side and avoid looking back at the circulation desk, yet I can already feel Roquelle's glare of irritation. One glance back is all I need to confirm that she's looking at me like she wants to strangle me. Maybe telling Ms. Maes about her consistent tardiness was too much, but a moment later, that's all forgotten as Ryan reaches down and snags my hand, pulling me along with him as we head out to the library parking lot.

"I just want you with me this weekend," Ryan says. "I know we're trying to avoid Lana finding out since she knows about the ... you know what." He pauses and I watch as something shifts in his expression. It's almost as if a darkness falls over him. I can sense the guilt ... and the self-loathing.

I squeeze his hand. "Don't you have football practice?" I remind him gently. "Or a game?"

Ryan's gaze finds mine as we reach his car. "I have a game," he tells me. "It's an away game. Somewhere where no one knows us. Where there are no school rumors and no Lana to stop me from kissing my girlfriend in public."

"You didn't seem to have much of a problem with doing more than kissing in the library," I say to him with an arched brow.

He barks out a laugh. "Don't worry. We were covered." He leans in and presses his face into the top of my hair, inhaling deeply. "I'd never risk your reputation like that."

"Yeah, well, it would've been better if you'd decided that before these rumors started," I comment dryly as he pops open the passenger side door and drops my bag to the floorboards.

Ryan pauses and looks back at me. "Will." His lips tilt down. "I meant it when I said that wasn't me. I wanted to make you hate me enough to avoid me so I wouldn't cave into my feelings, but I would never do something that could hurt you like that."

I stare up into his face, searching for any hint that he could be just embarrassed or ashamed to admit the truth, but his eyes are clear and filled with sincerity. I frown. "Well, if you didn't start that rumor," I say, "who did?"

He scowls. "I don't know," he admits. "But I'll find out soon, I promise."

I reach up and cup the side of his face, rubbing my hand across his unshaven jawline. Little prickly hairs scrape against the pads of my fingers. "Okay, I believe you," I say.

His shoulders sag as relief fills his features, but in the next moment, his eyes jerk to the side, scanning the parking lot. "I wish I could kiss you right now," he says.

"You can when we go back to my dorm," I suggest. "My roommate went home for the weekend."

He groans as if the thought is torture for him. "No, I wish, baby, but I can't stay. We've got to drive to Rinerville for the game tonight."

"You're going to Rinerville?" Sadness clutches at my chest. "Are you gonna be gone all weekend?"

Ryan gives me an odd look and then laughs. "Did you already forget what I asked you?" He shakes his head. "We're going to Rinerville," he says. "I told you, you're coming with me." He cups my side and drags me closer. We're almost there. So close, yet so far away. I can practically taste his lips again as he leans down, but he doesn't do it. He's been good. After what happened with us the weekend before and the promises we've made along with the truths we've revealed, Ryan has promised to keep the change of our relationship under wraps in case Lana finds out. It's just as much torture for me as it is for him.

"Don't you have to stay with the team, though?" I ask.

"Fuck no," he says. "Those fuckers can stay in that shitty motel the manager books for us. You and me—we're going high class. I've got a nice hotel booked, and I'm gonna make you scream my name all fucking night long."

My pussy practically drools at the thought. I tighten my thighs and reach up, fingering the curly strands of hair at the base of his neck as a smile lifts my lips. "Guess you better get me back to my dorm so I can get that bag packed," I say, acquiescing to his demands. Whenever it comes to him, I always seem to give in, whether to silly requests like this or carnal desires. All that I am is all that I can give to him.

Thirty-One

WILLOW

RINERVILLE IS HOME to the Riner University Forty-Niners football team and Trinity's primary college football rival. After Ryan drags me to my dorm and rushes me through packing a very small overnight bag, he hustles me into his car, and we're off.

Two hours later, we pull up to the Riner University stadium, and he hands me a card out of his wallet and the keys to his car. "I've got to go get changed and do all the before-game shit," he says. "But it starts at eight if you want to come see me. Just give the attendant your name, and they'll have a ticket for you at the front booth. If not, go to the Brookston Hotel, and you can hang out there until I get done. I checked us in online before we left, just go to the desk and give them my name. Game should be over by ten. I'll get a ride back."

I laugh and take the card, shaking my head. "I'll go drop my stuff off at the hotel," I tell him. "But I'm coming back to watch your game."

His face lights up like it used to on special occasions when we were kids—like birthdays with confetti cake since it was his favorite or Christmases where we both got new backpacks instead of old hand-me-downs. He leans forward and presses a quick kiss to my lips, and because we're not at Trinity, I can't help but return it even more enthusiastically. For once, it's like we're just two college kids in love. We're not Ryan and Willow Anderson, the unwanted foster siblings who are a little too close. We're normal to the outside eye, and it makes me heady even though it's a lie.

Ryan pulls away with a groan a little later. "I'm gonna fuck you so hard when we get to that hotel tonight," he warns me.

I giggle and push him towards the door. "Go," I say. "You can fulfill that promise later."

As he climbs out of the car, the look he gives me can only be described as a hungry predator being deprived of its favorite meal. Once he's gone, I clamber over the console into the driver's side and adjust the seat. I type the Brookston Hotel into my phone's GPS and follow the map until I pull up outside of a tall white building with a blue roof not far from the stadium.

It's not just nice, I realize, as I cut the engine, grabbing my bag and heading for the front doors, it's fancy. Expensive. My eyes are drawn immediately to the crystal chandelier hanging from the lobby ceiling when I step through the glass doors. Standing there in my scuffed converse and ripped skinny jeans, I feel way out of place.

"May I help you, Miss?" the front attendant asks, calling me over.

I blink and hurry forward. "Yes." I pull the card Ryan gave me out of my back pocket and lay it on the countertop. "My br—" I pause. "I mean, my boyfriend booked a room here tonight. He said he checked in online."

"Last name?" Her fingers are poised above her keyboard, expression expectant.

"Anderson," I state. "Full name: Ryan Anderson. We're here for the football game." I don't know why I added that last part, but my mouth seems to want to continue going. Perhaps it's because I'm viscerally aware that I almost called Ryan my brother rather than my boyfriend. These people don't know our relation, but in the time it takes for her to find the reservation on her computer, I've already worked up a whole background story in my head in case she asks. Though, I know she won't. No one cares. At least, I tell myself they don't and thankfully prove myself right when she looks up a moment later and gives me a bright smile.

"I've confirmed your reservation," she states. "You and your companion will be staying in the Princess suite." She gestures down the hallway to the left. "If you follow the gray markings along the floor, you'll find the elevators for the upper floors to your right. You'll be on floor eight. Here is your package, a brochure of Rinerville and the number to the front desk. A complimentary breakfast is provided in the mornings from seven to nine."

I take the packet she holds out and offer her a smile and thanks before heading in the direction she'd gestured to. Around the corner of the hallway, I find exactly what she'd told me to look for—a wall of elevators. I push the up arrow button in the middle of two of them and step back to wait. A few seconds later, an elevator descends, and the ding announcing its arrival is accompanied by the double doors sliding open and revealing an elderly couple holding hands.

The woman pauses at the sight of me, her eyes going wide. I step to the side to allow her and her partner to move past, but she doesn't. With a frown, the man turns his eyes from her to me, and then just as abruptly, he leans down and whispers into her ear. Together, the two of them hurry off the elevator, leaving me enough room to slip inside. Just before the doors close, I watch as the two of them turn and look back, their gazes full of curiosity and something else that I can't quite name. Something sorrowful.

Weird.

I shrug off the odd feeling and press the big eight button to ascend to the floor Ryan and I will be staying on tonight. The further into the hotel I go, though, the more suspicious I become. It's a nice place, way nicer than I'd expect a scholarship student to be able to afford, which is what I know he is. Ryan loves football for sure, but he's playing for his education, not just for fun.

How the hell can he afford something like this? I ask myself as I slide the keycard I'd been given in my packet and enter the room. My mouth drops open as it reveals a large suite, not just a standard hotel room. It's like a mini studio apartment, but hell, it's probably bigger than any studio apartment in Trinity.

To the left of the entrance is a wide doorway leading into a bathroom that's nearly half the size of my dorm room. A large walk-in shower with a seat that stretches across the back wall boasts perfectly aligned stone tiles and across from it is a double vanity with granite countertops and crown molding at the ceiling. Moving back into the main room, I spot a small kitchenette between the bathroom and bedroom areas. Across from the obviously king-sized bed is a long couch with a coffee table in front of it.

I walk to the bed and drop my backpack down before stepping past it all to the thing that's captured my full attention: a balcony. The sliding glass door opens easily and without resistance. I step out into the rapidly cooling air as twilight touches the horizon. White curtains flutter in the breeze behind me, touching the backs of my legs before I move to the railing and look down.

Rinerville is a smaller suburb of a big city—one that I can see in the distance, with its skyscrapers and flashing lights.

Still, my mind can't help but wonder ... *how?*

I turn back and survey the room from my place on the balcony. It's only been six years, and I know that Ryan wouldn't have gotten anything when he'd aged out of the system at eighteen. The only reason I have what I do is because of the McRaes. My fingers tighten around the railing and I suck in a deep breath. Ryan may have thought that this was a night to get away, to be together, and though I'm looking forward to that, this only makes me realize that it's time to face something else.

It's time to face the fact that these past six years have changed everything. Though our love hasn't changed, other things have. We're two different people now with different secrets. If we're going to walk down this dark and twisted path of ours, we need to be completely open. I do, and so does he. If I'm going to be with him, then I need to know who Ryan truly is now, not who he was in the past.

Glancing up as the orange and pink hues of the setting sun start to turn gray, I hear thunder roll overhead and watch as the sky darkens. It's going to be a wet game tonight.

Thirty-Two

RYAN

RAIN DRIBBLES DOWN over my helmet shell as I stare through the bars of the face mask at the opponent across from me. Above our heads, the countdown on the scoreboard hits a minute. This is it—last one.

My breath saws in and out of my chest as the padding of my helmet causes sweat to slide down my face. Johnson calls the play, and the ball slides between MacKenny's legs and straight into my grasp. I back up as my guys block the Forty-Niners defense. I back up some more, and there it is—an opening. I rear back and the ball goes sailing overhead.

Like a slow-motion movie, I watch as it goes up and up and then back down tilting straight into one of my wide receiver's hands. I pump my fist as he catches the fucker and runs straight for the fucking end zone. The second after he hits the goal line, the countdown hits zero, and the crowd roars—half in anger from the Forty-Niners fans, and half in excitement from Trinity fans who traveled for the game. Our points jump up six, just enough to put us in the winning. A win is a win, though, even if it's barely by the scrape of our teeth.

I look up and spot a familiar face towards the front row. Willow grins and waves my way. Just as I lift my hand in response, however, several bodies tackle me and dogpile my ass. My chest hits the ground, and an obnoxious laugh that can only mean one thing echoes in my ear.

"Striker!" I growl as I punch and kick my way free of the guys, laughing and shaking my head.

Tanner clambers off of me and reaches down to offer me a hand up. "Saw your girl out there," he says with a grin. "Guess now I know why you ain't staying at the motel with us."

I look back. "Nah, I got something else waiting for me."

Tanner claps me on the back as Coach blows his whistle, and Riner University's school anthem plays with the band moving across the side of the field. I follow the rest of the team back to the locker rooms and immediately start to strip. Coach begins his after-game speech, telling us how great we were and how we'll be even better next time, but I'm already clocked out. As soon as he's dismissed us, I take the fastest shower of my life—jumping in and then back out after scrubbing my body down.

I fly through the locker room with a towel around my waist, drop trow, and snatch an easy pair of gray sweats from my bag before yanking on a white t-shirt. The strap of my bag is over my shoulder and my tennis shoes are on my feet. I'm already halfway to the exit with my phone in my hand when I hear Coach's call. "Anderson!"

I pause and glance back. "Yeah, Coach?"

Coach Patel looks at me beneath the brim of his baseball cap. "You had a good game tonight, captain," he says. "Make sure to keep up the good work and don't stay out too late."

Tanner laughs as he passes through with a mop of wet hair and a towel around his waist. "No need to worry 'bout Anderson, Coach," he says. "He's not going out tonight. He's seeing his lady friend."

A bolt of something hits me when several heads pop up. "Anderson's got a chick?" someone asks.

I readjust my bag and send a glare Tanner's way. "Shut your mouth, asshole," I snap. If Willow finds out the guys are talking about her—Tanner knows, but the rest of the guys don't—she'll be upset. I turn back to Coach Patel. "Don't worry, Coach. I'll stay on the straight and narrow."

He nods. "You do that. Have a good night."

The second he's out of sight, I head straight for Tanner. "Hey," I snap, "you need to keep quiet about Willow and me."

Tanner pauses halfway into his locker. "Why?"

"Because we haven't told anyone yet."

Tanner pulls out a pair of boxers and jeans. "It's been a week," he says. "What are you guys waiting for?"

My fist tightens on the strap of my bag. "Just

don't say shit. She wants to keep it quiet."

Tanner drops his towel and slides his boxers on before taking a seat on the bench. "Is this because of the rumors and shit?" he asks. "If you just come out and say you're dating, people will leave her alone."

His words are a reminder. "About that," I switch gears. "Have you found out who started it?"

"A chick," Tanner says, shaking his head as he pulls on his jeans. "Though I don't know who yet. Still looking."

"Let me know as soon as you know; I want to talk to her," I say.

Tanner arches a brow as he stands back up. "Talk to her?" he prompts. "Or threaten her?"

I glare at him. "What do you think?"

"I think you've got it bad, man. That's what I think." He chuckles to himself. "But alright, I'll let you know what I hear. In the meantime, I'll keep my lips shut. Willow's the one who wants to keep it quiet, right? I'm guessing Lana still doesn't know?"

I glance down at my phone as it buzzes in my hand. "She's not exactly a Ryan Anderson fan," I hedge.

"Alright, I'll let Willow be the one to break the news then, but you should know"—Tanner pulls out his bag and shuts his locker before setting it on the bench and reaching inside—" the longer you guys put it off, the more upset she'll be."

He has no fucking idea, I think. "How about you take care of your girl, and I'll take care of mine?"

Tanner pulls out a shirt and slips it over his head before waving me away. "I got ya, go on. You know it's not right to leave a pretty girl waiting."

I turn and start for the door once more. "Catch you back at campus, Striker," I call back, pushing out of the locker room and into the stadium's underground hallway.

With a swipe of my finger across my screen, I unlock my phone and scan down the row of messages and texts. Half of them are from a few of the chicks I'd been fucking around with before last weekend, including Will's coworker. I grimace and delete them all before hitting block. The only one that matters is the one from her.

Willow: Congrats on the win! I parked in parking lot D, meet ya there.

It's cheesy, the smile that comes to my face, but I can't help it. Who would have ever thought we'd be here, her and me? Just two ordinary people head over fucking heels in love. I type a quick reply and pick up the pace until I'm practically jogging out of the stadium and heading towards parking lot D.

I spot her easily enough since mine is one of the last cars left in the lot. She's facing away from me with her hair pulled up into a ponytail as she leans against the front of my car. My feet slow to a stop a few steps away, and as if she can sense me staring, she glances back. The second she sees me, a big smile breaks out across her face, and she turns and launches herself into my arms with a squeal.

"You won!" she screams excitedly. "Congratulations!"

My arms close around her, and I bury my face into her neck, picking her up, and in a move that would give any corny romance movie hero a run for his money, I spin her around until she squeals again and laughs in my arms. That sound—the sound of her laughter and breathlessness—is one I've been craving since the day I got sent away. Since the day, I was stupid enough to think I could ever do anything that would keep us apart permanently.

Thirty-Three

WILLOW

"RYAN?"

"Hmmm." Ryan rolls across the bed and slides his arm around my side as he snuggles against my naked back. He presses a kiss to my shoulder blade. "Another round?" he asks. "Give me a minute, and I can make it happen."

I bite back a laugh and shake my head. It's been so long since I had a chance to really engage with playful Ryan since lover Ryan is still fresh. For a brief moment, I wonder if this is how he was with the other girls he's been with in the past, and a bolt of jealousy shoots through me. But just as quickly as it appears, it disperses. There's no room for jealousy between us now. The truth is out.

Ryan loves me just as much as I love him. No matter the circumstances of our birth.

I play with the corner of the pillow beneath my head. It's perfectly plumped, cool, and smooth with nice smelling sheets. The room smells like vanilla rather than the sharp stench of bleach and cleaning supplies which only speaks to the quality. As Ryan moves up further, he presses himself more firmly against my back despite the fact that our sweat has just started to dry after the intense sex we just had.

"Are you okay?" he asks when I still haven't responded to his comment.

"If I ask you something," I begin, "will you tell me the truth?"

His hands pause against my skin. After a moment of tense silence, he lifts up onto his elbow, and I roll onto my back until our eyes meet. "What are you talking about?" he asks, his brows furrowing. "Of course I will." His fingers move for a lock of my hair, lifting it to his lips as he presses a kiss to the end of the strands and continues to stare down at me with an expression that's a mixture of confusion and concern.

"This place," I prompt. "This hotel, it's …" *How do I ask?* "Expensive," I finish lamely.

A smile comes to his lips, and he arches one dark brown brow. "That's not a question," he points out.

I blow out a breath and narrow my eyes at him. "Okay, fine, then here's a question." I deadpan. "How can a college guy who splits a house with three other roommates and has a scholarship afford something like this?"

Ryan chuckles and shifts until he's no longer half-looming over me but is instead entirely over me, holding himself up by both hands on either side of my head. "Maybe this college guy," he replies, smirking playfully, "was smart when he was a little younger."

I scoff. "He's pretty freaking young as it is," I remind him. "What? Did he invest in the stock market when he was twelve or something?" *Had he even been interested in that kind of thing?* I think back and remember Ryan loving computers and tinkering with them, but he'd never said anything about stocks and money before we'd been separated. Like any other kid, he was obsessed with video games and the many things you would search on the internet. No future stockbroker genius that I could tell.

"More like nineteen," he says, answering my question.

"Nineteen!" I squawk. Ryan lowers himself down over me until his groin is pressed against mine, and I can feel the hard ridge of his revitalized interest, poking very insistently against me. "Ryan." I reach up and place my palms against his chest, not pushing but not letting him come down any further until he answers me seriously. "Did you really invest in the stock market?"

Ryan rolls his eyes. "It's not difficult to invest," he replies. "The difficult part is not to lose your money."

"Are you like … rich?"

He snorts. "I'm not a millionaire, but I've got some money—enough for a halfway decent hotel room. I started an online stock account about a year after I got out of juvie. Didn't have much money, but a couple hundred can turn into a couple thousand with the right market and understanding. I did my research. It didn't hurt that a few friends of mine started working for some pretty big private companies. They didn't give me any tips, but I thought it couldn't hurt to invest in the places they might be at, and they turned out alright."

"Wow." I blink up at him, stunned by this news. "And here I thought you've just been playing around like any other college guy."

Rough palms shoot down, grabbing my waist and then yanking me up and into him, as he flips onto his back and brings me up. My legs fall along either side of his hips, and his cock jumps up, slapping against his navel. The sheets twist around our lower legs, trapping us together. Not that being trapped against Ryan bothers me. If anything, it's a prequel to the coming pleasures.

"Who says I haven't?" he replies cheekily before quickly sobering. His eyes level on me. "But I think playing around has gotten old. I'm pretty sure that my newest conquest will be my last."

My heart jumps in my chest as I run my fingers down his. My tongue drifts out to swipe across my lower lip and his eyes follow the movement. Inside, my stomach clenches. I run my hands up and down his chest, scratching my nails right over his nipples as he jerks and hisses, his cock growing ever harder between us.

"Are you teasing me, baby?" he asks.

I stare back at him through my lashes. "Maybe

I am," I taunt just before reaching down and cupping his erection, squeezing and stroking the shaft. When a drop of precum wells up at the top, I smooth it over his head with my thumb and then reach up, staring down into his eyes as I suck my thumb into my mouth and lick it off before returning my hand to his cock. "What are you going to do about it?"

Ryan's groan fills my ears as I tighten my fist around his length and slowly stroke it up and down. "Fuck. That's good, baby. Keep that up, and I just might come," he pants, his cheeks flushing pink as his hips lift against my ministrations. Desire blossoms inside of me. It's been there for a long time, but I feel like this is the first time I've ever truly acknowledged what I feel for Ryan is something like this—something deeper, more meaningful. Something beyond the physical.

He's hot. There's no denying that, and I want him in every way a woman can want a man, but as I lift his cock up and position his tip at my entrance, I have to admit that this desire goes even deeper than that of sexual lust. I sink down on him, gasping as he fills and stretches me once again. Ryan's hands find my hips and start to guide me as I lift and lower myself back down, riding him.

I gave my heart to Ryan when I was too young to truly grasp what I was asking for, and as the flutterings of my pleasure bloom to life in my belly, I have to admit that he was stronger than I ever was. As much as it'd hurt, now I know that he'd only been so cruel out of love. He'd done it for me. Because now our lives are forever changed. In the future, people are going to judge us. They'll question us. They'll mock and reject us—and depending on where we end up, being together could even be a criminal offense. That's what he was trying to protect me from.

That's if they know the truth.

From now on, we'll have to play new roles. We'll cast off the old ones of brother and sister. No longer twins, but lovers. I moan as his cock hits someplace deep inside of me, sending new sparks dancing through me. It's so good it hurts.

"Ryan," I pant and gasp and call his name while all it does is make him clench his teeth and tighten his hands around my waist. He pushes into me more roughly, fucking up into my pussy until the deviant sound of his cock slicing through my juices reaches my ears. Wet slaps that prove to both of us just how much I want this.

Maybe that's why I never turned my back on him when he had been cruel to me. Because nothing could overwhelm the need for this. Watching his harshness, feeling the weight of his anger and brutality, had toughened me up—something, I have no doubt if I mentioned now he'd apologize for. It had shown me, though, that even if I still loved him, I wouldn't lower myself to being treated like that.

The truth is I'd been afraid. Afraid I'd have to walk away and cut all ties because I'd thought that the Ryan I'd loved had been nothing but a figment of my imagination. Tears spring to my eyes and slide down my cheeks as Ryan's cock slides between my folds, slamming into me with the same amount of brutality as his words had that night at the bar.

He'd told me I was poison. That I ruined everything I touched. Now, I know that it wasn't true. He was just as scared as I was—scared of this.

My head tilts down, and I meet his gaze as tears stream down my face. "Will..." He reaches up with one hand, cupping my cheek, and I can't help but return the call. I lean down, offering my lips, and he takes them. He sucks the bottom one into his mouth and nips it with naughty intent.

"Do you know how fucking sexy you look like that?" he asks. "Riding my cock with your tits bouncing."

I clench down on him at the dirty words that flow from his mouth into my ears, and he groans low in the back of his throat. "Oh, yeah," he says. "You know, don't you?"

Without warning, Ryan grips my arm and flips us once again until he's on top and my back's pressed against the mattress. He grabs my ankles and spreads my legs, lifting them up as he jackhammers into my pussy, slamming into that one place that seems to make the world go hazy over and over again until I cry out.

"Fuck, yeah." Ryan gasps out, dropping my legs as he continues to thrust into me. "You coming around my cock as I fuck you is the best feeling in the world, Will. Keep coming. Just. Like. That." He punctuates each word with a new thrust.

Hearing him praise me in such a deliciously dirty way makes my clit tingle. Without any shame, I reach down between us, sliding my fingers right over the button, and rub circles around it as my orgasm finishes crashing over me. My thighs tremble. My vision goes blurry, and I gasp as the wave of pleasure I've been chasing finally encapsulates me, taking over and rendering me wholly disconnected from the rest of the world.

It's only when I come back down that I realize Ryan hasn't come yet. As soon as he senses me moving again, he pulls out of me and fists his cock. "Watch me," he orders gruffly. My gaze falls to where his hand moves. His cock looks an angry red as he fucks it into his fist, hand flying down the shaft with lightning speed. Then, just as suddenly, his body tightens and cum shoots out of the head, splattering across my lower stomach and mound. Ryan pulls back and thrust himself back into me, mid-orgasm, groaning as he fills me once more.

My arms encircle him, pulling him closer as he shudders in my grip. His back rises and falls as he pants, trying to catch his breath.

"You're fucking perfect, Will," he whispers after a moment. "You know that, right?"

No one is perfect, but if he thinks I am, then I'm happy. I jump as he suddenly reaches between us and captures my hand. Dragging it down both of our chests, he stares into my eyes as he forces me to slide a finger through the cum at the top of my pussy and over the lower curve of my stomach. I blink as he pulls it back up and pushes it, with the white liquid covering it, into my mouth. My eyes open in surprise, but then the taste of him on my tongue actually makes me close my eyes with a groan as I close my lips around the digit and suck it clean.

Ryan's face breaks out into a grin, and as soon as my finger leaves my mouth, he takes it with a force to be reckoned with. He shoves his tongue into my mouth, seeking the last remnants of his cum that I just swallowed as he holds me tight enough to bruise. *This is what I like,* I realize. I always played the good girl, the smart girl—the girl who was perfect in almost every way. So perfect that I was able to get adopted on the cusp of aging out of the system. But now, I can be who I really am. I can be the dirty girl who likes to taste her boyfriend's cum and who loves it when he tells her just how sexy she is. I can be all of that with Ryan.

Thirty-Four

WILLOW

"YOU SEEM HAPPY." I jump at the sound of Lana's voice as I pack up the books of our literature class. Thankfully, we've moved on from Romeo and Juliet. Even though I'm not a big fan of Shakespeare, to begin with, that specific play makes me think of Ryan and me far too much and in the worst way. Forbidden love. It always seems to end poorly in books and movies. I don't want that to happen to us.

"I am," I respond as I finish shoveling my stuff into my bag and heft it over my shoulder.

"Any special reason?" she asks. "Any special someone, maybe?"

Her question makes me blanche. Not because she's right, but because she wouldn't be happy to know who the special someone is, mainly because she knows the truth about us. I've never really lied to my best friend before, and as the days pass and Ryan and I sneak around behind her back—trying as best we can to keep her from finding out—it's getting harder and harder. I don't *like* lying to her, but I don't want to lose her either, and I know if we tell her what we're doing, I inevitably will. I don't have many friends, but Lana is the oldest one.

I suck in a breath and plaster a smile on my face. "I'm just feeling good, is all," I tell her.

She grins back, the picture of trust and it literally makes my heart ache. "I'm glad," she confesses. "After what happened with that Jordan guy, I was kinda scared you'd be … I don't know, mad at me or something."

I turn and look at her as we reach the end of the staircase, and she moves to open the door leading outside. "Mad at you?" I repeat. "What for?"

"Well, I kinda pressured you into going with him," she points out.

I'm already shaking my head. "No, no, Lana." I reach out and grab her arm, pulling her to a stop on the sidewalk as other students and classmates spill around us, some heading off for the cafeteria and others heading to their next class. More than a few glance back and eye me before whispering to their friends. I resist the urge to roll my eyes. They should have moved onto something better by now than the stupid rumors circling me. I shake my head and refocus on Lana. "We've talked about this. I told you, it's not your fault," I tell her. "I don't blame you."

Lana's eyes don't meet mine. "I would understand if you did," she says.

"Well, I don't," I assure her.

She peeks up at me. "Is that because you and Ryan have made up?"

I stiffen. "What do you mean?" I ask cautiously.

"Well..." She takes a step away and turns to face me fully. "He was pretty mad about the experience you had, and he's been extremely protective of you lately. You've been hanging out more and ... are you guys becoming friends again?"

I look away. "What happened with Jordan made a few things clear, I guess," I hedge. It's technically not a lie. "We're comfortable with where we're at now." Again, not a lie.

"Have you forgiven him for spreading those rumors?"

I wince at the reminder. "He swears he didn't," I tell her.

"Really?" When I glance her way, Lana is looking at me with skepticism. I can understand that. It just doesn't make sense. If he didn't say that stuff about me, then who would?

"Yeah."

The two of us turn towards the cafeteria building and start walking. We're so late, though, that by the time we reach the entrance, the line is almost out the door. I glance at my phone screen and sigh. "I don't think I can stick around," I say. "If it's going to be this packed, I'll end up late for my shift at the library."

"Are you gonna go early then?" Lana asks. "Want me to bring you something later?"

"I don't know," I say, lifting my bag further up

on my shoulder as I turn away. "I'll text you and let you know."

"Alright, I'll see you later!"

I wave goodbye to Lana and head across campus. Not even halfway there, my stomach rumbles, telling me I'll probably be taking my friend up on her offer. I decide to ask her to bring me a sandwich from the stand in the cafeteria when she gets done with her own meal as soon as I reach work.

Ahead, the library looms, the parking lot half empty on a weekday. I enter the building through the front and spot Roquelle at the desk, actually early for her shift for a change. My eyes widen, but I offer her a bright smile. Maybe whatever Ms. Maes said to her had worked. Thank God. Working with someone who actually shows up for their shift will make everything so much easier.

I head into the back, drop off my bag, and clock in before shuffling out onto the main library floor. Roquelle stands at the front of the desk with her back to me as she types away on her computer.

"Hey," I offer in greeting.

She turns her head and scowls at me. "Thanks a lot, bitch," she snaps.

I start, taken aback by the venom in her voice, and before I can think better of it, I reply. "What the hell is your problem?" I demand.

She turns and crosses her arms over her chest. "You fucking ratted me out to Maes, and now I'm on probation," she growls.

"You were the one showing up late and hungover for *all* of your shifts," I point out.

"I was a few minutes late a couple of times," she says snidely. "So what?"

"You were almost an hour late *multiple* times," I correct. "I can't run the front desk by myself when it's busy."

"Yeah, well, it was a fucking bitch move. No wonder people think you're a psycho."

She moves to turn away, but I'm fucking furious. "*Excuse me?*" I snap. "What the fuck do you mean by that?"

"Stalking a football player and then staging a fake sexual assault on yourself for his attention?" she replies, lifting a hand to cover her mouth. I see it before she does—that conniving smile, almost as if she knows it's not true, but just wants to fucking point out what people are saying to piss me off. No … not to piss me off, to make me anxious.

My heart drops into my stomach. "*What did you just say?*"

"Everyone knows about you and Jordan? A football guy wasn't enough for you? You went after him too, and when he turned you down, you told everyone he drugged you and tried to rape you."

My mind is reeling. Acid sloshes in my stomach. No one knew about what happened with Jordan—no one except our closest friends: Tanner, Lana, me, and Ryan. And the police. They wouldn't have said anything, so how the fuck could she know about Jordan? Wait, Jordan's friend had been there.

And there's no discounting Jordan. Was he trying to spin the tale to stay in school?

I clench my fists at my side. "I don't know what you fucking heard"—I say the words slowly, so there's no mistaking them on her part—"but you're wrong. Jordan *did* drug me and he *did* try to rape me. Ryan stopped him. I don't have to defend myself, least of all to you."

"No," she agrees. "You don't have to defend yourself. I wouldn't believe you anyway." I stand incredibly still as Roquelle gets up from the desk and moves towards me, slinking like a snake. She stops just before reaching me, her head eclipsing mine with her height. Roquelle leans down until her mouth is right next to my ear. "You look all sweet and innocent, but deep down, you're just a needy whore, spreading her legs for any guy who pays her the least bit of attention. Ryan's so much better off without you."

I almost fucking punch her right then and there. I can see it happening in my mind's eye. I've never been a fighter, but then again, I've never been this angry before. I'm afraid, though. Afraid that if I hit her, I won't be able to stop. There's so much rage inside me—so much pain—and I know it isn't right to take it all out on her.

I'm angry about more than just her words. I'm angry at the rumors, at Ryan, and at Lana. At this fucking life. About the fact that the easiest thing to do to put a stop to half of my issues would be to admit that Ryan and I are dating, yet I can't do that because of what we are and because of what Lana knows.

It all collides inside of me, a bundle of vibrating wrath that's just begging to be released. One little slip, and I know I'll become precisely what she says I am: a psycho.

I'm thankful, though, that I don't get the opportunity to take out my anger on her because she turns around and walks away.

Of course, after that, my shift at the library doesn't pass in the blink of an eye. That would be way too convenient. Instead, it drags on. When the clock finally hits the end of our shift, I hurry through closing, grab my shit, and bounce—shoving out into the quickly cooling autumn air, leaving her behind as fast as my legs can carry me.

"Will!" I glance up at the shout of my name and sigh in relief when I see Ryan standing by his car, a light jacket hanging over his shoulders and his hands shoved into his front pockets, making his shoulders appear that much broader. I quickly change direction and head towards him.

"I thought you weren't going to make it tonight," I say as I approach, referring to the text he'd sent me before my earlier class.

"I wasn't sure if I would," he replies, smiling and pulling both hands out of his pockets so he can wrap them around me as I step up against him.

It's so natural now for me to tip my head up and back expectantly. He grins right before he obliges me—like we're two regular college students with no reason not to do this—and presses a kiss to my lips. I'd initially expected it to be nothing more than a kiss of greeting, a quick, chaste meeting of the mouths, but with Ryan, nothing is ever what I expect.

His hands tighten against my back, and move down until he cups my ass and drags me against him. I gasp, granting his tongue entrance as he shoves it past my lips and twines it with mine. The kiss drags, and by the end of it, I forget all of my earlier anger. All I can think of now is how much I want to go back to his room and climb on top of him and show him just how much I need him.

The revving of someone's engine drags both of us out of our reverie, and I look up in time to see Roquelle speeding past us and cutting out of the parking lot in her trashy white Buick. Just as she drives by, her eyes cut towards us, and there's a deadness there so void of anything but anger and resentment that it sends a shiver down my spine. Unintentionally, I move closer to Ryan, wrapping my arms around his back and pressing my front to his.

I don't say anything, but after a minute, I realize that Ryan hasn't said anything either. I peek up to see that he's followed Roquelle's exit with his eyes, and almost as if he senses my attention, his gaze turns down to me, and he smiles.

"Ready to go?" he asks, not commenting on Roquelle's rudeness.

I nod absently and then trail him as he leads me

around the side of his car and opens the passenger side door. I'm more than ready to be alone with him, and I want him to know it.

Ryan grasps the top of the passenger side door and his eyes widen as, instead of stepping into the vehicle, I move up closer to him and wrap one hand around the back of his neck. I lean up on my tiptoes and hover my lips right in front of his.

"We're going back to your place tonight," I tell him.

"Will?" He looks down at me like he's confused, but as I press my hips against his and feel the hardening of his cock—at the same time that I see his pupils dilate—I know he's not going to deny me.

"I need you, Ryan," I say, and that's all I have to say.

His eyes harden and his knuckles turn white over the top of the door. "Get in the car," he growls.

I take a step back and release him, turning and sliding first one foot into the car and then the other. The door closes rather sharply, but I know it's only because I've awoken the beast and my back straightens as he walks around the front of the car, his jaw tight.

Tonight, he's going to give me everything I crave.

Thirty-Five

RYAN

THE ENTIRE DRIVE back to my place, I keep glancing over at Will. Her eyes are trained on the road, though. Her face tight, and her hand on the door. I press the pedal down almost all the way to the floor, watching the speedometer arch up past the speed limit. I don't care.

She's not acting like herself, or maybe it's not her. Perhaps it's me, and how I'm so blinded by how much I fucking want her. Because I do. I want her like I've never wanted anything else in my fucking life. I want her more than water—more than air. I can feel the tension in the space of the car. Heat and something else I can't put a name to.

I careen into the driveway of my house, throwing the car into park and then jerking up the e-break. Before she can utter a word, I cut the engine and step out of the car, rounding the front. Her eyes follow me through the windshield as she unbuckles her seatbelt, and by the time I pull her door open, she's reaching for me.

My mouth slams down on hers the second she's out of the car and there's no patience left in me. I back her up into the side of my vehicle, my hands all over her. She moans into my kiss, driving me to insanity. Without thinking, I reach down, cupping my hands beneath her thighs and heave her up into my arms. My keys jangle in my pockets as I walk towards the front of the house without removing my lips from hers.

There's so much heat between us, it makes me dizzy with want. "Ryan..." she gasps my name when we make it up the porch. "Where are the keys?"

She can still fucking think. I'm not doing my job right, but she's got a point. As much as I want to, I can't take her out here, in full view of anyone driving by. Though that would be a thing, wouldn't it? To fuck her in front of a crowd. To have them all know how much she belongs to me as she screams my name and comes around my cock.

"Back pocket," I grunt, and she reaches down, fumbling for them as she drags them from their confines.

Seconds later, the door is unlocked and open. I slam inside, kicking it shut without bothering to lock it as I head straight for my room. Will's cell rings, but we ignore it in favor of focusing on each other. Each jerk and step makes her whole body slide against mine. If we were naked and my cock was inside her, we would never have made it, I think as I finally reach the bedroom.

Willow lets out a shocked gasp as I drop her onto the bed and come down hard over her before making sure the door is shut. I stand above her, my eyes locked on hers as I reach down and drag the shirt I'm wearing over my head and drop it to the side.

"Strip," I growl.

She doesn't resist. No, not my girl. Instead, she arches up and starts doing exactly what I tell her to. I wonder if I direct her to do anything else ... will she? I decide to test the theory the second she's naked and at my mercy. I look down to the front of my jeans and then to her.

"Unzip me," I order.

With a secretive smile, Will moves to the end of the bed and sits there as she reaches out towards my cock. Her fingers quickly undo my button, but instead of moving for the rest, she locks onto the sides of my jeans and holds on as she then leans forward, her eyes never leaving mine, and bites down on the edge of my zipper before slowly dragging it down. Holy ... fucking ... shit. This girl is going to be the death of me.

It's too slow. I push her back gently and then shuck my jeans and underwear. "Fuck, baby," I say, my voice breathless.

"I want you, Ryan," she says.

"Lay back," I tell her the second I'm free of all my clothes. "Legs up on the bed."

She gives me an odd look but does as I tell her, placing her feet on the edge of the mattress as I go to my knees before her, just where I'm supposed to be—the most beautiful place on Earth in front of me.

She moans as I spread her thighs wider with rough hands. "Look at you," I whisper, moving forward and shoving my shoulders between her legs to make room for what I plan to do to her. "So pretty and pink."

I touch her clit and her back arches off the bed. "Ryan!"

I shush her quietly, moving one hand up. I press my palm to the lower curve of her belly and then lean forward, blowing air over the wet flesh at my disposal. "Fuck, you're gonna taste so fucking sweet on my tongue, aren't you, baby?"

"Ryan, please … I can't … I can't..."

"It's okay," I tell her. "You just let go. I've got you." And I do. I'll always have her.

My head dips down and I press my tongue into the center of her, driving it into all of that wet flesh of hers and sucking down the juice that's dripping down towards her ass. Sweet. Divine. Heaven. She tastes like the last thing I ever want to have in this life.

Fuck heaven and fuck hell. If this is sinful, send me to the depths because I can't believe I've waited this long to claim it completely. That day in the library was just a hint. This is a full course meal.

I dive down and suck her clit between my lips, pulling on it as I swallow back more of her. I can hear her panting cries above me, feel the tremble in her thighs next to my ears. She's clenching down so hard, I know she's close to coming, but I haven't even started. I'm going to drive her crazy just as she's done to me.

I want her fucking back imprinted on my bed. I want her scent in my sheets. I want her. Forever.

"Ryan!" On the next pass of my tongue, a fresh wave of juice coats my tongue. I close my eyes and tilt my head back, letting it hit the back of my throat as I swallow.

When her trembling has calmed, and her breathing has gone relatively back to normal, I open my eyes and then stand. I can feel the wetness on my face dripping from my chin, but I don't care. I arch over her, grabbing her face in one palm and holding it steady as her eyes lift to meet mine. Then, I lean forward and kiss her. Hard.

My tongue thrusts forward just like it had into her pussy, only this time, it's against hers. She groans at her own taste, and my cock practically jumps at the sound. Too long. Getting inside of her is taking far too goddamn long. I release her face and reach down, gripping her hips and tilting them up as I lift her legs against my chest. I reach beneath and align my cock with the prettiest pussy in the world, and without any provocation, I slide home right into the place I belong.

Her pussy clings to me, welcoming me with all that soaking wet heat. "God, you're perfect, Will," I rasp. "So goddamn perfect. Keep squeezing my dick, baby. Just like that."

The dirty words that leave my lips have an effect. She clenches down once more, her pussy walls closing in on me and tightening until it threatens to drag an orgasm from my balls too soon. My head lowers as I hold her legs up, ankles crossed, bending her damn near in half.

"You like that?" I ask before opening my eyes once more. I look at her face and see the truth there. She does. She likes the dirty, filthy words coming from my lips. "You enjoy me telling you how fucking sexy you are?" She swallows, her hands clutching at the sheets, fingers digging into the covers. "You want more?" I pull back and thrust forward, watching with fascination as her naked tits jiggle with the movement. "You want to know what I see?" I ask, though I don't expect an answer. I'm going to tell her anyway.

"You're so fucking pretty like this, baby," I confess. "All spread out with your pussy clutching at my cock and your tits so ripe. Nipples hard like you can't even help yourself." I lean closer, pressing her legs almost into her chest as I do. "You know what I was thinking as we walked in the door?" I grin wickedly. "I was thinking that I'd like to fuck you in front of a crowd." Her pussy flutters against my cock as I drive in and out. "You want that? You like that idea? I'd hold you down and fuck your pussy so good. There'd be no fucking mistake. Every fucking guy in the room would know who you belong to."

"Ryan ... I-I..." She arches up on my next

thrust, her tits driving forward, almost as if they miss me.

"You wanted me to fuck you tonight," I tell her. "Well, I'm fucking you. I like fucking you, Will. I want to fuck you for the rest of my life. You and only you."

Her eyes widen and her hands release the sheets, reaching for me. Nails sink into my shoulders, that little bite of pain driving me to push her harder, faster. Her lips part and I can tell she wants to say something, but she doesn't get the chance. She can't, not with my cock buried inside of her, hammering home. Her body moves up, jerking back and forth and all she can do is moan.

"That's right, Will," I say, fighting back the need to come. It's almost there. I can tell. There's no way I'm going to do that until I watch her next orgasm. I want to feel her come apart around my dick this time, not just my tongue. When I do, and only then, will I let go. "It's you and me. You wanted this, and you got it. You wanted me obsessed. Well, here's the truth. I am. I've always been obsessed with you. You'll never have a chance with anyone else. I'm your beginning and your end. I'm the first and last man you'll ever fuck. Do you understand?"

She nods rapidly, her breaths coming fast and harsh. "Yes," she pants. "Yes ... Ryan. I'm gonna—oh fuck!"

I squeeze my eyes shut as her inner walls clamp down into a vise around my cock, squeezing me so roughly that there's no fucking way I can hold back now. I open my eyes and stare at her face as she throws her head back, her lips parting on a silent scream as she creams my dick. What a good girl. What a good fucking girl.

My own orgasm washes through me and shoots out of the head of my cock, bathing her inner walls. It's heady, the feeling of having her take everything I have to give. When I'm done and spent, I pull away, letting her legs fall to the side. Stepping back, I stare down at her ass, at the white cum seeping from her pussy and down her inner thighs.

Something comes over me—a dark desire. Something wicked. Disgusting. I reach down, fingering her hole as I catch a trickle of my cum and push it back into her. When I pull the digit free, I lean over her and grip her chin.

Her eyes open and meet mine. Her cheeks are flushed a rosy pink, and the sparkle in her gaze has dimmed with satiated pleasure. I press my finger to her lips, and when she parts them willingly, I push it inside. And like the fucking sexual deviant that she is, her lips close around my finger and she sucks me clean. Her cum and mine mixed. I watch as she swallows it all down without a single hint of hesitation.

She's going to kill me, this girl, I think. *And I'm going to die in the most exquisite pain I've ever felt.*

Will is exhausted, I did that to her. Even though looking at her makes my chest constrict, I don't feel bad. I feel proud. Like a fucking caveman who wants to drag her out and show the world and scream, *look at this! Look at what I did! This is my woman!*

It's completely ridiculous, and I have no doubt that if I tried, Will would kick my ass. She might like the fantasy of me fucking her in front of a crowd, but we both know the reality would be much different. No, she's mine and I'm hers, and we want to keep each other in this way. Just ours. No one else's.

As she turns onto her side and crawls up towards the head of the bed, I run into the private bathroom off the side of my room to grab a washcloth and wet it. I come back into the bedroom and quickly clean her up, tossing the dirtied cloth into the corner as I climb in beside her after turning off the lights. Seconds later, a phone buzzes and lights up the room from somewhere on the floor with our discarded clothes. I don't care and she's already asleep. My arms close around her, and I shut my eyes as well, relishing in this private space we've created. Where it's only ever the two of us and no one can tell us what's right and what's wrong, where everything we do is filled with nothing but love. Mine for her and hers for me.

If this is what's wrong, then I don't ever want to be right again.

Thirty-Six

WILLOW

I WAKE UP sore, but it's a soreness that I love. My thighs ache in the best of ways, but unfortunately, my back is cold. I roll over and note that the other side of the bed is empty. With a frown, I sit up, grabbing the sheets and drawing them towards my chest, wrapping them around my upper body as I slide from the bed and fumble around on the ground for my phone.

When I rise back up, still holding the sheet to my breasts, I double-check the nightstand to make sure I haven't missed a note, but it's empty and I also don't hear anyone puttering around in the bathroom. When I swipe my screen open, I grimace at the list of unanswered phone calls and messages—almost all of them are from Lana and a few from Tanner. I wonder if they got into a fight.

Before even opening them, I shoot a quick text to Ryan and then decide that it'll probably be better to call instead of checking the messages. I'm not sure how long my battery will last anyway since it'd been unplugged all night.

I press the speaker button and set the phone on the bed before dropping the sheet and reaching down, searching through the mess of clothes on Ryan's floor. I hear a click just as my fingers touch a relatively clean t-shirt.

"Will, where the hell are you?" I wince at the panic in Lana's tone.

"I'm, uh..." I start, but she cuts me off.

"Never mind, just tell me, are you at your dorm?"

"No, I'm out," I say, gripping the t-shirt and dragging it over my head. I stand and let it fall to my upper thighs before I start searching for my underwear. Thankfully, I find them discarded, but no worse for wear beneath Ryan's pants. "What's wrong?"

"Damn it," she snaps, and I can hear her moving on the other end. "Have you seen the university's student page?" she demands.

I snort as I pull my underwear on along with my pants, tucking the front end of Ryan's borrowed shirt in front of the button before scrounging for a brush or comb or something to tame the mass I feel on top of my head.

"You know I don't pay attention to that shit," I say. "It's full of dumb shit like gossip and stuff about the—"

"Yeah, well, it's full of you today," she snaps.

"What?" I freeze, after finding a comb on the end of Ryan's dresser, and turn back to the bed.

"What are you talking about?"

"I tried calling you last night," Lana continues. "Tanner tried too, but we couldn't reach you. I thought you were dead or something, but Tanner said you were probably with Ryan." My chest constricts at the tone in her voice and then even more at her next question. "Will ... what were you doing with Ryan last night?"

Shit. I really don't know how to answer that without outright lying to her. She's the only one I've told about mine and Ryan's real relationship—or rather, what we are. Siblings. Twins.

"He picked me up from work," I say. "Why is it important?"

The door behind me opens, and Ryan appears with a mug in each hand. Well, that explains where he's been. "Hey, baby—" I practically fly across the room and slap my hand over his mouth.

Ryan's eyes widen, and I gesture wildly to the bed where my phone lays as Lana starts talking again. "I really need to fucking see you, Will. You have no idea what they're saying. There are even photos. Will, tell me you fucking didn't. You and Ryan—"

I release Ryan and move towards the bed, snatching the phone up and clicking the speakerphone off. "I'm heading to my dorm now," I say before she can voice anything else. "I'll meet you there in half an hour."

"Will—"

"Gotta go. I'll see you there." I click the button

to end the call and then drop my phone to the surface of the mattress like it might bite me.

"Will?" Ryan steps further into the room, nudging the door closed, and sets the mugs of what I assume is coffee on the dresser before moving towards me.

"She knows," I say, inhaling sharply. Panic edges into my chest. "What am I gonna do?" His arms close around me. "Ryan ... she's my best friend, but she's ... normal. She won't understand."

"Are you sure?" he asks. "I mean, she hates my guts, but that's because she cares about you." I cover my face with my hands as I feel tears burning at the backs of my eyelids, and then Ryan turns me into him until my chest is pressed to his. "Hey, look at me." I shake my head even as he tries to nudge my chin upward with a gentle finger. Ryan, however, isn't the type to take no for an answer. Eventually, he makes me give in with his sheer persistence, and I'm forced to open my eyes and feel the hot trails of tears begin to slide down my cheeks when I tip my face up.

He frowns and wipes away the first streaks with his thumbs as he reaches up and cradles my face in his palms. "Whatever happens," he states, "it's going to be okay because it's you and me."

I shudder out a gasping breath as more tears fall harder. "I know," I say. "That's the problem—what if ... I mean what do they do to siblings who ... do this? Are they going to arrest us? It's illegal, but it's not like you're my dad or—"

"Hey, hey, hey, let's just slow down," Ryan urges. "You're not going to get arrested, Will."

"I don't want to leave you," I confess. "But Lana's been my best friend for years—since the McRaes died. I don't really have anyone else."

His brown eyes grow darker. "You know that's not fucking true, Will," he growls, pulling me closer. "You have me. Always. Whatever happens, we'll figure it out together. Even so, she's your friend. Do you really think she's going to try and get you arrested?"

"But what about you?" I reach up, sinking my fingers into the fabric of the shirt he's wearing. "Lana means well, but what if—"

"Don't think like that right now," Ryan says, cutting me off with a shake of his head. "We don't know what's going on. What was she saying before I walked in?"

I sink down and press my forehead against his chest, sniffling hard. "She was talking about the student social pages or something, but she didn't exactly explain..." Ryan pushes me back slightly and then digs into his pocket, pulling out his phone. "What are you doing? Are you checking them?"

"Of course, I am," he says. "I want to know what could get her so riled up or if someone..." His words drift off, and his eyes bulge as he flips his thumb up, scrolling. His expression turns murderous, and he utters a curse. "Fuck."

"What is it?" I try to lean over his arm and see what's on the screen, but he flicks it off and shoves the phone back into his pocket. "Ryan!"

He grits his teeth and then gently pushes me toward the bed. "Find your shoes," he orders. "We have to go. I'm gonna make some phone calls. I've got some friends in the IT department."

"What are you talking about?" I try again, but Ryan doesn't answer. Instead, he reaches down and snatches up a pair of sneakers from the floor, disappearing out of the room and leaving me—and the two quickly cooling cups of coffee he brought up here—behind.

Dread has me turning back to my phone, where it now lays like it's a snake waiting to strike. There was a reason Ryan didn't share what was on those pages with me. A reason why Lana had tried so hard to call me and why she now knew the truth, or at least suspected. I sink my fingers into the sheets, gripping them tightly. I have every right to know, but ...

With resolve, I reach for the phone and turn the screen on, pulling up a browser and typing in the students' social pages, clutching the edges of my phone with a strangling grip as I wait for them to load. Once they do…

"Oh fuck..." One of my hands automatically rises to cover my mouth as my panic reaches a new level. There are so many columns, forums, comments, but almost all of them have my name tagged.

Willow McRae, slut and liar.
Willow McRae Forces Football Player.

Willow McRae Secret Stalker.

What's worse is that there's a picture. A picture of Ryan and me from last night outside the library, me leaning against his chest, and it's obvious from the picture what we're doing. Though it's not clear by the graininess and the angle but still I know. And that means other people probably know.

I scroll, my eyes growing bigger and bigger as I read the comments. Vile, hateful things that they are. The cruelty is probably why Ryan didn't want me to see it. The photo is probably why Lana had responded the way she had.

I shut the screen off and set it down.

It's okay, I tell myself. People still don't know about anything else. They don't know the truth. This isn't as bad as I thought.

Almost mechanically, I reach for my shoes and pull them on. I don't even consider putting on a bra, I just want to make it to the dorms as fast as possible. There has to be something I can say, something I can tell Lana. A way to salvage our friendship because even if I don't want to admit it right now, I know the truth. She won't accept my relationship with Ryan. She's the type of person who sets herself apart from her own set of morals, and this is as far from morally right as one can get.

I scrub my hands down my face, wiping away the dried tears. I love her, but I love Ryan more. And that's the kicker; if it comes down between the two of them, I'll choose him.

"Will!" Ryan's call from the first floor gets me

moving. I quickly snatch my keys and anything else I think I might immediately need before leaving the room and shuffling down the hall towards the stairs.

I reach the landing and see him waiting by the front door, his own keys in hand. "I talked to my friend," Ryan tells me as I descend. "He'll try to track who circulated..." He pauses and winces, but it's okay. I know.

"The picture?" I clarify.

He looks at me with anguish, even though he doesn't seem particularly surprised that I searched the pages after he left the room. I step up to him and lift my hand, cupping his cheek. "I appreciate you trying to protect me," I say. "But it's okay. You're right, we'll figure it out."

Ryan turns his lips into my palm and presses a quick kiss to my skin. "They'll find out who took it and posted it," he assures me.

I nod, but even if they do, it won't take back the cruel and horrible things people are saying about me. I don't necessarily care what strangers think, but even I'm not naïve enough to believe that there won't be other repercussions. If enough people claim that I'm stalking Ryan and know what happened with Jordan, there will be more problems.

Right now, though, I have to deal with the biggest issue present. My best friend.

When Ryan pulls up to the front of my dorm, Lana is already there, and she's not alone. Ryan parks and gets out, and I follow, heading across the road to the sidewalk. "Tanner? What are you doing here?" I ask as soon as we reach them.

The corner of Tanner's lips turns down as he rubs the back of his neck. He glances between my best friend and me. I can feel her eyes on me, but I don't look. I'm not ready to yet. "Lana called and told me that she finally got ahold of you and that you were meeting her here," he offers by way of answer. It doesn't necessarily explain why he felt the need to show up, but I don't get a chance to ask.

"Tell me it's not fucking true!" Lana shouts, stepping in front of Tanner with a scowl as she glares at Ryan. She advances towards him. "What did you do to her?" she demands, waving her phone. "It's all over the campus pages! Everyone thinks she's stalking you!"

"I'm not!" I yell, stepping in front of Ryan as Lana comes to a halt as our eyes finally meet.

"You're not fucking him?" she asks. I can tell that it's hope in her voice, hope in her eyes. I freeze for a moment. *This is it. The pivotal turning point.* I can lie and tell her that all he did was pick me up, and we can come up with some other excuse as to why we were so close in that picture. The angle isn't perfect. There's no definitive proof.

But I'm fucking tired of lying.

My shoulders deflate. "I'm ... sorry," I tell her. That's it. That's all I have to say.

Lana's arm lowers to the ground, and I wince at the sound of her phone clattering against the rough pavement of the sidewalk. There's no doubt in my mind that when she picks it back up again, there'll be cracks in the screen.

"You told me you wouldn't," she says. "You said you knew that you could never ... that you were *over him*!" Her words are at a normal volume up until that last bit, when they rise and she's practically shrieking them. There's anger there, righteously so, because she knows that I lied to her. But more than that ... when I look at her, there's betrayal and hurt and concern.

"What Will and I do is none of your business, Lana." Ryan's arm encircles my waist, pulling me back against his chest. I glance up, noting the tightness in his jaw as he stares over me at Lana and Tanner. My gaze moves back to my best friend, who looks like she's ready to launch herself over my head and strangle him.

"What are you guys so upset about?" Tanner asks. "The picture? We can have it taken down—"

"No!" Lana snaps, cutting him off. "They're..." She swallows, her lips curling down in disgust. A shiver chases down my spine. Disgust. That's what I expected from other people for sure, but it's different seeing it come from her. "Together."

"Yeah?" Tanner looks at her like she's crazy. "So?"

Lana's brows shoot up and she rounds on him. "You knew?" she demands.

He crosses his arms over his chest and shakes his head. "Yes, I did, and Ryan's right, their relationship is none of our bus—"

"They're twins!" Lana practically screeches.

"Lana!" I scream and she turns on me, eyes wild.

"No, don't you fucking 'Lana' me, Willow McRae," she grits out. "You know it's wrong. It's reprehensible. It's—"

"They're not twins," Tanner interrupts, drawing her ire back.

My shoulders drop in half relief. Ryan's arms tighten around me. "It's okay," he whispers. "I tried telling him, but he doesn't believe it."

"What do you mean they're not twins, Willow told me—"

"Yeah, Ryan told me the same stupid shit," Tanner says, once again cutting her off. I can tell that it's making her angrier. Her face goes from tight to molten red, yet Tanner doesn't back down. He can be so easygoing and unassuming, but when I stare across the sidewalk, and he lifts his eyes to meet mine, there's a kindness in them and then a hardness as he looks back at Lana. "They're not twins. It's easy to prove. We can just go to the hospital and have them take a DNA test."

I stiffen in Ryan's arms. No, we can't do that. Almost as if he's thinking the same exact thing, Ryan's arms fall away from me, and he steps in front of me, steering the attention back to himself and away from that very idea. It's good if Tanner believes that it was a joke or something, but if we have to prove it ... well, they'll find that we can't.

Lana switches her focus on Ryan and me. "You really can't do this, Will. Please rethink what you're doing," she pleads.

I reach up and touch Ryan's back. "I didn't mean to lie to you," I confess. "But I knew you wouldn't approve."

"You're damn right, I don't approve," Lana says. "If you keep doing this, people are going to find out the truth, and then where will you be? What are you going to do?"

I shake my head. I don't know. I have no fucking clue what I'll do, or what Ryan will do. Will he turn away from me again? Go back to hating me to get me to leave him? I don't want that. My fingers clench against his spine, tugging on the back of his shirt. I need to make a stand. I need to convince her to just let us live our fucking lives.

If we don't now, we'll just keep hiding it forever, and I'm so fucking tired of hiding and stealing precious moments away from reality. I want to be normal. I want to be accepted. I don't want to have to shy away from expressing my love for Ryan. It's not fair to either of us.

Thirty-Seven

WILLOW

"THIS IS INSANE. Will, please tell me you're not serious," Lana continues.

For a moment, I don't say anything. I *can't* say anything. The disappointment on her face might have once been enough to have me shrinking away and denying everything that would've made her look at me like that, but that's not the case now.

"I can't tell you that," I say as I step around Ryan and face her. "Because it's true." My heart pounds against my rib cage because, just as I expected, my best friend's hope dies a fiery death and she shows me that expression of disgust once more.

Lana shakes her head, tears forming in her eyes as she stares at me as if she doesn't even know me anymore. Right now, I don't think she does. No one does—no one except Ryan. He understands just how messed up this is, him and I, but he also knows that deep down, there's no denying the attraction, the chemistry, and the love between us.

"He's your brother," she tells me, as if I need the reminder and she's hoping that I'd forgotten because to her, that's the only reason I would've allowed this to happen. "Your twin. It's wrong. It's disgusting. For God's sake, Will—

Her final statement has me barking out a laugh that cuts her off and makes her eyes go wide. God this, God that. I'd once believed in God, hoped he would cure me of my sin, of my love for Ryan, but now … I don't want to be cured. I don't want to be changed. "God?" I repeat sourly. "What the fuck does *God* know? I'm not doing this for His sake or anyone else's but my own."

"Will, I meant—"

"No, I don't want to hear it," I lash out. Ryan reaches for me. His fingers touch the back of my hand, but even that feels like too much physical stimulation. I pull away. "You think I wanted this?" I demand, glaring across the space between us until Lana meets my eyes. "You think I didn't struggle with my feelings? Didn't lie to myself? *I know!*" I scream the last words. "I know how fucked up it is. How wrong it is, but I can't stop." I press a hand to my chest as my emotions well up within.

It hurts. It's not fair. All of the anguish I've felt for so long comes pouring out. "So, fuck God!" I snap. "He should've never made me this way because I tried, Lana. I tried for you. I tried for me, and so did Ryan. He lied and he hurt me to drive me away. We both fucking *tried*." I can't emphasize it enough. "I tried for the sake of this world to deny my feelings, and that left me miserable and alone. I can't anymore. I love him. I never wanted you to find out because I never wanted to have to choose between you and him, but now I know that was pointless. I love you, but I choose him. I will always choose him." Lana may be my friend, but Ryan is my other half, my soulmate.

"Whoa, whoa, whoa, hold on," Tanner steps between us, holding his hands up in a placating manner, but I won't be placated. "Why don't we all just calm down," he suggests.

"Will, you don't know what you're saying," Lana says, ignoring his words. A new panic dawns on her face. As if she sees what's coming, Lana tries to stop me, but there's no stopping this tidal wave now that it's been started.

"I do," I say. "I know exactly what I'm saying. I'm in love with Ryan. Worse—I'm in love with someone who is not only my brother, but my twin. But if it's so disgusting and fucked up and wrong, then why does he make me feel whole?" I ask her. "Why does he make me feel like I can breathe even if the world is crashing down? Why does being near him make me feel safe?"

"He's not your fucking twin!" Tanner growls, but once again, his words go ignored.

"That's just your mind," Lana tries. "It's not real. What you're feeling—you're just confusing romantic love for—"

"No, she's not." This time, it's Ryan who stops her. He steps up, drawing her attention back to him.

"She's not confusing romantic love for familial love. Neither am I. I'm sorry you had to find out like this, Lana. I know how much Willow loves and cares for you, but I don't give a fuck who you are. You're not going to make her feel bad about loving me. Because it doesn't matter what you say, I'm not going to leave her, and she's not going to leave me."

"What are you going to do then?" Lana demands. "Get married? Have kids? What if someone finds out about what you are? You can't. Not only is it morally wrong, biologically, it's—"

"It doesn't matter," I say, cutting her off. Each word out of her mouth is like a dagger to my heart because I know she's right. That's what makes this hurt so much. I know that it's morally wrong. I know how society will view us. I know we're not normal, but the reality is that I just don't give a fuck anymore. I tried being the good girl. I tried to deny myself for so long, and all it did was leave me in a dark, black pit of pain and heartache. Now that I know the truth about Ryan and his actions, I can't go back. The door hasn't just been cracked, it's been blown wide open, and there's no shutting it now. "The only thing that matters is that I love him."

Lana shakes her head, tears streaming down her face. "This is a fantasy, Will," she says, sounding tired and broken. "I don't want to hurt you, but you have to know that you will regret this."

No, I think. What I regret is ever telling her the truth. Sometimes, the truth is too much for people to handle and if I'd only kept my mouth shut, we could've gone on, pretending to be normal. No one would ever have mistaken Ryan and me for brother and sister, much less twins, had I never opened my mouth. Hell, aside from our hair and eye color, we don't even look alike.

"Come on, Ryan," I state, reaching for his arm as I tug him away. "We're leaving."

"Hold on!" I turn away from Tanner's call and pull Ryan with me.

"Wait! Will!" Lana's yell pierces my ears as I yank Ryan back towards the street.

"Ryan!" Tanner snaps. Neither of us looks back. Tanner means well, I know he does, but he's wrong. He thinks with just a DNA test we can prove all of this wrong. I only wish that were the case.

Ryan's already got his keys out, but I take them from him and head towards the driver's side. "Will, I can drive," he says.

I ignore him. "Come on," I repeat. "Let's just go. I need something to concentrate on."

Ryan frowns my way. "Are you sure?" he asks.

"Yes," I snap. "Can we please just go?" I want to leave. I hate the feeling in my chest right now. Like the whole of my emotions is trying to crawl up my throat. I need to get away. "I want to leave," I tell him. "Please, Ryan, I want to go home."

His room at the house may not be our permanent home, but he gets what I mean. I want to be somewhere else. In bed with him, probably crying my eyes out until this tightness in my chest

359

eases somewhat.

Ryan's gaze softens as he gives me a small nod, letting me take the lead as I climb into the driver's side and he in the passenger side. My heart is pounding and my eyes burn with unshed tears. My chest feels like it's being ripped apart as Lana stops at the sidewalk, staring through the windows at us as I shut my door and turn the car on.

I tear my gaze away from hers and throw the car into reverse, backing out of the parking spot and then putting it into drive. We roll past her and I continue to avoid her gaze. All the while, I can feel Ryan's eyes on my face.

"Will..."

I shake my head, sniffing hard. "I don't want to talk about it," I inform him. "I just want to go back to your place, crawl into bed and forget this ever happened."

Ryan's quiet for a moment, and then, "It's not something we can forget forever," he tells me. "She might still tell people about us. She was quick to say something to Tanner."

"Then we'll move," I tell him. It hurts to think that Lana might ruin our chances for a future here at Trinity, but I don't know what she'll do now that she knows the truth. She might very well tell people. And as I pull up to a red light, I have to wonder if I wouldn't do the same.

This isn't exactly a situation anyone is prepared for. The further away we get from campus, the more I think that maybe ... Lana isn't just doing this to be cruel. It's hard to accept. It's something that not very many people can do. Tanner acknowledges us, but he also never believed Ryan when he told him the truth. So, is it even real acceptance?

"Will?" I jerk out of my reverie at the sound of Ryan's voice and realize the light's turned green. I press down on the gas, and the car starts forward. "Will!" I jerk my head to the side at Ryan's shout.

Ryan's eyes go wide as horror descends. I follow his gaze back around before realizing there's a truck barreling right for us, headlights blinding my vision. It's only a moment, but it's too late.

It's all too fucking late.

Glass shatters. I scream, but the sound is lost to me. The world spins—around and around. I can't count how many times it goes, like some fucked up merry-go-round that won't stop long enough to let me off. I can't see anything but lights. I can't hear anything but the blaring of horns and shouting and metal crunching under metal. Something pierces my side, and I feel the warmth of my blood flow down my side. Sharp agony burns through me.

I reach for Ryan, but I can't feel him. I can't feel anything.

Finally, the car stops, but I can't move. The lights cease shining so brightly, growing dimmer and dimmer until there's nothing there at all, and I'm lost in the dark with nothing but the sound of a broken car horn blaring to keep me company until I pass out.

Thirty-Eight

RYAN

LIFE HAS A FUCKED up way of coming at you full speed. One moment, you're walking along, thinking everything is fine—even happy—and the next, it body slams you into the ground and makes you regret ever being born. It's always when you least expect it too. The world waits until you feel somewhat safe until you're on the verge of happiness. Oh sure, sometimes, it's not always complete perfection, but it doesn't give you any warning when it fucks you over. You're just fine, and then … you're not.

I scream Will's name, but it's adrift in the noise of metal crashing into metal. The screech of tires against the pavement sounds in my ears. Glass shatters, raining against my face and chest. I try to reach for her, but it's like trying to punch through a wall. The vortex of space and speed that spins us out of control has us both in its grip. Fighting it is insane; it's a test of wills, and nature always wins.

The car careens one way and then another until

it catches on something, and suddenly, the whole world turns upside down. If Will is screaming, I can't hear her. Again, I try to reach for her—to touch her arm, her hand, do *something* to let her know that I'm here, that she's not alone. And again, I fail.

Gasping for breath, my head slams to one side and then the other. The roof of the car above us caves inward, and something crashes into my temple, sending me into a terrifying nightmare of darkness. When next I open my eyes, the world is no longer spinning. I blink and wince as water drips down my face. Rain, I realize, as it patters against what's left of the glass and the roof of the car. It's coming in through the shattered pieces of the car around us. Outside, people are shouting. The loud whir of a machine reaches my ears a split second before the car door is pried from its hinges, allowing light to spill into the interior of the vehicle.

My head slumps to one side as I crack my eyes open even further, finally getting my first look at Will. Blood runs down the side of her face. I wince at the sight of it, and when I try to reach for her, I realize my arm is pinned by something. I croak out her name, but it's stolen by the sound of EMTs and other workers flitting around the vehicle. I watch as she's cut from her seat belt and pulled out. However, when someone comes to my side, I try to move my arm again, and the pain that shatters my mind sends me right back into the darkness.

Light invades the darkness a second time, and

this time, I remain awake but in massive amounts of pain. My arm feels like it's been ran through a shredder. Every time I try to move it, the nerves send spikes of agony through my muscles. That isn't the worst part, though. The worst part is that even though I've been pulled from the car and can tell I'm in the hospital, I don't know where Will is.

"Sir! Calm down! You need to calm down!" the nurse over me yells as she shoves me back down onto the emergency room bed I'm lying on.

"Where's Will?" I demand. "The girl I was with—where—"

"She's in the operating room," the nurse tells me. "But you can't go see her until we get your arm reset and she's moved to a room."

My arm? I think. Fuck. My arm can't get fucked up. If it's fucked up, I can't play. If I can't play, I lose my scholarship. I've got some cash flow from my stocks, but I'd worked hard for that damn scholarship. I curse as I shut my eyes and feel fingers along my shoulder, prodding exactly at where it hurts. The fear of losing my scholarship fades, however, when I think of Will. *Operating room? Why is she—*

A nurse cuts off my train of thought. "We've given you something for the pain. As soon as it kicks in, we'll—"

"Just do it," I grit out. "Get it over with."

"It's going to hurt," she warns me.

"It already does," I counter. Besides, the faster this is over with, the faster I can get to Will.

The nurse calls for someone, and within a few minutes, another man strides into the small room, sliding a curtain down as he steps inside. I hear lots of yelling on the other side of that curtain and crying from both adults and children. Talking. Phones ringing. I tune it all out as the man steps up alongside me, and just as I feel the pain start to fade from my arm, he and the nurse move towards it. Hands grip me and I feel the unnatural shift of my arm as the joint pops back into place.

Agony races down my arm, burning bright and fast. It's there and then it's gone, leaving behind the worst ache I've ever felt, but the sharp pains have finally ceased. Sweat drips from my brow and into my eyes as I pant and wheeze and lay back against the starchy, plastic-covered pillow behind my head.

The nurse and doctors are talking over me, telling me things and I think I nod while making the appropriate sounds at the right times. Eventually, one by one, they leave the little room and disappear beyond the curtain, leaving me alone with my agonizing thoughts and wondering if Will is alright.

It feels like hours later when the curtain is once again drawn back, and someone steps into my room. The pain meds have finally kicked in, and I don't quite feel like I'm being pulled apart, so when I see him, I immediately sit up.

"What are you doing? Stop. Lay back down." Tanner steps up next to the cheap emergency room bed I'm lying on and pushes me back down. "You're going to hurt yourself again."

"Will?" I demand, grabbing his arm. "What do you know about Will? Is she okay? Is she out yet?"

Tanner's face blanches and my stomach drops. "She's still in the operating room," he says quietly.

I'm still for a moment, and then, "Get me out of here," I say. "I need to see her."

"They're not going to let you in the OR, man, and you're pretty fucking banged up yourself …" He shakes his head when I refuse to be pacified and finally gives in enough to let me sit up. "What the hell even happened?"

"I have no fucking clue," I admit. "Will was driving, and there was another car…"

I wince as I shift my position, and a bolt of pain shoots through my arm. I open my mouth to tell Tanner to go get the doctor because I want to get the fuck out of here, but a moment later, my request is fulfilled all on its own when the curtain is pushed back a second time, and the doctor walks in with a clipboard.

"Alright, Mr. Anderson, we've got some news for you—"

"When can I be released?" I cut him off.

The doctor gives me a look. "I don't recommend it," he states. "In fact, we'd like to keep you here overnight. Your shoulder was dislocated, and I'd like to run a few more x-rays—"

"If I let you run your damn x-rays, will you release me?" I grit out.

The doctor moves across the small space and sets the clipboard in his hand on a nearby counter.

"Mr. Anderson, your friend here tells me that you're an athlete. You play for Trinity, correct?"

I swing my gaze to Tanner, but his sole focus is on the doctor. "Why the fuck does that matter?" I demand. "I don't care about my damn shoulder. I want to know about the girl I was with. How's Willow?"

"Your girlfriend is in surgery," the doctor answers. I don't correct him. As far as he or anyone else knows, she should be my girlfriend. Tanner doesn't say a word. Not yet.

"I want to see her," I say.

The doctor shakes his head. "Listen, son, I understand you're worried about her, but you should be more worried about yourself right now. We're taking care of her, and you should be—"

"You better fucking be taking care of her," I snap, cutting him off once again. "And I'm not your damn son."

"Ryan." Tanner's voice is calm and collected. I am anything but. I'm freaked out. I'm angry. I'm fucking panicked. I want to see her—no, I *need* to see her. It's a compulsion. She's not in front of me and I can't tell how hurt she is.

"I'm going out of my fucking mind," I mutter, shaking my head.

Tanner reaches forward and touches my shoulder. I shrug him off, feeling a violent surge inside me at the mere touch, and scrub my non-injured hand down my face.

"I'd like to put you in a room for the night," the

doctor states.

I already know my answer to that. "No," I say with a shake of my head. I don't want to be apart from her when she gets out.

"Then you'll have to sign a waiver," the doctor replies.

"Fine," I snap. "I'll sign it. Just get me out of here. I want to see Will."

"It may be a while," the doctor states. "Your girlfriend has lost a considerable amount of blood, and we typed her as O negative." I sense Tanner stiffening next to me, and then he sighs, but I don't have the energy to concern myself with him as the doctor keeps talking. "We're looking to have some driven in from a local clinic since we don't have—"

"I'll donate," I interrupt.

The doctor stops and blinks. "So—" The doctor catches himself and stops himself from calling me 'son' again with a shake of his head. "Mr. Anderson, O negative can only take O negative. You'd either have to have that blood type or be a close relative with a high probability of that type."

"Ryan, it won't work," Tanner says before I can say anything.

"I'm her fucking twin, Tanner!" I yell. "I know you don't want to believe it, but I fucking am, and if she needs blood..." I turn back to the doctor and jerk out my good arm. "Take it. However much you need."

Tanner sighs. "Can you give us a moment?" he

asks the doctor.

My hand clenches into a fist, and I have to withhold the urge to punch him. We're wasting precious time. The second the doctor said that Will needed blood, my mind had gone into overdrive. The doctor doesn't even look at me; he merely nods and steps out of the room, closing the curtain as he does.

I turn to Tanner. "What the fuck are you doing?" I growl.

"Keeping you from making a fucking mistake," Tanner replies in a cold tone. I frown at the look he gives me, as he steps in front of me and takes me by the shoulders. I grit my teeth as his hand on my injured shoulder causes a twinge of pain. "You heard the doctor. If she has O negative blood, she can only take O negative blood. Even if you were her twin, you'd be fraternal and there's—"

"*If?*" I repeat. Anger boils through me, and I shove him back, ignoring the agony in my shoulder and arm as I stand up. "I am her fucking twin, Tanner. I don't know why you can't seem to get that, but yes, I'm her brother. I'm her brother, and I'm her fucking boyfriend."

"You may be her boyfriend, but you're not her brother, you fucking idiot," Tanner snaps, glaring at me as his palms squeeze into fists at his sides.

"How the hell would you know?" I demand.

"Because I'm her fucking brother!" he yells. "*I'm* her twin! Not you!"

Silence. Cold. Dead. Silence. It echoes around

us in the shocking wake of those words. Then slowly, the rest of the world starts to filter back in. The sounds of phones ringing and people walking by beyond the curtain reach my ears, but I can't focus on them because everything inside of me is focused on the man in front of me and the almost anguished expression on his face. It's full of pain but also anger and frustration.

"What the hell are you talking about?" I demand.

Tanner's hands unclench and his body relaxes as if it's forced to. The curtain opens and a petite framed nurse peeks in. Her eyes bounce between Tanner and me and then refocuses on the man across from me. "Mr. Striker?" she prompts. "We're ready for you."

"Thank you," Tanner says without looking her way. "I'll be right there."

"What are you doing?" I ask as the nurse steps out and lets the curtain fall back into place.

Tanner runs a hand up his face and then through the hair at the top of his head, stopping and clamping down on it before tugging it hard. "I promise I'll explain everything," he says. "But right now, I've got to go donate some blood."

It hits me. "You're donating to Will?"

He nods. "It's going to be fine, Ryan. Just..." Frustration mounts on his expression once more, and he shuts his eyes as if he can't stand looking at me anymore before turning away. "Stay here. I'll be back."

With those final words, he steps out and lets the curtain fall, and I'm left alone to deal with that fucking bombshell in the only way I know how. I turn and grab the clipboard from the counter and throw it as hard as I can against the wall, hearing the wood splinter and crack right before I fall to my knees and clutch my arm as bolts of pain shoot through me.

He can't be right ... can he? He's her twin? How the fuck is that possible? My mind swarms with confusion and ... worst of all, with hope.

Thirty-Nine

RYAN

A NURSE COMES into the room I'm in to draw some blood before giving me paperwork to fill out. Once that's done, I'm fitted for a sling and moved to an empty waiting room filled with fabric-covered chairs, a small table stacked with children's blocks, and a collection of health magazines. It feels like forever before I hear footsteps from down the hall, and Tanner comes around the corner.

My eyes zero in on the bandage attached to the inside of his arm before slowly lowering to the papers in his hand as he strides across the room and takes a seat. Tanner drops the papers on the table right in front of me and motions to them.

"What is this?" I ask.

"Proof," he says, sounding tired.

I glance at him and then back to the papers. "Proof of what?" I say. I have a suspicion, but I'm scared for the first time since I left Willow at fifteen. Terrified of what those papers might say.

Tanner sighs. "I'm sorry," he says, drawing my

attention back to him and away from the stack on the table.

"For what?"

He groans and leans back. "For not saying anything before now, I didn't ... I didn't know how." He laughs, but the sound is anything but amused. "I mean, can you imagine? How the fuck was I supposed to walk up to her and just tell her, 'Hey, I'm Tanner and I think I'm your fucking brother?'" He looks at me, and his lips tilt up in a self-deprecating half-smile. "How well do you think that would've gone over?"

My gaze returns forward and I stare at the white sheets until the air conditioning clicks on and the top page lifts and flutters to the ground right between my legs. Almost as if it's taunting me, daring me to pick it up and read it.

"I asked the doc to run a DNA test while I was back there. For Willow and me and for the two of you, so you'd know."

"You've already looked at it?" I clarify. "You're sure?"

Tanner is quiet for a moment, and then he speaks. "I've been sure since I saw her, man," he says. "She looks just like my mom did."

I shake my head. "This is ... insane." I reach down and lift the page, squeezing my eyes shut before reopening them and turning my attention to the words on the page. My name is there and so is Willow's. Then there are a bunch of numbers, but all I can look at are the zeros, the percentages. Then

I reach forward, grab the next paper, and see Tanner's name alongside hers and the change. 99.99% match.

"How ... the fuck..." The words slip out of my mouth. I feel like I've been punched in the chest and shoved off the edge of a cliff all at once. "How could you do this without our consent?" I ask.

Tanner sighs. "My family donates a lot of money to this hospital," he says quietly, looking at me out of the corner of his eye. "We get ... privileges."

His meaning is clear. It's probably not legal, but money goes a long way. I look back to the papers in my hands.

"You're not twins, Ryan," Tanner says after a prolonged moment of silence. "You're not even related. You never have been."

I've never believed in God. Hell, I cursed His name as much as Will had for putting the two of us on this Earth and forcing us to be so close and yet destined to be so far away, but this ... this is a fucking miracle. The paper crumples in my grip as I bend over and hold them to my face.

It's true. Will isn't my sister. She's not my twin. My eyes itch and burn with unshed emotion, and it's only Tanner's voice that draws me out of my internal thoughts.

"What do you know about the Striker family?" he asks.

I sit up and look at him, still holding the papers in my fist. "Nothing," I tell him. "What does this have to do with us?" Then I realize how stupid that question is because, if what these tests say are true, then it has everything to do with us—with Willow, with me, and with him.

"The Striker family has had a set of twins almost every generation, at least every other generation," he confesses. "Twenty-one years ago, my mom and her best friend got pregnant together. My mom had twins..." He drifts off and glances my way before saying, "my sister and me." Willow, he means. I nod and wait for him to continue. "Her best friend had a boy," he says. My back stiffens at this news because I already sense where this story is going.

Tanner faces forward again and stares at the wall across from us as if he's looking into the past. "They threw a party to celebrate—people who come from money always like a chance to throw a party."

I shake my head. "What does this have to..."

"Just let me finish," Tanner says. He sucks in a breath and then blows it out. "Like I said ... money makes people do things. Those with money want to spend it, and those without ... want to get it. The night of the party, one of the hired caterers snuck in and kidnapped what they thought were the Striker twins."

My chest clenches at this news, but I keep my lips pressed firmly shut.

"I know you've noticed, but Willow and I don't look anything alike," Tanner proceeds. "We'd been placed in the same nursery while the adults had gathered together. In the same fucking crib apparently, and the kidnappers only noticed that I had much lighter hair than my sister. They took the wrong boy."

He sounds guilty. Tormented, almost. Yet, at the same time, determined to see this story through.

"The kidnappers requested a million dollars in ransom, and my parents paid it to get their daughter back as well as the son of their friend, but ... even after the ransom had been paid, the children weren't returned." He finally looks at me. "I was raised thinking my sister had been lost forever. There was really no way to track her down. To be honest, we didn't even know if she'd still be alive."

"But when you saw Will..." I surmise.

He nods. "She looks just like my mom did. At least, what I can remember of her. Funnily enough, my grandparents came to that game we had at Riner—they don't live far from there, but they came into the city and stayed at a hotel. I think you ran into them because my grandma called me that night, after the game, and said she swore she'd seen my mom ... it was Willow."

My head feels like it's going to fucking explode, but all of this is just the background behind what's important and what's important is that Willow isn't who I thought she was. Neither of us is. We're not twins, not siblings, and that means that we can just be ... us.

"I love her," I confess.

Tanner barks out a laugh. It's so loud it makes me jump and look at him. He continues to laugh until he's bent over in his seat. "Yeah," he finally says, shaking his head as he calms down. "I fucking know, dude. You're not exactly discreet. I'm shocked that it took Lana that long to pick up on things. I think she was in denial. Just like you were for a while there."

"Will told her that we were twins," I explain.

He nods. "Yeah, that would do it then. That'd explain why she was so pissed." He looks down at his pocket as it vibrates and shakes his head. The vibrating pauses and then starts up, and once it does, it doesn't stop. "She's been texting me nonstop when she heard you two were here. She didn't want to come because she's afraid of Willow kicking her out when she wakes up."

"If Will doesn't want to see her, I don't care if she's your girl, she's not coming," I state.

"Yeah." He grunts as he places his hands on his knees and stands, pulling out his phone. "I figured you'd say something like that."

"I meant what I said," I inform him. "I love Willow, and I'm going to marry her."

Tanner arches his brow and then steps around me, heading for the hallway. He lifts a hand as he goes. "You'll have to invite me to the wedding then, brother," he replies. "Oh, and the rest of the fam—you can do it when they get here."

"What?" I bark.

Tanner pauses at the corner and lifts the phone,

grinning. "You didn't think I'd keep it a secret, did you?" he asks. "That I'd found my long-lost sister? Ha. No, motherfucker. They're on their way here. You better prepare yourself. The whole Striker family is about to descend ... along with a special guest star of your own. Your birth parents, Ryan. Now, gimme a few minutes to calm my girl. I'd appreciate it if she didn't show up only to have you strangle her. Even if you've got a gimpy arm, I doubt she'd stand much of a chance in the face of true love."

With that, the fucker leaves me. Sitting there like an idiot. I sink back into the seat and drop the papers to the floor as I stare at the ceiling. I'm about to meet my parents ... my birth parents ... people even Stone couldn't find. I laugh, and once I start, I can't seem to stop. I'm sure anyone passing by must be wondering who the hell that dude in the waiting room, laughing his ass off, is and why he isn't locked up in the local psych ward, but I can't seem to help myself.

This is too much, and it's honestly too good to be fucking reality. Willow and I are free. Free to do what we want. To be who we want. To love who we want. We can be *what* we were always meant to be. *Together.*

FORTY

WILLOW

WAKING UP AFTER a car wreck is like waking up after a nightmare that you still think you're living. My body tenses as I crack my eyes open, half expecting that the world will still be flipping around and around, but it's not. It's like one moment I'm driving and then the next, I'm flying and not in a fun way.

Now, I'm motionless and it's disconcerting. Everything is quiet and I'm cold. The thin hospital sheets covering me aren't enough to keep me warm. They feel cool to the touch and almost flimsy—like little more than air covering me. The only spot of heat I can genuinely feel is spread out along one side of my body from my shoulder to my feet. When I turn my head, I realize it's because that heat is Ryan. He's asleep, his head pillowed between what appears to be an uninjured arm and my shoulder. The other arm, however, is locked to his side in a sling. He doesn't look comfortable like that at all.

But as I look over at him, my sudden memory

of the wreck reminds me that I wasn't the only one at risk and makes me search over what I can see of him with worry. I notice he doesn't seem any more worse for wear. There are some bruises and scrapes, but he's not in his own bed, which means that he either refused one or the doctors released him. Either way, I'm glad to see he's alright.

"He's been like that since they moved you here," a quiet voice says, startling me. I nearly jerk and accidentally bump Ryan, barely managing to stop myself before I do as I turn my head towards the quiet voice.

"Lana?" My voice comes out a raspy croak, and I wince at the tight dryness in my throat. She moves to the bedside without me asking and picks up a white cup with a lid and a straw. She leans down and offers me the end of it. I look at her over the rim of the cup, but I find that I'm so thirsty I don't quite care who's holding the cup. I lean forward and take a drink. Water flows onto my tongue and down my throat, soothing it, and I release it a few moments later with a sigh.

"Better?" she asks.

I nod before asking a question of my own. "What are you doing here?"

Lana sets the cup back down on the bedside table before bringing her hands in front of her. "I can't be worried about my best friend?" she asks in a whisper.

My fingers twitch, and I resist the urge to look at Ryan, but I don't think I need to for her to get my intention behind my next words. "I wasn't sure we were best friends anymore," I tell her honestly.

She winces but doesn't disagree. Instead, she surprises me. "Things are ... different now," she says.

"Because of the wreck?" I ask. Did I almost die or something? I wonder.

She shakes her head. "No, Tanner ... explained things."

"He did?" What did he explain? How we wrecked? How did we wreck anyway?

Lana's head bobs up and down. "I mean, it's still weird to me. You two ... together." *Still?* I think, *as in not anymore? What the hell happened while I was unconscious?* "I mean, you grew up together. You still thought you were twins your whole lives, and you basically grew up as siblings every day."

"Um ... well, before this semester, I technically hadn't seen Ryan in six years," I remind her, confused by her words.

"Right, yeah, I know ..." She drifts off, looking away.

I shake my head. "Wait, what does that have to do with Ryan and me? Are you saying you're okay with us?" That was not what she'd claimed previously, just before the wreck. Why do I suddenly have the sneaking suspicion that I've entered *The Twilight Zone*?

"I mean, I guess ... it's fine now," she says with a shrug, obviously still uncomfortable from the way she won't meet my gaze. "After everything …"

I frown. "After what?" I ask, finally. "Are you talking about the wreck?"

Lana's head turns and her lips part. Her face pinches as she looks at me. "No, not the wreck," she says like that should be obvious.

"Then what…"

"She doesn't know, Lana." This time I do jerk and hear Ryan's intake of breath when I accidentally bump him. However, instead of looking at him, my eyes find the man standing just inside my hospital room door.

Lana looks back to Tanner with raised brows. "What? I thought you said—"

"Ryan knows," Tanner interrupts her with a shake of his head as he steps further into the room. "But she's been asleep."

"Oh." She flushes guiltily, looking back at me as Ryan yawns and sits up.

"How long have you been awake?" Ryan asks, touching my arm and drawing my attention to him finally. "You should've woken me."

"Not long," I assure him with a smile, reaching for his hand and noting that he's not the only one with scrapes and bruises. My arms are covered with them. I feel a little queasy, and there's a giant bandage wrapped around my middle; it crinkles when I move.

Ryan looks into my eyes, and I can see all of the fear that I first felt upon waking reflected in his expression as he leans into me, pressing his forehead to mine briefly before closing the gap completely and stealing a kiss. I jerk back. "Ryan!" I gasp, turning to look at Lana and Tanner. But though Lana doesn't look comfortable, she doesn't say anything.

"It's fine," Ryan tells me, pulling me back towards him as he slants his lips over mine once more. I want to resist, truly I do. It's rude to do this in front of Lana and Tanner. Still, Ryan has a way about him—an all-consuming domination to him that burns through all of my resistance in a heartbeat, and I find myself returning his attention.

When he pulls away, I'm left feeling lightheaded and woozy. "Are you okay?" Ryan asks.

I nod. "Yeah ... just fine."

"Here." Tanner is suddenly by my side, replicating Lana's earlier actions as he lifts the cup from the bedside table and holds it out for me. I take it gently from him with an apologetic smile and sip slowly.

"Will?" Ryan takes my hand in his once I'm done. "There's something we have to tell you."

"I'll ... ah," Lana says quickly, "go to the waiting room. I think I should leave you guys to explain alone." Before I can ask what she means, she disappears into the hall, and the door swings quietly closed behind her.

I turn to Tanner and Ryan, looking between them with curiosity. "What do you have to tell me? What's going on?"

Tanner turns and leans against the hospital bed. "We need to tell you a story," he says seriously. His eyes are focused on my face, and for some reason, I know this isn't just any story he's about to tell me.

"Okay," I say, sensing that this is something bigger, something more. "What is it?"

Tanner's lips part, and I feel Ryan move closer, sliding an arm around my back as his friend tells me about his childhood and the sister he lost. It's tragic and strange. I'm not quite sure why he wants to tell me this, or why now, until he finishes.

"And then I met you," Tanner says.

I blink. "What? Me?"

Tanner nods. "Willow Tree," he teases with a gentle smile. "There's a reason I wanted to hang out with you so much. I wanted to get to know you—to know who you were, who you'd become and because … you remind me of our mother."

"I look like your—wait, did you say *our* mother?" My bewilderment turns to outright shock. I yank my head around and look at Ryan, but he doesn't look particularly surprised by this. "What the hell is going on?"

"This, Willow Tree," Tanner answers as he withdraws a wad of papers from his back pocket. He unfolds them and then hands them to me.

"What is this?" I ask, staring down at them.

"DNA tests," Ryan explains. "Yours and mine, and … yours and Tanner's."

"Why would…" My words drift off as I read the names atop the first page and scan down to see the correlation. I would have been less stunned if ice had suddenly formed on the ceiling and dropped onto my head. "This..." I shake my head, an overwhelming mix of confusion and hope suddenly forming within me. "Is this true?" I look between the two of them before refocusing on Tanner, who seems to be the one in charge of this shocking revelation. "Ryan's not my brother? *You* are?"

Tanner grins. "Yeah, it's true."

I feel almost numb and overpowered by my emotions at the same time. How am I supposed to respond to that? How am I supposed to react? How would a normal person react?

I don't know. All I know is that my reaction is to cover my face with both of my hands and break down into tears like an embarrassing sloppy mess.

"Will?" Ryan's arms close around me. "Will, it's not a joke!" he says quickly as if he thinks I would believe that these two men would play the cruelest of pranks on me just when I wake up in the hospital. No, I know it's not a joke. It can't be. That's why I'm crying.

"There's one more thing," Tanner says after what feels like several long minutes of me crying.

"Oh fuck," I mutter, sniffing against Ryan's shirt and making him chuckle. "What now?"

"Well ... um..." I look up to see him scratching the back of his head. "Our dad and grandparents are out in the waiting room. They were hoping to meet you when you woke up."

My eyes widen. "What? Right now?"

"You don't have to," Tanner says rapidly. "I can send them back to my place, but if you want to meet them, they're here."

I bite down on my lip hard before turning to Ryan. "W-what do you think?" I stutter.

He grins, lifting his good arm so that he can cup my face in his palm. "I think I can't blame them for wanting to meet you," he says.

"But what if they don't like me?" I demand, panicked. "What if they're disappointed in who they think is—"

"Will. Will, no. Stop." Ryan cups his hand over my mouth, stopping me, and stares into my eyes. "They are going to love you," he swears to me. "They'll love you as much as I love you."

My heart melts a little bit right then, and after a moment between us, where I take strength from the unwavering seriousness and unspoken oath that I see in his eyes—where I know he'll stand by me no matter what I say—I turn back to Tanner.

"Okay," I say, my voice trembling with nerves as I make the decision. "Yes, I'd like to meet them. I'd really like to meet … my family."

Epilogue

WILLOW

6 weeks later

IT'S FUNNY HOW, in a whole twenty-four hour period, life can turn upside down and you find out you're living in a Spanish soap opera. Then in the following weeks, you're left to pick up the pieces, except you find that the pieces aren't as broken as you thought, and finding out the truth makes you feel whole for the first time in your life. Or rather, *my* life.

Tanner Striker is my brother. Not just my brother, but my twin brother. And although Ryan and I share our age and past, there's nothing else. According to Thomas, Tanner's dad … and I guess mine too, sorta, though it's still hard to call him that—as well as Maryanne and Richard, Ryan's real parents, Ryan's real name is Corey. Seeing his face when he learned that had been priceless. He's going to keep his name, though. I believe his exact words were, "not fucking happening." Mine was supposed to be Heather. I like it, but I'm too used to Willow now. It's who I am, just as Ryan is who he is.

As much as I respect and am grateful to have found Tanner and Thomas, especially since it led to me finding out that not only were Ryan and I not twins, but we're not even related, and that has been the biggest blessing of all—I still think about the McRaes. Though I didn't have them for long, my adoptive parents had been the kindest people in the world. When Tanner and Thomas mentioned possibly changing my last name, I told them I'd prefer to keep McRae. It's almost like a tribute to the elderly couple who took in a young teenage girl when she didn't have anyone else.

"What the fuck is she doing here?" Lana's sudden curse draws me out of my thoughts and to the present.

I turn my head and follow the direction of her narrowed gaze. Sure enough, Roquelle is sitting front and center at the end of the bleachers as the announcements are made. It's Ryan's first game back after rehabbing his dislocated shoulder.

"She's just on academic probation," I tell Lana. "That doesn't mean she can't go to the games."

"Yeah, well, she shouldn't even be showing her face around here," Lana continues as she grabs my hand and pulls me after her. A few kernels fall out of the bag of popcorn I've got pressed to my chest. "She should be ashamed of herself. She's the reason you went through so much trouble with those rumors."

I roll my eyes. She's not wrong. I'd been less

than surprised to find that she was the one behind the picture and the rumors circulating about me when Ryan's friend at the school IT department tracked down the IP address of the picture poster.

"She got fired from the library," I pointed out, "and is on probation. I think that's punishment enough for a few rumors."

Lana glances at me over her shoulder. "You're too nice," she tells me.

"Yeah, I get that a lot." I laugh.

We make it to our seats, high up enough that we're away from the general crowd of students, faculty, and other game attendees, but close enough that I can still pick out who is who. When the announcements end and Trinity's school team comes running out of a big ass banner at the crack of a loud boom, the crowd goes wild, cheering and throwing their hands in the air. I spot Ryan almost right away because he's got his helmet off.

He jogs along with the rest of the team at a slightly slower pace, turning his head and scanning the bleachers. I know who he's looking for, so I stand up, passing the bag of popcorn to Lana as she chuckles, and wave my arms to get his attention. The second he sees me, he smiles and waves my way.

"Okay, okay, lovebird," Lana teases, reaching up and tugging at my shirt—a jersey with Ryan's matching number. "Come on down, the game is about to start."

I grin down at her but relinquish and clamber

back onto the floorboards of the bleachers and retake my seat. She passes me the popcorn and I grab a handful, shoving it in my mouth as Ryan, Tanner, and the rest of the team line up on the field, facing off against their final team before the championship.

"So..." I say after I swallow. "Are you and Tanner still..."

Lana's face scrunches up slightly, and a light pink shade touches her cheeks. "We're unofficial," she says quietly.

"But you're dating?" I prompt.

The pink shade darkens. "Kind of ... He says he wants to see me," she says. "Exclusively."

I grin. "Wouldn't it be cool if you two got married?" I ask. "Then we'd be sisters."

"Will!" I laugh wildly as Lana turns and snatches a handful of popcorn from my bag and tosses it in my face. She's so embarrassed her face is practically tomato red. "It's too early to be thinking about m-marriage or weddings."

"Yeah, yeah, I know," I say. "But it's a nice idea. My best friend and my ... brother."

"Your real brother," Lana says with a shake of her head as she settles down. "Yeah, I can't tell you how relieved I am that Tanner's actually the one who's your brother."

I know she is. Though we haven't really spoken about it since the wreck, and we've acted like everything is back to normal, there's still a small bit of distance between us. Turns out when you're ready to give up everything—including your friendships—for love, it leaves some people a little driftless. Some people being Lana. I have no doubt, though, that we'll get back to where we were. After all, Lana isn't like me. She didn't grow up thinking that Ryan was my brother. She doesn't have years of guilt built up. She also isn't the one who said, 'fuck that guilt because I love him anyway.'

The two of us turn back and watch the game, passing the time with small commentary and talking about class until the timer buzzes for halftime and the team makes their way off the field. I lean back, lifting my arms as I stretch, nearly falling over when Lana suddenly jerks to her feet.

"Come with me," she says, reaching down and grabbing my arm. My now half-empty bag of popcorn falls over and spills across the bleachers, but she ignores it.

"Lana? Where are we going?" She doesn't answer me as she pulls me behind her, nearly sprinting down the stairs as we make our way to the front. "What's going on?"

"Almost there," she calls over her shoulder.

"Almost where?" I gape at the back of her head like she's lost her mind.

Lana jerks both of us to a stop right at the front of the bleachers, next to the railing that separates us from the field. "What are we doing here?" I ask. "Is Tanner meeting you here?"

She turns to me, features tense. "I just want you to know," she says, ignoring my question, "I wasn't really sure about this, but I know that this may be my best way to apologize."

"Apologize?" I repeat. She's not making any sense.

Her face softens. "It's weird," she admits, reaching down and clasping my hands in hers. "You and Ryan. I'm still not completely comfortable, but I've come to realize it's not my life. It's yours. It doesn't matter if you grew up together, thinking one thing. The fact is, you guys are happy together and that's all I've ever wanted for you—to be happy."

"Okay?" I tilt my head, still not sure what she's trying to get at.

"I think this is the best way I can offer my apology and show you that I stand behind you," she continues. "To be honest, if things had turned out differently, I don't know that I'd be here right now. I don't know that I could've supported you. But I don't want to think about what could've happened. I want to focus on what is."

"That's great..." I nod as though I'm understanding, and a part of me is, but another, much larger part is more bewildered by this sudden confession than anything else.

"Is she ready?" I turn at the sound of Tanner's voice as he appears on the other side of the railing.

"Ready?" I repeat. "Ready for what?"

Lana releases my hand, and without answering my question, Tanner reaches over the railing and grips my waist. "Come on, Willow Tree," he says. "Help me out here."

"Are you crazy?" I ask, but I do as he asks anyway and hop up on the railing, just enough for him to drag me over to the other side and set me down on the grass.

"Completely," Tanner replies with a grin. "Let's go."

"Good luck!" Lana calls from behind us as Tanner grips my hand and starts running.

"Good luck with what?" I try to ask, but Tanner doesn't answer. Instead, he throws his head back and laughs.

We don't stop running until we reach the center of the field, and I can feel all eyes on me. I turn in a circle when he releases me. "Tanner? What's going on?"

"Just stay right here, Willow Tree," he says. "Your knight in shining armor is on his way."

"My what?" Once again, though, Tanner doesn't stick around to give me a straight answer. Instead, he jogs off to the side of the field, leaving me there. Alone. The center of attention.

"Will."

I turn at my name to see Ryan standing a few feet behind me. Thank fuck. Maybe he'll tell me what the hell is going on. "Ryan? What's going on?"

He takes a breath and moves towards me. "Will, you know I love you, right?"

My face flames bright and I spin, nervously, to see that the crowd is watching and ... "Why the hell are we on the screen?" I ask, panicked.

Ryan chuckles and then grabs my hands,

pulling my attention back to him. "I love you," he confesses, staring into my eyes.

I blink, startled, and then I soften. "I know," I tell him. "I love you too."

"Good," he says. "Then will you answer a question for me?"

"A question? Yeah, I guess, but that doesn't explain—what are you doing?" My jaw drops as Ryan goes to one knee in front of me, and then it clicks. It all makes sense. Lana's words. Tanner's laughter. The big screen—probably something Tanner set up since I doubt Ryan would be behind asking me in front of the entire student population.

"Willow McRae, will you marry me?" I stare down at him as he withdraws a small box and opens it, revealing a ring with the prettiest green and white stones.

I start to cry. I can't help it. Big, fat, embarrassing tears come streaming down my face.

"Will?"

"You're such an asshole," I cry, gasping.

He chuckles. "Is that a no?"

"You damn well know it's not a no!" I half yell, half blubber. "But did you have to ask me in front of *everyone*?"

"I thought it'd be a good way to put any of those lingering rumors to rest," he says.

"I don't care about those rumors," I tell him as he gets up from the ground and cups my face.

"You still haven't given me your answer, Will," he says.

I slap his chest. "Yes, you big dummy!" I yell. "There's my answer."

Before I can hit him again, Ryan lifts me up and his mouth crashes down on mine. There are cheers, and I can hear Tanner yelling, "get a room!" like the fucking idiot he is.

I don't care about any of it. Not the people. Not the place. Not even the fact that I probably look like a hot, tear-streaked mess as Ryan claims my mouth again and again.

"Are you really that mad?" he asks when he finally breaks away long enough to let me suck in a gasping breath.

I reach up and touch his face. "No," I tell him seriously as I let my eyes fall shut, relishing in the feeling of him against me, even if it's slightly blocked by all of the football padding he's wearing. "I could never be mad at you."

"And you don't hate me?" he asks.

I laugh and reopen my eyes, tipping my head back to meet his gaze. The gaze that once looked at me with contempt. "No," I say again. "I couldn't even hate you if I tried."

His arms squeeze around me. "I love you, Will," he says. "I think I would've found you, and I would've chosen you, no matter what."

I smile so hard that it makes my cheeks ache. "I don't think you would have, Ryan," I say. "I *know* you would have." He pulls back and stares down at me. "I fell for you in spite of the circumstances because we were meant to be." We weren't twins, but we were each other's other half. "In a thousand years. In a thousand lifetimes. It would always have been you and me."

ABOUT THE AUTHOR

LUCY SMOKE, also known as Lucinda Dark for her fantasy works, has a master's degree in English and is a self-proclaimed creative chihuahua. She enjoys feeding her wanderlust, cover addiction, as well as her face, and truly hopes people will stop giving her bath bombs as gifts. Bath's get cold too fast and it's just not as wonderful as the commercials make it out to be when the tub isn't a jacuzzi.

When she's not on a never-ending quest to find the perfect milkshake, she lives and works in the southern United States with her beloved fur-baby, Hiro, and her family and friends.

For more information, please visit Lucy's website at www.lucysmoke.com

Printed in Great Britain
by Amazon